God's
Fool

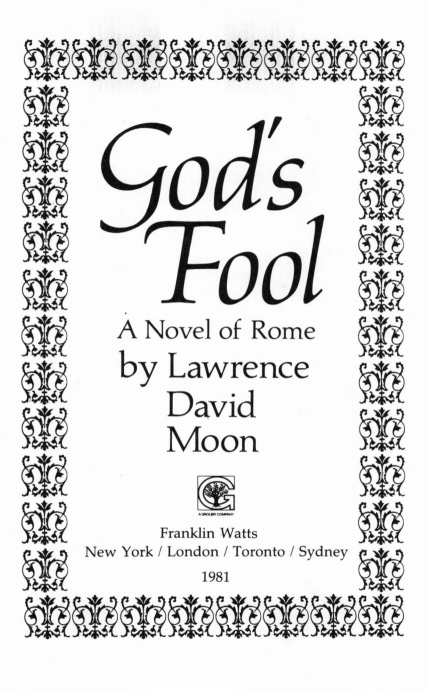

God's Fool

A Novel of Rome

by Lawrence David Moon

Franklin Watts
New York / London / Toronto / Sydney
1981

Under no circumstances can it be said that any character in this book is patterned after any human being alive or dead. The characters are fictional, invented by the author.

Library of Congress
Cataloging in Publication Data

Moon, Lawrence David.
  God's fool.

  I. Title.
PS3563.05616G6   813'.54   80-29113
ISBN 0-531-09946-6

In loving memory of Anna

Acknowledgments

For the many encouragements that made this book possible, the author would like to thank Vivienne Browning, Lesley Guthrie, Victoria Huxley, Willis Joel and Ruby Lee Moon, Margaret and Elena Byrne, Kirk Saint-Maur, Susan Gould, Eva Vedres Carocci, Bernardo and Tita Seeber, the Reverend Anthony Davies, the Reverend Harry Reynolds Smythe, the Reverend Brother Dominic Walker, Brother Jerome Cox, the Right Reverend Peter Ball, Marchesa Laura Corsini, Marchesa Nannina Fossi, Marchesa Alberta Serlupi-Crescenzi, Principessa Maria Concetta Barberini, and the family of the late Conte Donato Sanminiatelli.

Perhaps one day or other, I may attempt some work of fancy in prose, descriptive of Italian manners and of human passions.

—GEORGE GORDON, LORD BYRON
Letter to John Murray,
dated 2 January 1817, Venice

Foreword

Cardinal Arcadio Monsignani and I were kidnapped by the Brigade, on Sunday the third of July. The cardinal was to have officiated at the baptism of the son of his niece, Principessa Aurora Collemandina, at Castelangelina, her estate east of the Holy City. But as we were being driven out of Rome, our automobile was ambushed just after it reached the countryside.

Our chauffeur was killed. We were taken to a subterranean prison which, we learned later, lay beneath a villa in the ancient Appian Way. After six weeks of cruelty and deprivation, His Eminence was martyred before my eyes.

The cardinal was the goal of the kidnappers, because of his having been one of the main financial experts in the Vatican. His knowledge of the global economic network of "the smallest state" was augmented by the contacts of his own family, which will be described later.

My relationship with His Eminence stemmed from

my position as Personal Representative of the Archbishop of Canterbury to the pope. In this ministry I also functioned as the sole Representative in Rome of the whole Anglican Communion. As for executing this ministry, it was not altogether fortunate that I, Rupert, Marquess of Broxbourne, also was a peer of the realm. As a young lord, I rose within the Anglican Church with certain insights denied other priests, but with privileges that forbade much suffering along the way. Yet, as God oversees all works, so He must have seen it necessary that I witness, and go through, what is described in these pages.

I have had the honor to know the Archbishop of Canterbury all my life. Our family seat is in Kent, located a few miles south of Canterbury. I must say, though, that I was startled when His Grace suggested that I should go to Rome. The Anglican ambassador to the Vatican recently had died, so the post was open and everyone had assumed it would go to a dean or a much older priest of proven tenure. My own position, as vicar to a South London parish, had been in effect only one year.

But that year had been a very difficult one for me. I had recently lost both my parents—they had been young. Mother and Father had died within a matter of months. Therefore, our ancestral title had come to me prematurely. I can hardly say that I had been prepared, though I was twenty-eight years old.

As a vicar, my prayer life and ministry, thank God, had kept me busy, but inside I was eaten by doubts about my being a man of the cloth. Family problems, involving inheritance and the managing of our large estate, kept nagging me. So when the archbishop's request that I relocate to Rome had come, I accepted gladly.

But I must confess that my desire to accept the position coincided with the growing realization that I was incompetent to perform the Lord's will. I didn't fit in with my working-class parish, my background being alien to most of those with whom I dealt. After one year it seemed to me that I was failing completely. Thus I requested an audience of the archbishop, who knew my family situation well. But had His Grace known all the factors at work in my mind, he never would have decided to commit me to some other duty of the Church.

If I'd only had the courage to tell the archbishop why I was failing as a priest! The Archbishop of Canterbury knew that I was setting out for Rome to propitiate some unstated error, with his prayer that my work further Christian Unity, but I journeyed to the Eternal City concealing a truly mortal sin.

Yet now, as I have survived, and a cardinal—my friend—rests with the heavenly hosts, I feel it a duty to God to publish this confession.

Broxbourne
Dexter Mote
Nr Canterbury
Kent

Part One

1

On August fifteenth, the Feast Day of the Assumption of the Blessed Virgin, Cardinal Arcadio Monsignani was murdered in my presence—then I too was shot, and left for dead. The Brigade had done all they could with us, had tried to extract the maximum of information out of us; when they were through with us, after six weeks of nightmare, we were shot. I hardly knew where we were—I was delirious by this time—and to recall it today is very painful.

For me, the horror of the event was lessened by the spiritual strengthening I received toward the end of our captivity, which kept urging me to become a Catholic, a conversion I did accomplish with the cardinal's instruction during the last days we were held together.

In Italy the reaction to the shootings was mixed. There was outrage and mourning for the loss of a familiar, albeit controversial figure of the Vatican bureaucracy, the Curia. But there was also joy—that for the first time somebody survived, someone who could tell the government and

3

secret police what it was like to be held captive by the Brigade.

Needless to say, such joy did not occur to me till recently, as I contemplated this book. My first reaction after regaining consciousness in hospital was that I never again wanted a thing to do with the Church, with Italy, or with politics of any sort. But this initial anger was sublimated somehow, just as fear of the Brigade was sublimated in their captivity.

Even at the outset of recuperation I was not allowed to rest, but was thoroughly interrogated by Italian ministers, NATO officials, and Special Branch and Scotland Yard investigators. All this transpired the first four days in hospital.

His Holiness The Pope had been a very dear friend of Cardinal Monsignani. Prior to the Holy Father's election, many in Rome felt that Monsignani was one of the three being considered to become the next Pontifex Maximus. And because of the deep love the pope had for Monsignani, His Holiness intervened and withdrew me from the interrogations, even though I still was under heavy sedation. The pope had me transferred to Castel Gandolfo on the nineteenth of August, and for the next four days I was totally at peace, seeing His Holiness for brief interludes throughout the period of convalescence, and drawing strength from the sanctity of my host.

I have mentioned that prior to departing from England and assuming new duties in Italy (I arrived the nineteenth of June), I seriously debated whether or not I was spiritually fit to remain a priest. During captivity I expressed these doubts to Cardinal Monsignani. By the time I arrived at Castel Gandolfo, I was convinced I was incapable of saving the souls of others because my own soul seemed so lost. I wept when I had to confess such misgivings to the Holy Father, when I had to tell him that I must withdraw from Holy Orders, but this was the inevitable step.

4

I did effect this four months ago, by having directed a letter to the Archbishop of Canterbury. But even now, at the beginning of this new year, when the six-month period of waiting will soon be up (tradition dictates that after six months Lambeth Palace replies and asks if one still wishes to relinquish one's vows), I am torn by the irrevocability of saying that the Church is not my true calling.

Each of these failings His Holiness listened to with awe-inspiring calm. I was given his assurance, that last day I saw him, that should I choose to remain in Holy Orders, my training in Rome would be permitted; but since leaving Italy, I have accepted the fact that I lack the spiritual reserve to become a Catholic priest. His Holiness also said that to be spared the scrutiny of the public eye, which would follow my career because the kidnapping had placed me so much in the news, I could be given a post within the Vatican itself once I became a priest. I wouldn't need to be sent back to a parish where the Brigade might kill me, should they feel inclined.

Let me say that the Brigade had no wish to kidnap me—their goal was Monsignani. The cardinal and I were busy discussing Unity between Canterbury and Rome, as he was one of seven members of the Vatican's Secretariat for Promoting Christian Unity; the Brigade wanted *him* because he was an expert in Vatican finance.

The information the Brigade extracted from the cardinal is not the point of this book, however. Understand, though, that few facts unavailable in recently published exposés of Vatican investment policy were yielded by the cardinal. Moreover, he was not a man to relinquish key information easily, even under torture and threat of worse. Monsignani truly died a martyr, with the Church of Christ's interests in his heart until the last.

The Brigade wanted to understand none of this. Better to explicate the story of this terrible tragedy, please allow me to reconstruct events as they occurred, beginning with my entry into Rome.

2

I was born an earl. As if that stigma were not enough, people often tell me I look, and act, like Rasputin. In London I have a horrid reputation—that I know—nonetheless for the tragedy in Rome but mainly because I went against the advice of all my friends, and father's friends, in choosing to become a priest of the Anglican Church. It would be dishonest not to admit here that I chose to leave the temporal world of Britain for the spiritual one simply to be rebellious. For some reason, I always have been dissatisfied with myself—yet those who think I'm evil are convinced I was only trying to show off, to prove something to the naïve who might be impressed by a young lord who could abrogate centuries of upper-class inculcation. But I was not out to convince a soul, since I realized immediately after commencing divinity studies what agony it was to "leave the world" and "turn to God." Whether or not God ever called me, I still don't know, but perhaps in analyzing why anyone ever becomes a priest, I must admit I was running from my family, or from some part of it, with which I felt I could not cope.

My mother Louise died not even a year and a half ago, just before Christmas before my arrival in Rome. She was a renegade, as un-English a Lady as a Lady could be—being Greek and being a stage performer. Mother was detested by Society, though she had a following, one might say, of "fans" who proved faithful till her cancer possessed her. She was a cabaret singer, not unknown, and she was cantankerous, difficult, and melodramatic. Born Athenian, she was a true comedienne of the Aristophanic sort, meaning that beneath her mask there was tragedy. Mother kept her Greekness very private. She took a French name, Louise Senlis, when she left her homeland for Italy and eventually for Paris. Father told me he met her when she was thirty-five years old, in Las Vegas, where her career somehow had taken her. He said Mother was on her last legs, that her voice was gone, and that she was on drugs. But others who knew her were equally emphatic in denying anything of the sort. They claimed my mother's "torch song" never had sounded better.

My father Aldous, sixth Marquess of Broxbourne, was twenty-five when he met, proposed to, and married this woman. Everyone was scandalized, though Father was not the eldest son and few feared such a "low woman" would triumph as Marchioness of Dexter Mote, which she did, to everyone's horror. I do not exaggerate this in the least. Admittedly, Mother never was a shining example of femininity no matter how much everybody loved her. Perhaps my affection for her was only shocked awe. I didn't really like the fact that I found myself applauding her anti-Society ways. But, I followed her example. I've always enjoyed laughing at convention, which is why I felt that I, least suitable for the priesthood, might just as well join it, to show my father's world it damn well could be done.

Poor Father. He was young and foolish to marry the likes of Louise Senlis. He regretted it for the rest of his life. The second son and the last child of six, Aldous became marquess at thirty, for his brother was killed in a plane crash and Uncle William produced only female issue. Father—he never did a thing but be jaded and adored . . . except *one* thing, and that was to me, and to that I must return later.

My grandfather Nicholas, fifth Marquess of Broxbourne, did not die until I was fifteen years old. Nicholas was deeply mourned, and very much beloved, not just by the gentry but also by the common people. He always was cited in my family as the example par excellence of a *noble* man. It is due to Grandfather, verily, that I was considered for the position of Anglican Representative to Rome.

7

My father hated his father, because he knew he never could live up to the Victorian ideal set by Nicholas Broxbourne. Father knew he need not try to realize himself as Knight of the Garter, and never did so. Perhaps because opposite generations attract, I always was drawn more to my grandfather, in moments of weakness, as my own father's faults seemed so glaring. Grandfather was pious and devoted to duty. God alone knows how he did it.

Grandfather was a marvelous man, and I loved him dearly. He, of all the men I ever have known, influenced my thinking toward the pursuit of the Good. If one can ever analyze oneself, I believe I went into the Church more to please my dead grandfather than to shock those relatives still alive.

Grandfather had always been involved in high echelons of the Anglican Church. This is why I've known the present Archbishop of Canterbury all my life, though he has not been in the See for twenty-eight years. When he was a young bishop, we saw him frequently at Dexter Mote. Like a devilish schoolboy, Grandfather always was delighted to show clergy round our moated isle. He loved to boast that our home had been a "recusant house" for centuries. I recall how shocked the Cardinal of Westminster was when he was told, in no uncertain terms, that Grandfather had *been* a proud and practicing Catholic, just as his ancestors had, *until* 1929. The cardinal became disgruntled when told that Grandfather became an Anglican in protest against the Lateran Pacts which, he felt, "sold the Vatican to the Devil," meaning Mussolini. Be that as it may, Grandfather stuck firm to his decision. All family members to this day have remained Anglicans, except for myself who recently made the return to Mother Church.

While Grandfather was still a Catholic, he was involved behind the scenes with one of the major encounters between the Churches of Rome and Canterbury in this century, that is, with the Malines Conversations. Even scholars hardly remember them now, but in the years between 1921 and 1925, breakthrough discussions between the two hierarchies were held in the Belgian city of Malines. These were principally between the Catholic Cardinal Mercier and the Anglican Viscount Charles Linley Halifax, a close friend of Grandfather's. Although there was a great difference in age—the viscount being over seventy and Broxbourne in his early thirties—the two men often met to discuss Church Unity. Halifax would poke my grandfather for advice about "how best to deal with these Catholics" as the Conversations were about to take place. Twice, Grandfather went along privately to Malines. Given his connection with these important dialogues, I believe the Archbishop of Canterbury felt that I too might be of some use, diplomatically speaking, on a similar assignment to discuss Ecumenism at the Vatican.

When the archbishop dropped this bomb in my lap, in the middle of last May, my life was at its worst point ever. Only twelve months before I had assumed the title of marquess, as my father had died the previous May, just seven months before Mother passed away. The death of both parents left me increasingly dispirited. This was aggravated by enormous death taxes. Too many affairs had to be managed in Kent, none of which was I prepared to handle even had I *not* been vicar of a parish in which I felt myself an outsider. Suddenly, I'd become a Lord Temporal in a poor London parish which regarded me for some odd reason as its Lord Spiritual. My parishioners kept rallying round me, though I could not fathom why. This bizarre attraction, this magnetic power I appear to have (which manifested itself in my church by attendance and activities) kept getting stronger and stronger as my desire to remain in the parish kept getting weaker and weaker. Whatever I possessed, though, was frightening—and, I believed, diabolic.

This force compelled me to confess to the Archbishop of Canterbury that I doubted I could remain a priest. Although I retained within me a terrible secret—which I shall save till it needs be told—my confession convinced the archbishop that he must send me away, soon. So I was ordered to Rome, for propitiation, to assume less conventional responsibilities for which my personality and upbringing were suited.

Thus, after one month of eight hours per day and seven days per week of tutoring in Italian, to refresh what I had learned at Cambridge, plus numerous briefings in Ecumenism, I flew to Rome on the nineteenth of June, a Sunday. As I viewed the Eternal City roasting beneath a summer sun, how little did I suspect that these next two weeks would be a countdown.

3

The previous Anglican Representative to the pope had died in the chapel of the Anglican Centre, located in Palazzo Doria, late in the evening of the tenth of May. It had been very hot that night, and the priest suffered a heart attack. Six weeks later, when I arrived in Rome, the weather was even more stifling. Given that my arrival was at the least likely time of year for conspicuous entry into the Holy City, I decided to get through the summer by sending letters to contacts necessary to continuing the dialogue between Canterbury and Rome. Honestly, I was praying for as little business as possible, so that I would have time to get to know that part of the populace which remained in the steamy capital.

The pope had not yet retired to Castel Gandolfo. I had no message to deliver to His Holiness from the Chief Commoner of the United Kingom, so it was decided by the Prefettura della Casa Pontificia that during my first two weeks I should meet with the Secretariat for Promoting Christian Unity, and *basta*! The sole cardinal of the Secretariat available, or still within the walls of Rome, was the late Cardinal Arcadio Monsignani, whom I met the twenty-third of June, only four days after my arrival. My first audience with the pope was scheduled for Monday, the fourth of July, at Castel Gandolfo.

Having been briefed at Lambeth Palace on the Curia cardinals whom I likely would meet, I recognized Monsignani immediately and sensed that we would get along well. I shall never forget the elder's face when he saw how young I was, as he snapped: "You must shave that impertinent beard! If only to survive our summer." Then he forced a great clerical grin and sat me down in his library. I particularly remember the music of a piano filtering through the walls from somewhere distant in the cardinal's private residence.

The cardinal spoke English—no small help—and joked that it was only due to his knowing the Queen's English that Paul VI had chosen him to be on the Secretariat for Promoting Christian Unity. But he countered this by saying, "It's about time you rebellious northerners sent us some new blood." I wondered whether those penetrating black eyes beneath that tanned and bald pate were making fun of me. This cardinal was shrewd, but deigned to acknowledge my discomfort by saying, "Well, Rome will be the change you've been hoping for."

Such remarks, and more to follow, left me wondering what the Eternal City did have to offer. So overwhelming were the contradictions of Rome, especially as her beauty stewed in brutal heat. There was nothing to do but give oneself totally to her. I couldn't help thinking it was a dream come true to have been sent to work in Rome.

Monsignani lived in a palazzo, whose address was one of the most impressive in the city. The edifice faced the little-seen eastern flank of the Palatine Hill, in Via di San Teodoro at the corner of Foro Romano. The palace filled the block between Via dei Foraggi, and its smallest end faced the ancient Forum of the Caesars. I must admit being impressed.

It was love at first sight with this sixteenth-century structure. I felt at home in it. Its plushness reminded me of our own moated house near Canterbury. Needless to say, though some historians have labeled our home "grand," it's not nearly as luxurious as this palace of Rome, which her own historians have labeled "simple" and "not overly ornate."

Arcadio Monsignani, receiving me in full crimson ceremonial, made an operatic gesture toward his window with an ostentatious amethyst ring. "Look," he declared defiantly. "Out that window lies the Palatine, rotting in notoriety, her brown bricks sprouting verdancy and dreams. And here we sit . . . but two human beings . . . seeking to unite two thousand years of mortal foibles. How . . . do we possibly do it . . . how can *two* succeed?"

A nun, skinny, middle-aged, and very severe, brought us coffee at that moment. We took it on the balcony off the cardinal's library.

I was very much moved by the cardinal's poetic turn of mind. There was not much that one could say. The past, so present, wafted upward from its moldering below. The glory and excrescence of Rome was so aromatic, enough to kill the fumes from our small cups of espresso.

With no pertinent comment to make, I suddenly was overcome by fear that I didn't know what I was doing in Rome, in an ecclesiastical position, in the presence of someone so august—who undoubtedly saw how paltry I appeared.

After putting the golden cups on the ledge, which was graced by terra-cotta pots and white dahlias, His Eminence excused himself for being undiplomatic. "I know what the Anglican Centre looks like, that it's comfortable and accommodates the Representative, its Director, but I wonder if you feel at home there?"

I had to admit I did not. It wasn't as if Palazzo Doria was displeasing—being so central and commodious—but I didn't like living behind the door of my office, though the office was open only Monday through Friday.

The cardinal spontaneously took my hand, patted it, let it go, and gestured toward his house, saying: "Then move in here! We've a fair-sized flat available, and we shall lend it to you . . . for the pleasure of your company." He was beaming. "Not that I wish to score a coup against other members of the secretariat who wish to make Your Lordship's acquaintance."

"Please, just call me Reverend. I needn't be addressed . . ."

My response made the old man laugh, as he pointed to the palazzo's three storeys below us. "I'm a boarder here, too—my sister's husband's family, you know—so one more cleric won't collapse the roof. They should be honored. To accommodate the Archbishop of Canterbury's ambassador to the Holy See is no little thing . . . something the family can boast about."

So more out of vanity of being a *cause célèbre* within the Catholic community (tongue in cheek though this be) than being just another prelate amidst Anglicans, I decided then and there to accept the cardinal's offer. I moved to Palazzo Roseazzini the next day.

4

Cardinal Monsignani was seventy-one years old. He stood five feet eight, was corpulent, and had no hair on his head. His thin face was dominated by a very large nose. His right hand, which usually exhibited a very large jewel, invariably shook, because of his age, but it wasn't so noticeable as to be undignified, and it lent a certain élan to his person. His parents had lived in Fiesole, above the city

13

of Florence, but because his father, during the first quarter of this century, was a prominent professor of Renaissance literature at the University of Florence, the cardinal was able to overcome his bourgeois status.

Only two of the nine Monsignani children survived into this decade, the cardinal and his sister Aurora. One of the great, albeit legendary doyennes of Roman society, Aurora, four years her brother's senior, still flourishes in Palazzo Roseazzini as the dowager principessa of the house's name. Although she was not a *nobildonna* by birth, few in Florence or Rome objected when she wed Principe Ermenegildo Roseazzini in 1922, for her intelligence was very acute and her father's scholarship universally recognized.

After moving to the palazzo that Friday, I had my first evening meal in the cardinal's apartments. The principessa joined us and His Eminence joked with his sister and congratulated her fondly for having made it possible for him to become a member of the Vatican senate, the Curia. At such a dinner, I could not tell if the man was being outré or if he was admitting truth. The more I got to know him, though, the more I sensed that what the cardinal stated only could be taken lightly by the naïve.

The cardinal's sister was one of the most fascinating women I ever have met. I shall never forget my first sight of her—menacingly impressive in an anachronistic mourning gown of black silk and jet. Whenever I would see her thereafter, she would always be dressed in the same garments.

Principessa Aurora Roseazzini had mothered seven children, three princes consecutively, then four princesses. The eldest son, Guadagno, now head of the family, also resides in the palazzo with his wife Dulcinea, and this nuclear family will become important as this story develops. Of Princess Aurora's other sons, Giovambattista died young and Averardo, who never married, lives in Paris. But it is due to the four daughters, I realized quickly, that the cardinal was not joking about his sister's having enabled him to become a Prince of Mother Church.

Through the four nieces, Monsignani was linked by marriage to all the major houses of Roma Nera, the nobility of the Eternal City deemed "Black Rome." The eldest, Licia, wed Principe Orazio Ferrucci; Tecla wed Conte Teseo Civitali; Onesta wed Marchese Zanobi Mimabue; and the youngest, Aurora, wed Principe Melchiorre Collemandina. It was to the christening of the firstborn child of this last couple that the cardinal and I were going when we were kidnapped.

Need one say such powerful family ties did not hurt Monsignani when he was still a *monsignore*. Prince Ferrucci and Marquess Mimabue today still function as consultants to the Consultore dello Stato della Città del Vaticano, founded in 1968 to ameliorate the running of the Vatican as a modern temporal power. More important, three of the families to whom the cardinal was related—the Roseazzini, the Ferrucci, and the Collemandina—produced popes. Anyone who lives in Rome realizes how much import this carries, even today after Vatican II and its consequent social reforms, for the fact remains that these papal families are valuable links to the Vatican's past and they buttress the Apostolic See from the too rapid changes of this era. Even after the reorganization of the Papal Household in 1968, few people not involved with Roma Nera realize the extent to which these families contribute to the functioning and the perpetuity of the papacy. When one does hear of Black Rome these days, all too often it is in the pejorative sense.

"You see," the cardinal emphasized at dinner, "the principessa my sister is not only mother-in-law to four important noblemen of Rome, but the families of the four, by marriage, unite this house with the principal palaces of the city. Such a system, this aristocracy, has no counterpart anywhere else on earth."

"I just pray the papacy appreciates it," stated the

princess, but the cardinal chose not to acknowledge his sister's remark.

"This aristocracy is unique: its service isn't simply solidarity to itself; its service, quintessentially, is to the Holy Father—and thus to God."

"Do you *really* believe so?" asked the princess rather hotly.

"Even the majority in Italy—our own country—fail to grasp this; they label the whole system antiquated, when they understand nothing of the benefits it accrues. The reason the principessa and I thought it worthwhile to invite you to reside here was to give you the chance to see the system for itself."

"That's correct," the princess declared, "but the cardinal my brother is probably the last of his sort; cardinals don't proliferate from noble houses these days."

"In the long run," the cardinal continued, oblivious to his sister, "who knows? What you might see might be more beneficial to our dialogue to unify our two Churches than had you continued to reside in the Doria, where of course you'd get invited *into* the important homes of Rome . . . but you wouldn't come close to understanding them."

"And," the principessa added, "your background in Canterbury is similar to ours in Rome, which is why, I'm sure, the archbishop decided it was time to send somebody such as yourself to get to know us."

At this moment, the short, attentive butler in gleaming white scurried round the table without making a bit of noise. He replaced our service with dessert plates topped by crystal finger bowls. It was then, from afar in the palace, that I heard again the same faint sound of a piano. The cardinal and the princess smiled at each other briefly, then dipped their fingertips into the lukewarm water as if blessing it for a High Pontifical Mass.

5

Later, alone in my sumptuous flat, I pondered my first evening at the Roseazzini palace and worried. Being ever prone to introspection, the words of the two people I had dined with suddenly sounded so pompous, so staged to me—to say nothing of the tension between the brother and sister. It struck me, though, that the two were testing me, baiting "the Anglican" to see if he'd hold up. I felt laughed at—as if they thought I had never dined in a house of means before, had never held a silver spoon. Perhaps I was overreacting, caused by their exquisite *chianti classico* and the excruciating *romano* heat.

Instead of letting these suspicions, no doubt unfounded, fan themselves undirected, I tried to content myself with the principessa's declaration that by residing in Palazzo Roseazzini, I still would have the flat in Palazzo Doria to utilize for what entertaining was deemed necessary by the Anglican Centre. "Two abodes are always more civilized than one," the lady had offered with a gleam in her eye, as if she ever wanted for a place to stay. "Anyway, if one is bored here, one can always stroll past the Forum. In a second one's in Piazza Venezia for one's work."

Yes, this reflection did make it seem too good to be true. A stroll past the Forum and in a second. . . .

Those terribly tiring, never-ending chores of being a vicar at last were behind me. Yes, at least those were over. I wished I could have said the same about family tribulations. Though I rarely spoke of them to other people, my brother and sisters always were on my mind. Nicholas, thirteen, was at Eton but was growing so fast I hardly knew him. And the girls. My sister Samantha, twenty-five years old, recently became engaged. She and I never correspond and very rarely talk because the difference in our ages is a mere three years and our thoughts are too alike for comfort. But Louise, who's twenty, and I are close, yet nowhere near as close as I feel to Amy, eighteen, who's the Greek in the family and the most moody of us all, the one so very much like Mother. Poor Amy. She was the hardest hit by our parents' deaths coming seven short months apart. Amy's constant stream of letters to me record nothing but tenderness turned to despair.

Yes—soon taxes would have to be paid on Dexter Mote, our home in Kent. Society in Rome certainly didn't seem paralyzed by death duties. Rome looked so much better off, even with the violence, even with the ubiquitous fear that, again, a new Dark Age cannot be prevented from descending, slowly, from somewhere north in Europe, down . . . into Rome.

This thought brought me back to reality. I rose from the easy chair in the drawing room, in this residence I was trying to accept as "home," and walked to the double doors giving out onto the garden.

In Rome *la vita* could be *dolce* I thought, as I deeply breathed in the perfume from a trellis of golden roses. A little fountain, constructed round an ancient statue of a nymph being fondled by a tumescent satyr, bubbled benignly in the tepid Italian night as the moon cast a palpable glow on lush potted plants.

The atmosphere that evening moved me as few I ever have known. I wiped my eyes, then plunged wet fingers into the warmth of the fountain.

Just as I did so a cat from beyond the wall fell into a tangle of ivy and squalled bitterly at its clumsiness in the night. A simultaneous rustling on the balcony above gave me fright. Someone in the cardinal's family was watching.

A male voice chuckled behind a column of stone, then shadows and stillness resumed dominion. There was no sound of a door closing. I looked for the cat, but the animal had vanished from sight. Feeling eerie, I hastened inside, away from the nocturnal garden, and my mind mocked me: "Welcome home!"

Good old withdrawing room, all in brown hues, veritably reeked of aeons as did the dining room, the pantry, and the kitchen. It all seemed strange. And these Romans: who were they? How could I ever relate to them?

Evil thoughts often do possess me. Did Monsignani and the old princess lodge me here just to steer my mind *away* from Unity with Rome? Perhaps they'd "Rome" me to death, give me such a dose of palazzo hospitality, let me be catered to—at the drop of a *cat*. Was I a fool to accept their offer? What if I'd refused? The Curia must know of this move. Was the Curia the agent of it? And what about Anglicans in this "religious" city? Would their recent party for me, paid by All Saints in Via del Babuino, now be judged a waste of money, of time? Would Anglicans say I've "poped," gone to Rome forever?

Why was I paranoid? It must be that blasted Tuscan wine!

I realized at that moment the least advantageous thing to do was cogitate, so I left the pantry via the corridor to my room and retired. Where would this so-called "job" in Caesar's city lead me?

6

Palazzo Roseazzini was quite the workable establishment. Unlike many palaces in the *centro storico*, this one had no shops on the ground level, freeing lots of space for dwelling. I resided in apartments at the western end of the building, off the second and far smaller courtyard. Access was via one main portal giving onto the first court; to find my rooms, one turned left and passed under a colonnade protecting a series of partially damaged ancient marble statues.

I grew to prefer the *piano terreno*, though I must admit being disappointed at first at not having an upper floor with the magnificent views to the Capitoline and Palatine, the Forum and Colosseum. If one craved a view, there always was the second floor, inhabited solely by Principessa Aurora, or the third storey, by the current head of the family, Prince Guadagno, or the penthouse utilized by the cardinal, which afforded one of the best vistas in all of Rome.

The first storey was not lived in permanently but set aside as three separate apartments for relatives and friends; it also contained state rooms for receptions. The staff lived in various rooms about the first courtyard, and they functioned for the whole palace.

I was woken at eight the next morning by a very timid though handsome young butler from Sicily who handed me a note from a silver tray. He requested it be read and answered. It was an informal invitation for breakfast at nine with Princess Aurora's daughter-in-law who signed it simply "Dulcinea."

The boy hurriedly explained, at my request, that his mistress was eager to meet me, that she regretted not being able to dine last night. He ended by admitting: *"La signora principessa è molto bella,"* and with one hand drew what he thought represented a buxom femme fatale while the other hand still held the tray.

I grimaced and said I'd be there. He said he'd return to my room at five to nine to lead me to the princess's *appartamento*.

It seemed extracurricular, but I put on my clericals anyway. It was beastly hot, and I longed for a swim instead of a meal with someone I never had met. Too promptly, the boy called to fetch me before I was ready.

I was led three flights up a grand staircase, and

couldn't help noticing that the halls seemed to have an inordinate amount of ancient Roman nude sculpture of atrocious aesthetic quality. As antidote to this, again I heard that same repetitive piano, closer now, distinguishable this time as a melody by Chopin.

The boy now led me through a series of deluxe salons; then suddenly he opened a door and announced me to Principessa Dulcinea. The woman, who was lolling in bed, flung off a pale green satin sheet and held her hand to be kissed.

"No, no, it's all right," a truly melodious and low sultry voice stated. "I'm just getting up."

Her English was as perfect as her looks. For an instant this thought arrested my hunger as well as my eyes, which had dropped onto my cheekbones.

"My," she cooed, "you do have a gorgeous beard!"

I flushed. The cardinal, likely out of foresight, had not said a word about what his niece looked like, but her footman certainly wasn't joking. The principessa was stunning, and I gaped unashamedly as she sashayed to a green marble table set for two. The silken lines of her turquoise peignoir swayed left and right.

"Do sit please, Rupert," she commanded in a mocking tone. "No don't—feel free to call me Dulcinea."

As we breakfasted on orange juice and eggs, the woman's volubility and tendency to gossip increased, but never to the point of vulgarity. Like others in the house, it seemed she too was testing me, but for something a man could identify. I liked her approach, as if a lady of her standing and attractiveness could do no harm to any total stranger, even in her own bedroom.

She already had made up. Despite the collar round my neck I wanted to reach for her hair so fastidiously arranged. She looked as one pictures Livia, wife of Caesar Augustus. My eyes couldn't stop returning to the flesh

21

that I could see, two barely covered breasts, fine white wrists and hands, a long slender neck supporting such a face as to make a babbler lose communicability. But I couldn't get over her hair, so black, so unnaturally high above her forehead, brushed and gathered in a chignon.

"I knew your mother, you know," she stated as she wiped her lips.

That completely nonplussed me. "No, I didn't . . ."

"Louise . . . she was a very shy child deep down," the princess said and stood. "You know, she came to Rome before going to Paris, where she was a sensation. But—it was Rome that convinced her to be an artist. Thank God the inspiration stuck with her, it fades from so many so quickly, as soon as they leave this city. But not your mother! Oh she *was* an artist, a great one, Rupert. You likely haven't met a tenth of the people she knew."

This made me wonder about the princess's age. She looked no more than thirty, but such a remark meant she might be fifty.

"Do sit over here," she pointed to a stuffy silver chair. "Smoke?"

"No, thank you," I replied. "How did you know her?"

"In Paris. It wasn't Rome at all. I wasn't fortunate to have known Louise before the war. My mother-in-law did, though, and it was through my husband's mother I met yours, in Paris, her favorite place. Poor Louise . . . she always went there to sing, to run away from the frightful snobs of London."

We both laughed. I felt more at ease, though I was startled that my thoughts were fixed on the princess's body.

"What are you doing this afternoon? Intending to bring Saint Peter's closer to Saint Paul's?" she asked, then added, "Lots of luck!"

"Nothing really." Then I recalled it was Saturday. "I've nothing planned. I'm not required at the office till Monday. I must say mass Monday."

22

"Well, come with me today. Rome's not half so boring in June as the cardinal and my mother-in-law like one to believe. Granted, it's no *banquet du roi*, but Rome doesn't curl up and die."

"What do you have in mind?"

"I'm making a movie at Cinecittà. Do you know it?"

"The film?"

"No, Cinecittà. Our so-called Hollywood—it's such a farce. Nothing happens there for months, then a director begins something and every *cretino latino* flocks there, begging to be hired as an extra. I'm no extra though."

"A principessa in a film?" I asked sarcastically. "What does your family say?"

"Don't be tedious. What did they say when your dear mother Louise, a marchesa, strutted onstage and sang the blues!"

"Touché, Dulcinea. You know me head to toe."

"I'd like to."

I laughed, glad to have found someone so quick, so quickly, with whom I could jest.

"How did Louise die? Excuse me for changing the subject, but I read it in *The Times* of course. Well, everyone in Rome who loved her said—"

"She killed herself, Dulcinea."

"*Madonna mia!*" A look of horror spread over the princess's face, and she crossed herself.

"In a sense it was suicide. Mother had lung cancer the last year, or two years. It was so quick, no one really knows. She was in awful pain toward the last so . . ."

"But your father just died too! What was it, six months before?"

"Seven."

"How terrible it must have been for you."

"I'm no little boy."

"Anyone who loses both parents—even if he hates them both—can't but help . . ."

"Father died very mysteriously."

23

"How?"

"I'm in no position to say."

"Oh my God. Did Louise do it?"

"Please . . . don't. Perhaps later when . . . but please not—"

"It must have been horrible for your brother and sisters."

"Yes, for Nicholas and . . . Amy took it the worst. She still writes me the saddest things."

The conversation was getting to me. The princess sighed and pressed her hair. "I'm terribly sorry. It's just that I knew them both, your dear mother especially."

"She was addicted to distalgesic. A very dangerous pain-killer . . . it comes in tablets. At the end she took too many and that was—"

"*Porca miseria,*" whispered the woman. She crossed herself again and quickly changed the subject. "As I was saying, at Cinecittà they're making a movie and I've a very wicked part. I play an 'easy woman.' Well, if Elizabeth Taylor can do it for an Oscar, why can't I? I entertained her right in this house when she was filming *Cleopatra,* so it's not as if we're in competition. I only act for the fun of it. Other ladies of Roma Nera paint, garden, entertain, but though I succumb to those temptations, I hate them all, so I act to keep my wits in order. The cardinal's not at all amused; neither are my relatives and friends."

The princess was rambling obviously to cover the pain she felt for Mother. "I'm deeply grateful for the cardinal's offer of hospitality," I said to alter the mood.

"Unlike most cardinals in the Curia, he's one who truly *likes* Anglicans! I think it's a wise move—your moving out of the Doria and coming here with us!" She laughed and gave me an ironic smile, overly dramatic, which reminded me of my mother and made me shiver.

"Yes . . . I think I'll enjoy living here," I said, trembling as a presentiment of danger rippled through me.

"Don't let my uncle or mother-in-law monopolize

24

your time. I'm telling you, set yourself apart, be aloof. You'll get what you want."

"Redemption?"

"What does Canterbury expect you to get out of Rome anyhow? You're awfully young, you know, to be dealing with Vatican fossils old enough to be your great-grand-father."

"Anglicans aren't as simple . . . to say they want this or want that. Questions of Unity are complex and legion. The most important thing is to keep the dialogue moving."

"Well, it's summer now. Nobody gives a thought to anything but parties, beaches, and villas. Why, I should be moving this very moment! But—you know you *are* frightfully young for the Vatican."

"I shall manage."

"Do dine *en famille* with us at one o'clock. And come for a drink, Rupert, at half past twelve. The prince will be here, and my children—even the one constantly at the piano."

"How many children do you have?"

"Three. Then we'll drive to Cinecittà—no siesta to-day—as I'm needed on the set at three o'clock. It's ghastly, this life I lead."

"What's this film about?"

"Nothing much, just the fall of ancient Mexico. It's a spectacular—one of the wildest ones since Fellini's *Satyricon*."

"Hmmm. I've a friend who wrote a book about the last days of Mexico City."

"Every idiot writes novels nowadays."

"Whose film is it?"

"It's based on some book—wait a minute!"

"Not Alexander Pella's book?"

"You know him? Lord Luxborough?"

"Know him! Is *his* book—God, that's right—I read about it months ago . . ."

25

"In *The Times*. So did I. Well, now it's being shot, and I'm in it."

"He's in town? Alexander? He's one of my best friends."

"He's the guest of Conte Pietrolomini, a cousin of ours by marriage. The count's producing the film. How else do I get in movies? Nepotism is Rome's middle name."

7

Dulcinea Roseazzini was a crepe suzette flambée. So rich a dessert was this lady that I felt giddy leaving her boudoir and had to be led back through the palazzo by her boy. On the way down, a transfer of thoughts made me recall the nun who had served coffee to the cardinal and me two days before. Strange . . . when the house had a doting staff already. I asked the lad about this.

He replied, "The Order of the Annunciation sends two sisters to the house each day, to tend the cardinal's office and help the occasional guest. But nuns *never* wait on table," he told me and laughed nervously, as if the mere thought of such domestic labor were blasphemy.

I was dying to ask the boy if Dulcinea was only curious to get to know the new *straniero* in her house or whether his mistress had more up her sleeve. The fight between my manly attraction to her and my priestly need to resist her forced me outside for air. A foolish idea, for the atmosphere in the street was enough to gag a heart-and-lung machine.

Stubbornly, to punish myself for leaving the house, I turned right in Via di San Teodoro instead of going left toward the ancient Forum, which was what I really wanted to see.

Rome's morning heat was so obnoxious that I only got to the Circus Maximus at the end of our road. I sat on a stone bench to catch my breath. The heat continued to bake me—so much so that, contrary to Anglican conscience which kept telling me "Such a thing shouldn't be done!," I stripped off my collar and oppressive black shirt and exposed my chest to the sun.

I lay back and slept, dreaming about the job I had to perform. We were in the Circus Maximus, and Rome was the fulcrum of the Caesars. There were Christians then, chained together in a long row, awaiting martyrdom. They were chanting some unintelligible language, and shaking their heads and trembling as they watched a race witnessed by no one but themselves. The customary tens of thousands, the *populus romanus*, were nowhere to be seen, and the sun beat down on the prisoners with enough force to kill them. Those who were racing round and round the gigantic ellipse only sped round once, but were added to constantly by newer participants, each wearing a costume more and more contemporary, from all the lands that Christ's gospel ever touched. This race of time's travelers kept advancing closer, closer, closer to the present, in machines ever more meaningful to today. The racing continued, but the Christians in the swelter were hardly at peace and were now fighting with each other to win some moment of glory they'd never see, for each one vanished after completing one lap. But the uproar continued ever fiercer, the machines now of iron and steam, propelled through portals to the dusty arena, chasing each other, causing chaos, virtual war. The noise became deafening, the chained martyrs were weeping, there was absolutely no peace amongst those who professed the same creed. Then the brutal wagons of the twentieth century stormed in, busting walls made of stone, wreaking havoc, polluting, shooting at each other with lethal weapons. Then, the chained line of humans began to wail, then let out a horrible, piercing screech which blasted from the carved stone seats upward to high heaven. . . .

27

I woke in a sweat—staring at the sky—to see a huge jet fire all of its engines. It screamed into the clouds above Rome.

When I checked the time I panicked, for it was after twelve and I certainly did not want to be late for my first lunch with the Roseazzini family. Pushing the curious dream from my mind, I rushed to the palace I now thought of as home.

8

Hardly had I entered my sitting room when the buzzer sounded. It was the footman, announcing *la pranza*. We took a different route and I soon found myself on the main balcony of the palazzo, where the air was miraculously refreshing.

Our march through the third floor had startled me. I had been led past two young people, who were surely Princess Dulcinea's children. The girl was so beautiful I all but bumped into a settee as I gaped at her. She sat at a grand piano, practicing Chopin, and I realized that *she* was the pianist whose playing I'd heard filtering through the walls. Needless to say, she was far more entrancing than the unshaven boy, a year or so older—nineteen perhaps—who was slouching in an armchair. He was clad in the briefest of briefs, a garish black and red floral print, and one of his powerful legs hung loosely from the arm of the chair. His hands were cupping his groin. *"Ciao, Padre,"* was all he said, albeit derisively. The girl said nothing.

The servant looked at me after closing the door behind us, as if he pitied me for ever having seen the two.

He apologized and said: "Ercole always gets through the hot months dressed for the sea."

As I stood on the splendid roofed balcony admiring the view and enjoying the pleasantries exchanged with Prince Guadagno and Princess Dulcinea, and their eldest son Oduardo, the vision of the daughter was foremost in my mind. She looked remarkably like Vivienne . . . the woman to whom I'd been engaged five years ago. Vivienne had been an actress, very much "into" Jayne Mansfield, whose image she tried to resurrect. Strange—as I walked away from Dulcinea's daughter I couldn't help thinking of both the woman I used to love—the woman who died by taking her own life—and the Hollywood star from the 1950s who died so horribly. Thus, to clear my mind of these morbid thoughts, I heard myself asking about the young *principessina* who was still playing the piano.

I was surprised that her father was pleased by my interest. "She's just eighteen," he stated and toasted her with his martini rosso. "Serafina studies at the Accademia di Santa Cecilia. She plays well. She recently began composing."

"After years of pleading with her, we've finally talked her into giving a concert this autumn," her mother admitted proudly.

"If you should be here, Reverend, we'd be honored by your presence," Oduardo added.

"Rupert's sidetracked already, can't you tell?" Dulcinea laughed softly. "I'm taking him to Cinecittà this afternoon. I think it'll do him good to see the *other* side of Rome."

"Not that our film world is booming, as it was ten years ago," the prince countered. Guadagno seemed to be tolerating his wife's interference in my affairs, but he cautioned, "You mustn't let such activities occupy you too much, especially now, as I find my best work's done in summer, when everyone's left the city. It's the only time

29

Society calms down enough to let one think a creative thought."

"Rome's frightful for mental pursuits," the princess retorted. "Guadagno's right. *Some* try to plan next year's strategy this summer."

"But as soon as autumn comes . . . the Church, diplomacy, Society, and government—when there is one—fight for one's attention." Oduardo joked.

"And it takes a saint to withstand it all," Dulcinea declared.

"Now we have the extra worry—no small one either—of this violence and . . . *revolution!*" The prince stated the last word with such loathing nobody dared to speak. He was staring at his heir.

At twenty-four Oduardo obviously was a gentleman. Not much younger than myself, I realized. He was properly dressed in a light linen suit, and his brown hair neatly parted and combed back. At that instant Ercole walked in, looking obscene in nothing but those tight briefs. The contrast between the brothers was embarrassing, and Oduardo turned his back. I couldn't help noticing how weak, how almost pitiful, the elder appeared against the virile strength of his nearly nude brother.

The prince reacted immediately: "How dare you come out like this! If you wish to join us, put on something decent instantly, or find yourself a workers' *trattoria!*" He glared at Ercole, who patted Oduardo teasingly on the behind then turned and left us in peace.

Guadagno apologized to me. His wife was acutely embarrassed and stated: "Ercole's been troubling us for years. Thank God Oduardo shares our ideas."

The prince continued: "You've seen already that the princess and I are tolerant, but many in Rome find us too tolerant. We try to live in this century, but the longer you stay in Rome, the better you'll understand how much tension this causes in families of standing. But we're not a house to take tradition lightly, even though one of our sons has strayed."

The episode on the balcony set an insalubrious tone for the meal. Suddenly, everything was serious. Conversation was delicately polite, most painful. It reminded me of England, those multifarious dinners where one dare but ask the most impersonal question—but where everyone always seems to ask the question considered most private!

"Ercole used to be the *bel-ragazzo* of Rome," the prince said over his prosciutto and melon, "but now he exemplifies Rome's futile attempt to pave the way to the twenty-first century. Such assininity. Let New York lead the world astray. I can do nothing with Ercole; I've all but lost my patience."

This statement made me most uncomfortable, not because it sounded like my late father but because it reminded me of Father at all. I looked quickly from face to face, from the prince to his wife to Oduardo to Serafina. The lovely girl seemed so exceedingly shy. The combination of sandy blond hair, hazel eyes, and olive skin was irresistible; I could not help staring at her. Beauty is such a tonic for deadly conversation.

"What do you actually plan to *do* with the Vatican?" Princess Dulcinea asked unceremoniously, mentioning the first thing that came to her mind to change the subject.

All ears were tuned, so I risked stating: "Rome still does not recognize Anglican Orders as valid. This is juridical and runs through centuries of debate between Canterbury and Rome. The 1896 bull 'Apostolicae Curae' stated that, '*We pronounce and declare that ordinations performed according to the Anglican rite have been and are absolutely null and utterly void.*'"

"Yes, but," the prince countered, "there has been quite a reversal of opinion, and the said bull now is recognized as not having arisen with international diplomacy high in the Vatican's mind. Much progress between the two hierarchies has been seen of late."

"Granted, but it still remains for the Vatican to recognize Anglican Orders as valid," I repeated, keen to make the point to this prince of Rome who, until its recent abolition, had been a member of the papal Noble Guard. I sensed that the man was a supporter of honest dialogue and was gladdened that a smile crossed his face.

"To Unity," he responded and raised his glass of *vino bianco*.

"But how can this young man hope to penetrate the thick skull of the Curia?" demanded the princess. "He's only a child—look at him."

"Don't be absurd, Dulcinea. Anyhow, youth has ways forgotten by those of us no longer in our prime," countered Guadagno. He smiled broadly and let it be known to all that he was only teasing his wife.

"What ways?" The princess was angry, not playing lightheartedly at all. "You, you, and you," she pointed from Oduardo to Serafina to myself. "What can three youthful sprites like you *do* to change this impervious world? Look pretty, flatter your way through Society, through the Church, right through the Pearly Gates? How streamlined."

"At least we're not like Ercole, Mama," Oduardo stated, then beamed across the centerpiece to his sister. Serafina, visibly unnerved by the discussion, looked down in distaste, as if the words had spilt too much salt on her *cotoletta milanese*.

"Well, one thing which would amuse everyone in Rome, and in the whole Anglican Communion, would be to do what the pope did in 1965 when he withdrew the anathemas and curses against the Eastern Orthodox Church after nine hundred years of rupture." The prince, obviously in his element, took great pride in exposing his penchant for the obscure anecdote.

His wife suddenly lost her rancor when she sensed how humorous her husband was being, pulled at a strap beneath her cream satin dress, and began playing with her pearls. "Do tell us, Guadagno, *how* to amuse such a large part of the world."

"There are two ways," the prince informed us. "First, one could convince the Vatican to give England back to the English, since it has belonged to the pope since 1213."

"*Cosa?*" Oduardo practically shouted. "*Que buffo!*"

"Theoretically. But King John did give England to Pope Innocent III and England has never officially been returned."

"That could be arranged," the princess laughed. "Make note of it, Rupert. It could make you Archbishop of Canterbury, not to mention win you the Nobel Prize for Peace."

The whole table laughed. I especially noted Serafina was smiling kindly at me.

"Secondly," Guadagno continued as the table was being cleared for the *dolce*, "I think the pope should send a Golden Rose to Queen Elizabeth the Second."

"What would Her Majesty do . . ." I tried to ask.

"This would signify that the anathemas and curses directed against the British Isles since 1570, when Pope Pius the Fifth officially 'excommunicated and dethroned' Queen Elizabeth the First, were now a thing of the past and 'committed to oblivion.'"

"And a rose made of gold would *do* all that?" Oduardo asked.

"A *rosa d'oro* is never given lightly. It would signify much—as it need not be given in silence."

Principe Guadagno's cultured wit was impressive. Having the chance to discuss things with him informally at table was to become a joy I looked forward to greatly. In many ways, he reminded me of my dear grandfather, though Guadagno was only fifty years old. Such casual urbanity and demeanor made me all the more thankful I had chosen not to reside alone in Palazzo Doria but had accepted the cardinal's kind offer.

9

Everyone in Rome was petrified of terrorists, so people traveled about the city as unostentatiously as possible. This surprised me at first, accustomed as I was to London's thousands of grand limousines. I must say, I was disappointed that our drive to Cinecittà was neither chauffeured nor in a car big enough for a man to stretch his legs. The automobile, what the Italians call a *cinque-cento* (a "500"), was red and no bigger than a Mini.

The princess drove, gossiping all the way along Via Appia Nuova and Via Tuscolana, till we passed through the gate to "the Film City." She was wearing the same satin dress, but had exchanged her double strand of pearls for costume jewelry. Her bright red lipstick and the way her upper lip came to a virtual point were most interesting to watch as she spoke. As often as she could she turned to me, and her blue eyes were animated and large. We discussed Canterbury and love—two incongruous topics—as if my answers and her questions about my "adventures in Kent" were bandied about by human beings other than ourselves.

"But love for the Lord is in no way connected to love as it still flourishes in high society," Dulcinea stated cattily.

"Yes, but Canterbury was *founded* by Rome. During the Crusades it was a favorite watering place between London and the Continent. People called it miniature Rome."

"The Crusades certainly didn't teach brother to love brother! Look at this film I'm making. The Conquest of Mexico *was* a Crusade and look what it did! You know, you'd be perfect for the Spanish priest who plants the crucifix in Mexican soil."

"What? Have me signify the downfall of the Aztecs?" I asked.

"But the priest hasn't been cast yet," she retorted. "Yes, it's you—you and that devilish beard." And the princess stopped by the studio and opened the door. "I'm getting you a part in this movie. There'll be no objection if you're as good a friend of Luxborough as you claim to be. How you could be though, I can't figure out. You didn't even know he was in Rome!"

As soon as we were allowed in the huge studio, people rushed toward the princess from all directions. "Get your paws off me," she shouted half seriously. "Luxborough—where's Lord Luxborough? Bring him to me immediately!"

The change in her personality was total. A moment before, the woman had been giving all her attention to me, but the sudden activity about her turned her within seconds into "the star." It was all *la signora principessa è arrivata,*" and she turned cold as ice to me, or so it seemed.

"*Vieni qua*—we must make you up—*Signora Principessa—Principessa.*"

Everyone was shouting at once, like sports fans lurking round a lottery.

I spied a blond and handsome mop of hair making its way toward me. My childhood friend, Alexander Pella, the Earl of Luxborough, suddenly noticed me, and we ran and embraced like lost brothers. This set the throng about Dulcinea gabbing more raucously than before.

The rest of the afternoon went by in a blur. Alexander, as delighted to find a familiar face in Rome as I, poured out a torrent of worries, as if making confession. Principally, he was upset about Conte Pietrolomini who was producing the film. Though Alexander had written the film script from his novel *Moctezuma* he was nervous about the book's "vision being lost." He complained it would have been, had he not found a brilliant set designer and, above all, an empathic director.

I was totally captivated by this world of ancient Mexico re-created for the film *Moctezuma*. The huge causeway leading across Texcuco Lagoon to the Aztec capital had been constructed in miniature for special effects. With no difficulty one could see the fabulous city called Tenochtitlán rising from the water like a primordial Venice, steaming as Mount Popocatépetl smoked in the distance.

The suicidal mentality of Moctezuma himself had been fiendishly well re-created by the uncanny crew; walking through the emperor's private chamber in the Aztec palace gave me the creeps. Actors kept slinking about on tiptoe, rustling rare exotic feathers, wearing garlands of priceless orchids, belts of heavy gold.

In this sultry atmosphere of degradation, the wanton culture that allowed such a monster as the Catholic conquistador Cortés to ruin what had taken centuries to bring to such eerie flower, my thoughts turned toward *Roma catholica*, to the papacy's macabre past. I confessed to my friend that I'd been sent to the Vatican as a diplomat but admitted having doubts about being able to do my job with any success. "I only had a month of training for this. Much more qualified priests spend lifetimes in Ecumenism, yet I beat them all. The jealousy, Alexander, the gossip in London about me was bestial. I begged the archbishop to consider a more mature man. The huge amount of historical material since Henry the Eighth seemed totally beyond my means. Thank God I'd read a bit of Italian at Cambridge. Speaking the language at least is one point in my favor."

"How noble of you to admit it, Broxbourne. But, you're far more intelligent than your reticence lets you say. Gossip and scandal, what do they do but stimulate you? You haven't changed that much—just because Your Lordship's now an Anglican priest!"

"I've doubts as to my ministry, Alexander! If you just knew half of them . . ."

"No thanks, I've my own. Life goes on, to change the subject. Anyway, I know you don't really *believe* in Christ."

"Don't be blasphemous. *You're* the pagan. You always were. Those discussions we had when you were at Westminster . . ."

"And you at King's Canterbury . . . proved what? So, my father was murdered, and so was the woman I loved. What little faith in Christ I had before Marina died was shattered totally at Heathrow that night. Ah, but wasn't it you who always said, 'Death is what unites us'? Your fiancée drowned herself, didn't she? Well, mine—mine was shot. You're perfectly right, Broxbourne: I'm *pagan*. I knew someday I'd arrive in Rome. Now, alas, so have you. Yet we must ask, What are we doing here? Tell me, tell me about this Christ you pledged to love."

For the first time since ordination, I was totally at a loss to express anything resembling belief in Jesus Christ. Was Alexander too sincere, too beloved a friend? Was it that he saw through me? Why was I suddenly afraid to give voice to any faith? Was superstitious conscience warning me against my God? The spiritual reserves I retained for my job—had they been lessened by speaking so frequently about them? This was so unnerving, this film set of total Aztec paganism. My thoughts kept trying to turn to the eventual meeting I'd be having with His Holiness the pope.

I sensed that Alexander was grappling with a dangerous spirit in himself, which I felt incapable of coping with. I wanted to shy away, to return to my rooms near the Forum.

Luxborough sensed my dread when I couldn't verbalize the simplest answer to his question. Each second crawled by and I seemed all the more inadequate, not only as a priest but as a friend.

Finally, after he had stared through me for what

37

seemed an eternity—as all I kept seeing were flashes of gaudy plumage and masks of beaten gold—Alexander put his hands on my shoulders and said, "I'm sorry. I do understand. Rome hit me very hard at first, too. I've been here eight weeks. The place is very strange."

"We'll have time to talk, I hope."

"Of course, Rupert. I look forward to it. I need somebody with a brain, an English one, with whom I can exchange a few profundities, as well as an even greater amount of inanities. But, I've also an idea for you. Tomorrow . . . are you free?"

"I am. Why?"

"We're shooting tomorrow and we do need a bloke like you to be our conquistador priest, to—"

"You want *me* in your ruddy film?" But this expression was instantly checked in my mind. Since I had failed to give my friend a valid answer about my faith, it only was civil to do him this small favor. A peace gesture, at any rate. Maybe my "priestliness" could be of some use to him, even if it was only playacting. I accepted.

"Smashing! It's simple, really. All you'll do is be the first Spaniard to step on Mexican soil. You'll carry a great jeweled cross and plant it in the sand of the beach. You'll signify the commencement of the Christian Conquest."

The young author beamed strangely, but my mind was far away. The responsibility of carrying the Cross *anywhere* suddenly terrified me. All I could say in reply was, "You hardly can realize . . . what it is you ask of me."

10

I spent the rest of the afternoon immersed in the catholicization of the Aztecs and watching Dulcinea Roseazzini posturing as a bawd in fight after fight with Cortés, in take after take. I was totally exhausted and even more unsettled when the principessa came out from under makeup and looked on dazedly as she proceeded to invite a huge cast home to dine. Why she wasn't tired from brawling so with Cortés, who kept saying her morals were worse than any Mexican heathen's, I'll never know. The real-life social hostess just wallowed in it. The shooting had invigorated her.

As the princess drove us home I asked if she minded playacting the conqueror's tart, when everyone who read *Moctezuma* realized the author wasn't historically accurate. She laughed. "So it's not historically accurate; *nothing* is in Rome. That's the first thing any Roman learns."

Two hours after leaving Cinecittà, everybody reassembled in Palazzo Roseazzini. Aside from Ercole, the whole family and many others—were present, this meaning a salient mélange of the film world and *Roma Nera*. The princess had let all her friends at the studio but me know that this Saturday evening was the Dowager Principessa Aurora's seventy-fifth birthday. The Ferrucci, Civitali, Mimabue, Collemandina, Roseazzini, Monsignani and Pietrolomini families had turned out in force, not to mention many other members of the aristocracy and two dozen cardinals who came to show their respect to the sister of Cardinal Arcadio.

I daresay I wasn't in the least prepared for such an evening. Contrary to what everybody told me in London— that the Roman worlds of Celluloid and Society never mix—Dulcinea mixed them and mixed them well.

The staff managed to feed a hundred on the huge third floor balcony. It was illuminated by large mediaeval torches, and the space easily could have held more. Another three hundred and fifty guests passed through the house before midnight.

The evening was marvelous, and I mention it only because I was honored to have the chance to speak alone, for the first time, with Serafina, the lady who soon will be my wife. That night I understood why she had been practicing the piano so industriously. Her father had asked her to play the larghetto of the First Piano Concerto by Chopin for her grandmother, as it was one of Princess Aurora's favorite compositions.

The gathering of people in the frescoed music salon, the second largest reception room on the palace's first floor, was truly majestic. The faces were distinguished and attentive, as into the lovely beige chamber walked the girl. It was at that moment that I fell in love with Serafina

Again, on seeing her, I couldn't help but think of hapless Vivienne. Damn—why must I think of the dead right now? I tried hard to focus on the beautiful form before me, but there was Vivienne walking across the inlaid marble floor, a spectre from a past I never would forget.

I'd become light-headed from the wine. The blood was all in my feet. I backed through the crowd and leaned against a pilaster of malachite to catch my breath, never once taking my eyes off Serafina.

Her figure was so sensual I almost couldn't bear it. The 1950s-style glittery gray gown squeezed her tightly and very nearly bound her ankles together. Thank God she stopped moving and sat at the piano and, after what seemed an eternity, began to play. I held my breath, afraid her playing would be less than I expected. However, so consummate a pianist was she—truly of the highest caliber—and such a hypnotic one, that she held the audience in a spell. The majestic harmonies of the melancholy composition were not lost on anyone in that room.

When the long burst of applause subsided, Principessa Aurora, gowned in black as before, formally received her guests and their birthday wishes. In the commotion, I sought out the cardinal as I felt I must speak with him about his beautiful niece. There was something almost tragic about this girl who played so masterfully, this woman so young yet so mature, so protected by her family—sequestered, one might say, or so I surmised.

When I did find His Eminence, he was walking up the main staircase with my friend Luxborough. "Oh, here comes the marquess," Alexander stated to annoy me, and it did tremendously. I retorted that I didn't want one word mentioned in Rome about my title, and that was that.

Alexander smirked, so out of politeness to the cardinal I apologized. I reminded my friend that I hoped he'd join me after the filming tomorrow, so that we might go to the Basilica of Saint Paul's-without-the-Walls. Mass was to be celebrated by His Holiness.

Out of revenge against Alexander's last remark and also to deal a blow to his purported paganism, I mentioned that His Eminence also would be attending. The cardinal was glaring at Alexander, whom he had been interrogating about Dulcinea's "dramatic activities," so the poor chap hardly could refuse to accept to attend mass with me, pagan or not.

I had all but forgotten that I wished to tell Monsignani something, when he invited us to his penthouse "for the view and a touch of Gemma d'Abeto." The Abbot's Gem turned out to be one of the most superb liqueurs of the Continent, a delicious delight which the cardinal had been given by the monastery of Santissima Annunciata of Florence, which produces it at one of their properties in the Tuscan countryside. The drink helped my memory considerably, and I recalled I wanted to ask His Eminence about his talented niece.

For Alexander's edification also—no male could be blind to the girl's charms—the cardinal said that even though Principe Guadagno was well-intentioned and convinced that he was a modern father, it was common knowledge in Rome that the prince was one of the very few who refused to let their daughters go out unescorted.

"Escorted by whom?" Alexander couldn't help asking.

41

"By a mature woman," the cardinal replied sternly. And to lighten the message, His Eminence gave us another shot of the Gem. "With his boys he's even worse. It troubles me greatly. I say the rosary every night for those two, but God works in strange ways. Oduardo is turning into a well-rounded man—not gifted, but capable. His father's training him to take over the family's not inconsiderable assets. This, of course, has displeased young Ercole all his life—that his father, being of the old school, believes in primogeniture. But Ercole is the smartest this family's ever produced. He always sees through the prince's ruses. Right now, though, I daresay I'm greatly at fault. Ercole and I used to be like father and son. He always came to my rooms to talk, but suddenly . . . two years ago . . . he stopped."

"Why?" Alexander asked boldly. "Did your being a cardinal have anything to do with it?"

"Probably. Of course two years ago he still was in school. Then he entered the University of Rome, though now he doesn't attend. Every single time I've attempted to discuss things with him, he's become ruder and ruder. I fear to say this, but I almost think the boy's soul is *possessed*."

"Possessed? By what?" Luxborough couldn't help asking.

"Something's lethal in the air in Italy now. Nobody yet, though, has dared to say it's demonic possession, but evil can and will abrogate all the goodness built up through the centuries. God knows, the concept of the family as institution has been undermined irreparably since the war; yet our nobility at least is the greatest defender of family life, simply because the family must continue or else the whole network of estates we hold will fall into the hands of—well—communists! The *nobiluomo* or *-donna* still own vast amounts of Italian territory and serve as a buffer against changes forced on the land by mechanization. And this is to say nothing of the even more stupid changes attempted by the government . . ."

42

"These demons you mention," Alexander was keen on pursuing his point. "Are they rejuvenated spirits from pre-Christian times, or new forces at work, whose origin no one knows?"

"I think they're both, for Christianity—not just Catholicism—certainly is on the wane in this country," replied the cardinal gravely.

"And when Rome falls, so falls the world," I heard myself saying though I was shocked at my words, which seemed to slip off the balcony and fall amongst the rubble of the Imperial Palatine of the Caesars.

"Something definitely is creeping toward Rome. The more I study the Scriptures, the more concerned I get. I think we're witnessing the slow buildup preparatory to the coming of the Antichrist." The cardinal crossed himself and said, *"Santa Maria, abbi pietà di noi."*

"How do you mean?" I asked incredulously.

"Prophecies—Daniel and Revelations—hold the key. Satan must come, incarnate in man, and this evil being will be the Antichrist long foretold. He will rise to power in Rome. He will not be pope but will completely destroy the Church as we know it. Abolish it, illegalize it! Europe again is on the ascent—America has lost her chance. These terrorist activities and rumblings of violence are but the merest premonitions. Europe will be forced to unite, the center will be Rome, and the leader will die, then rise from the dead—literally!—as the incarnation of the Devil. United Europe, bound in chains, will be marched toward Jerusalem, but by this monster, and there will occur, without the holy walls, the forecast war: Armageddon. The archangel Michael will lead the Lord's hosts, and Christ will vanquish the Fiend. The Bible foretells this. Read Daniel, read Revelations."

Alexander and I were dumbstruck. Never in my life had I heard such things spoken by someone of such ecclesiastical authority. It suddenly hit me we had heard just too much. I looked from Alexander to the cardinal to the Col-

43

osseum across the ruins of the Forum, and felt a chill shake the whole of my body. I wanted to leave the balcony, to rejoin the party downstairs, but could not make my legs move. Likewise Alexander was unable to say a word.

"We must pray; we must wage war together," His Eminence continued, "so that the teachings of Christ are not subject to derision or worse. The Antichrist will be far more shrewd, far more intelligent, far more suave than *any* Machiavelli—due to his really being Satan become man—and thus he will move toward his wicked goal easily, destroying all that we cherish in this world."

"My God," breathed Alexander, speaking for me, too. "Is there any chance that the Holy Spirit which protects the Vatican could become so weakened by the current decrease in worship of the Lord that it could lay the pope himself open to demonic possession? Perhaps the time could come when the Holy Father himself could become schismatic and heretical, yet nobody would dare—would you cardinals dare?—utter words of reproach to him, out of fear of provoking an even more rash encyclical than any ever passed down from the papal throne. Perhaps the pope could try to excommunicate the *whole* Church, laymen, priests, bishops, everyone of the whole wide world!"

As I listened to this shocking statement, I felt Alexander was trying to outrage Monsignani but was surprised that the cardinal kept shaking his head. I felt that the two had carried the conversation beyond the limits of possibility, but since they both refused to act as though they were beyond the edge *I* suddenly felt that I was the one off balance, that I had missed the vital thread of the argument and had been left behind.

"But," Alexander kept on, to my distress, "perhaps the whole Church has been sinning against its Self incessantly—and thereby against God—ever since the idea of Petrine succession and papal infallibility first was conceived. Perhaps these ideas *are* an affront to the Holy Spirit. Yet, if these ideas are sins but have been allowed to perpetuate, then who, may I ask, who is the spirit of the Church? Is God . . . or the Devil?"

"Oh, Alexander!" This last remark revolted me and I retorted: "Ever since childhood you've been asking vile, idiotic questions. Where have they got you but nowhere?" To the cardinal I explained, "Luxborough's always felt it necessary to pose queries as insane as these for no apparent reason than to air his insecure vanity."

But His Eminence wiped his forehead and looked worried as he said, "No—no, my young Lords. Such questions are vital and most necessary. Someone has to pose them. It's just that today . . . so few seem to care."

11

As I looked for the still-full moon, which momentarily hid behind a cloud, a soft voice came round the corner of the terrace. I was both relieved and excited to see Serafina, whose arrival took the eldritch edge off her uncle's words. The cardinal in his crimson robes, which in the dark seemed the color of coagulating blood, suddenly made me fear the man more than I feared his message. Yet the touch of the lovely girl's hand, offered to all of us, drove any sort of fear from me.

Again Alexander and the cardinal retreated heavily into the discussion of the Antichrist, so I seized the opportunity to talk with Serafina. It didn't seem rude that we moved a short distance away, to a stone bench beside an ancient sarcophagus filled with geraniums. Immediately I found myself sincerely praising her performance of Chopin and asking how long had she been studying the piano. I ached to speak to her in Italian, but she was eager to demonstrate her command of English. She laughed, admitting she'd once had a nanny from Salisbury.

In my nervousness, I asked her about the rather eccentric dress she was wearing. I couldn't help wondering if it was a sign of haughty lèse majesté or merely rebellion against her family. She giggled like a schoolgirl and said: "I found it in some junk shop. It really *was* made in the fifties."

"It fits you perfectly," I commented, then turned away in embarrassment.

"He's the novelist—the one who wrote *Moctezuma* which Mama's acting in—isn't he?" Serafina changed the subject and nodded toward Alexander. "He's an earl, isn't he? I haven't seen him before."

"Someday he'll be Duke of Brendon."

"He's beautiful. His profile is so classic."

"He's even got brains, sometimes."

"So why does he write?"

"Why do you play piano?"

"Why are *you* a priest? That's the silliest of them all! You're a *marchese*." Serafina used the Italian form of the word as if reproaching my ever becoming ordained. "You're strange."

I didn't know what to say. Italians were so brash at times; no wonder Alexander hadn't offended the cardinal. But this girl's questions, I felt, were not really condemnatory but simply nosy. Her interest in me made me rather excited.

"You were mum at table today," I said.

"Papa makes us all that way. Ercole didn't even show. He . . ." she started, but checked herself.

"Do you like your brother?"

The woman looked at me oddly wondering what prompted such a personal question, but did not answer. Instead, she asked: "Why did you really come to Rome? Are you hunting a wife?"

This startled me. Serafina quickly stood and giggled. "Anglican priests can marry! It's sinful! How can you be a man of God, if you soil yourself with the blood of a woman?"

46

With that last question, which left me speechless, the girl hurried toward Lord Luxborough and the cardinal. She held out her hand to say good night, and I was green with envy when Alexander squeezed it too long, then kissed it. The cardinal let himself be kissed on both cheeks, then raised his right hand as if giving benediction. He watched till his niece vanished from sight.

I ambled slowly toward the two, hoping they would now return to the party. Coming into their discussion cold, I heard His Eminence dramatically say: "Man said that he wanted to go to the moon. Man believed that he could do it. Then man went to the moon to show that he could do it . . . for man didn't believe in himself."

The silence on the terrace was commanding. After those words nobody breathed a sound. Then, a truly horrifying thing happened.

A colossal swarm of bees—improbable at this hour of the night—descended from nowhere onto the house. The horde—making a terrible buzzing noise—seemed to swoop from the Palatine, perhaps from some lost subterranean room of the palace of Caesar Augustus. The twisting ball of insects, a good thirty feet in diameter, tumbled toward us through the moonlight, a mass of glistening wings like great sparkling flakes of hard-driven snow. With a dash, we three rushed to the cardinal's library and slammed the sliding glass door. As we did so, I heard ladies screaming on the main balcony below and doors closing all over the palazzo.

When the swarm was out of sight, I ventured to the terrace and was taken aback to see the bees flying like mad about a chimney midway in the cardinal's roof. The noise was alarming, and I knew instinctively that something must be done quickly to prevent a rush of bees into the house.

Hastening to tell His Eminence, I suggested we build a fire to smoke them away. But he was blanched, seated on a chaise, and kept ringing for a butler. However, the cardinal quickly was becoming livid, so I asked if he'd been stung. He pointed to his right hand above his priceless amethyst ring, which he was trying to remove with difficulty. The hand, already swelling, had just been bitten. Alexander was stepping on a bee.

"Don't—don't kill it!" the cardinal gasped. *"Porta male!* Don't you see it's an evil omen?"

"But . . ." Alexander did not finish; the bee was already dead. More were buzzing inside the fireplace.

An old valet, one I'd never seen, rushed in and appeared to revive His Eminence with his presence.

"We must leave at once—this is dreadful—I need ointment—where's Dulcinea?" Arcadio was in a state. "Roberto, a fire. Build one immediately—hot as the devil. These monsters must be removed tonight. *Porta male."*

The cardinal stood, smarting from the sting and the situation, and held his swelling hand. "On Aurora's birthday—it's a sign I tell you—a sign! What else could do the unnatural? Bees don't fly at night! It's impossible—unless they were goaded by evil spirits . . ."

We were leading the Prince of the Church through various chambers, then down deserted marble stairs. "Only once in my life have I heard of it . . . and then it boded no good. My poor grandmother, God keep her soul, I shall never forget her though I was such a little boy. Aurora was eight and I four, yet this very thing happened in Fiesole. We had a house with a view of all Florence and one summer night—the arrival of bees in daylight bodes fortune—they arrived in a terrible swarm, just like now. And dear Grandmama had a fit and kept shouting, 'The end of one of the family is near! Someone must die!' Of that she was certain. Shortly thereafter, perhaps a month, perhaps more, *she* died—dear Grandmama died. Oh, God help us! *Santa Maria e tutti i santi.* What force of blackness is at work this strange night?"

12

The bizarre events of Saturday kept me awake long toward dawn. I had been so preoccupied with the inhabitants of the Palazzo Roseazzini as well as my part as a conquistador priest, that I all but forgot my promise to celebrate the Eucharist at All Saints near the Spanish Steps next morning. So, before retiring I arranged for a taxi to pick me up early Sunday, and for the same one to fetch me once Communion was over in order that I might reach Cinecittà in time to playact whatever nonsense Principessa Dulcinea had arranged.

As I stood at the altar of the Anglican Church, the words of Cardinal Arcadio came back to haunt me, words of preoccupation with forthcoming doom, words of unmitigated superstition. Contrary to doctrinal teaching, the fact that the cardinal wasn't the sort of man of the cloth one assumes a member of the Curia to be made me trust him more. Yet that didn't lessen the impact of the weird experiences of the day before.

Cogitation always makes me feel unsettled, and ever more so as I gazed from the altar to the group of English-speaking communicants so properly seated in their pews. The thought of being an actor—even as a priest—struck me forcefully; I felt doubly conscious, standing before this "audience," as I raised the Host to the Lord.

The old notion that I wasn't fit to be in such a privileged spiritual position once again began to plague me. For a moment, with the ciborium aloft, I thought I was back in London, my relationship to Christ spinning in ever more dizzying circles. But thank God this sensation vanished when I partook of the Bread and then drank of the Wine.

Without allowing myself the proper interval after Communion to chat with parishioners—there were a few important ones I hadn't met—I dashed out and taxied through Rome to Cinecittà.

Luxburough met me promptly at the door. With him was the film's director—a tall, exceptionally handsome, curly-haired chap from the New Wave of Berlin, named Boch-mann—who gave me a five-minute summary of my "action." Simple it was; all I had to do was walk down a gangplank and plant a great gem-encrusted crucifix in the soil for Spain.

The director was one of those excitable types I found sickening in London, the hyperenergized "artiste" who falls all over one with praise for the purpose of putting one in the mood he wants. Alexander, though, looked on with great delight as Bochmann kept saying my black beard was "perfect," and that I had "outrageous, evil-looking eyes." He even had the gall to ask if I seduced boys by hypnotizing them! Then he came out with the ultimate cliché: that I looked "just like Rasputin." To that I snapped, "I didn't realize you were that old."

Alexander led me away as the director laughed; I'm sure he thought my line was meant in jest. I asked Lux-burough, as soon as he guided me to Makeup, where he ever found such a character. He didn't apologize but only said the German was very talented and was "doing wonders interpreting my book." So be it.

The makeup crew was Roman, so as I stripped and dressed and was painted amidst a chorus of chatter, I felt a right fool. Alexander stayed to chat. Something weighty was on his mind. He admitted pondering the cardinal's words, too. "I even read Daniel last night."

"You mean you allow a Bible in your house?"

"It's Pietrolomini's. I'm his guest. You know his wife, Roxanna—she's my agent. Anyway, I've been wanting to speak with you again about your spiritual beliefs, Rupert."

"I don't have any," I joked.

"Rubbish! But they are quite tenuous."

"So."

50

"I *hate* Christianity, Rupert! I can't tell you how much it revolts me now. Being in Rome's been torture to me."

I smirked. "Only because you're being pulled to Christ all the time. It *is* the Apostolic See."

"Don't be glib. I wanted to tell you the last night in London when we saw each other—at Covent Garden when my lover Marina Novikova was dancing her last performance—that I wanted to arrange to see you then. But after her funeral, when I went back to Somerset and Shrove Tor to recover, I telephoned you and . . . where were you?"

"I was preparing for my ordination. Why didn't you come to that? I invited you. You see, we're even."

"Why did you become an Anglican priest, Rupert?"

"Oh just for the dress-up of it all." Just then I glanced at the makeup mirror and saw that a diabolic transformation had occurred. The reflection sent a shiver down my naked back.

"You're a deviate, Rupert. Just like I am. I don't mean because we're titled, but both of us are cursed by some inexplicable need to translate our spirits' transgressions." Then he paused, and took me by the shoulders: "Rupert, admit something to me. I only ask this out of love for you. Did . . . did you *kill* your father?"

No one was in the room at that moment, but I looked about anyway, then uttered: "Mother did. Mother poisoned him. It wasn't a stroke as everyone was made to believe."

"But why?"

"Heavens, Alexander, stop plaguing me!"

"Why did she do it?"

"Jealousy, Luxborough, jealousy! Dear God and it . . . it was aimed against *me*."

"You?"

Just then a pretty director's aide stuck her head in and said, "The Reverend Broxbourne has five more minutes. Please come to set thirteen."

"Come, let's find it." Alexander spoke warmly and

51

put his hands on my head like a father. I followed him to set thirteen.

As a sedative for the worrisome questions posed with no warning, the young earl thought he would calm me by switching to the battle between the Christian and pagan, which his own roving intellect was fighting. Again he condemned the former as having harmed more than helped the civilized world.

As we were walking through the unused set of Moctezuma's private apartments he admitted: "I embrace the pantheon of ancient Greece, and I haven't come to do this simply by poetics, though I do draw inspiration from the Hellenes, but I now *worship* the gods. From most mortal eyes . . . they stay hidden . . . and never once deign to show their faces."

"You've *seen* these gods, I suppose," I asked sarcastically.

Alexander answered boldly: "In Greece, where I ended up after Somerset. I had to flee somewhere to restore myself after watching the woman I loved be buried. Yes, Rupert, I saw them in Greece."

"*Explain* them then!"

"I can't put it into words, Rupert."

"You call yourself a writer, an explorer of the soul, who interrogates the beliefs of others and sets them down in print, yet you can't even describe what's happening inside you?"

"Give me time, please . . ."

"That's what they all say."

"Oh, sod off with your fake Christianity. Scoff, spout rubbish, I don't care. I'm telling you, Greece gave me something alive, though this something was being written about thousands of years ago. And truly, my friend, what Greece gives *isn't* your God the Christ!"

13

After ten useless takes, we broke for a crude box-lunch, which was served on the set. It did nothing to alleviate the anxiety that the shooting of the film produced in me. I hated it, felt I was wasting my time and everybody else's. Furthermore, the "simple" task of walking down a gang-plank with a weighty cross of gold was not as facile as I'd imagined.

I was pressured into speaking with a slew of uncouth people who badgered me with personal and ridiculous questions. The worst of the lot was the director, Boch-mann, who should have known better but obviously did not—or didn't care. He was the type who wanted to know everything about one at one sitting.

In this jungle of arc lamps, huge black cables, crates, props, boxes, and rubbish, sat about twenty people, all of whom ate like hogs at a feed. Apparently, bad manners were not in the least bit offensive. Talking nonstop, their mouths stuffed with pasta, they appeared fanatically interested in me. Their interrogation of me was egged on by Alexander, who kept feeding the crew bogus information when I refused to answer. None of them believed I was a priest, which infuriated me. I began to wonder if I had gone too far this time for the sake of friendship. Perhaps I should have been more aloof, more "priestly" with my old friend.

Bochmann reinforced my doubts by taking great pride (after I explained as hastily as possible my mission in Rome) in denouncing my professional intentions. He said, "As far as I'm concerned, your two Churches of Canter-bury and Rome—plus the whole Lutheran Church of Ger-many—are all useless as tits on a bull."

53

Then an actress dressed as an Aztec slave added, "'At's right—a *papal* bull."

"Unity won't do a single soul a bit of good," Bochmann, with all his Nordic erudition, continued, "since it's what the individual believes inside that guides his life and not what senseless organizations such as churches seem to preach."

"Yah," posited twenty freethinking voices.

"Anyhow, if this Unity rubbish comes to an 'ead, when all the bleddy Anglicans and all the soddin' Catholics and all the flippin' Buddhists and flamin' 'indus are at the point of being one, I wanna referendum, 'cause I don't know if it's such a good thing after all. I wanna be *consulted*—if it's to 'appen," the same Aztec slave girl added with great illogical gusto, in a cockney voice from a pugilistic part of London.

"Well, give us a self-addressed envelope, luv, and we'll stick you on the list and post you a bleeding form," I replied and stood to leave this heinous group.

"Pooh pooh, Father's upset. Aw, I'm awful sorry," the girl whined and stood to try to stroke my beard. "Wot's a matter, Gorgeous and Well-Hung Winston, you fancy the touch of a boy, ay?" Everybody chortled as she slinked away melodramatically, vanishing behind lamps of the set to the cheers of adoring fans.

"See?" Alexander persisted. "See what the masses think of Unity and your work?"

"Don't spout rubbish, Luxborough! She and the rest of them here"—and I made a sweeping gesture of Old Testament defiance over the open-mouthed lot—"would use the same tactics against saint or sinner. Anything but a truly edifying discussion! Just lampoon anything which smacks of being the least bit constructive to society, because anything constructive is seen as *elitist* and therefore ripe for attack. Right?" I glared from eye to eye before me, irate at the interminability of human idiocy yet simultaneously pitying them for the anxiety that caused their souls to quake.

This fury I felt at least was good for one thing: Bochmann called a new. "take." The group broke apart and headed off in twenty directions.

This time, as I came down the gangplank, whatever childish notion Bochmann wished my face to project obviously was being projected, to his immense satisfaction. It occurred to me that my anger was very useful to him, and I began to feel that the luncheon episode had been shrewdly provoked by him to get me, his guinea pig, to act as he wanted me to. This insight into the director's ploys and filmmaking on the whole calmed me somewhat, as an Aztec lackey in plumes and gold led me away so my makeup could be removed.

Suddenly a loud *"Rupert!"* was shouted my way. A gaudy dash of blood-red cloth and silver jewelry rushed toward me. Princess Dulcinea, planting two affectionate kisses on my cheeks, pretended she hadn't seen me in years. Then she put the two tickets for the papal mass in my hand. "They said you were saying mass—no wonder I missed you this morning. I'm glad I caught you, though. My mother-in-law told me to ask you to dine with her tonight. Are you free?"

"Yes, I believe so. Are you going to be there?"

"No, not tonight. We're invited to the American ambassador's. How did you like it last night? Did you enjoy yourself? Sorry I didn't tell you beforehand it was a birthday party."

"I enjoyed it very much. Are the bees gone?"

"Yes and so is the cardinal."

"Isn't he attending the papal mass today? Thanks for these tickets."

"That's right. He leaves for Palermo this evening. Sorry I'm in such a flutter but I'm late and must make up.

I'll be glad when this silly movie's over. I'm going to retire!"

Before I could tell the princess she was far too young
to retire, she vanished. The aide and I were almost to the
dressing rooms anyhow, so I asked him or her (I couldn't
tell) if Lord Luxborough could be found and sent to my
room.

When Alexander arrived, I was dressed. It was three
o'clock, and I was looking at the tickets we would need
to enter the Basilica in order to see *il papa*, when my friend
entered in what appeared to be torturously tight jeans and
a ridiculous orange T-shirt. He looked peeved, and asked
why I wanted him. "What're those?" he asked, pointing
to the tickets.

"To let us in to see the pope. Have you forgotten?"

"Is that today?" he gulped.

"Of course; it's Sunday. You promised Cardinal Monsignani last night, or were you too sober to remember?"

"I wasn't sloshed at all."

"You can't go looking like that!" I declared and
pointed to the bulge in his jeans. "How'd you fit into
those?"

"But they're shooting Dulcinea's main scene!"

"She just gave me the tickets, so of course she doesn't
expect you to stay here all day."

"Oh."

"Come on, Luxborough. We'll have to take a taxi
to . . . Where *are* you living anyhow?"

"Palazzo Pietrolomini, Via dei Banchi Nuovi. I'll have
the aide telephone for us, to have tea ready, then ask to
have the taxi return for us in half an hour. What time's
this thing start?"

"Six."

"We've time."

"Not much. Let's find your aide and run."

56

14

Conte Guido Pietrolomini and Roxanna, his contessa as well as Alexander's literary agent (she was originally from London), had left the country that morning. She was visiting relatives in England, and he had business in Tangiers. The Earl of Luxborough, their guest during the filming of *Moctezuma*, had retained the services of the cook; the rest of the staff were on holiday. The count and countess were not expected to return to Rome for some time.

Palazzo Pietrolomini was quite different from Palazzo Roseazzini—much smaller for a start. It rightly should be called a deluxe town house. Whereas everything about the cardinal's residence exuded age, tradition, and mellowed opulence, the Pietrolomini house felt recently restored. The priceless leather-bound books looked the same, oils on the walls were equally old, but the edifice itself somehow seemed new, though it must have stood a good four centuries. Much more time had been given to arrangements. The way things were placed in the rooms Alexander led me through was different from the Roseazzini establishment, noticeably so, as if this house expected a photographer from *Vogue*. Nothing was askew. Everything, in fact, looked perfect.

Whilst Luxborough changed, I waited in a parlor that was all shades of yellow, and scanned a back issue of *Apollo*. Tea was brought promptly by a hefty girl of my age, with orange hair and miner's shoulders. I said, "Cream first." She frowned, poured as if it were drudgery, then took her leave.

Luxborough appeared in a severe gray suit—far more presentable—and said: "You're bloody lucky you did read Italian at university. It's likely what pulled you that job."

"I'm beginning to think the Devil pulled it."

"Your grandfather's connection with Halifax . . ."

"Helped some. Even the cardinal mentioned it, the first day we met."

"A bit superstitious, isn't he? Those bees! There's certainly a pagan streak in him."

"He *is* Roman."

"Tell me, Rupert, what're you doing about death duties on Dexter Mote? Can you manage your inheritance here in Rome—as a priest—with those vast responsibilities you now have? I'm concerned for you, I must say."

"You've never been concerned . . . in your life. I should turn the estate over to my little brother. He's . . . well *Nicholas* is my responsibility now too."

"Do you regret becoming a priest?"

"Do you wish me to lie? This new post, though, has given me assurance. I think I shall perform good for a change," I said and laughed.

There was silence, save for the noise of china on china. We finished tea and looked at each other, seeing for the very first time that we were adults whose visions of life weren't the same. It was a sad moment, though of import to our friendship. Before, when we had known each other too well, our visions of life had been childish, merely alike.

"Come," I said softly and put down the tea. "Come and let us go see the pope."

We left the house in silence, each enveloped in thought. Such uncanny quiet from one I'd spent so much time with bothered me considerably.

The taxi sped along the Tiber toward the Basilica, and Alexander said nothing till we turned off Via Marmorata past the Pyramid of Cestius, whence he gazed back quickly through the fence to the Protestant Cemetery. "Keats . . ." he said in a faraway, forlorn voice.

I realized he must have been thinking about literature, about his own pursuit of the elusive Word. I wanted to communicate something special to this friend, not just sermonize. I wanted to tell him how much meaning Christ had given my life, but I knew the mention of the word *Jesus* would alienate him in an instant. It was easier, far easier, to speak with dullards, to explain something important within, than to reason with a truly creative mind which had no need for dogma of any kind. *Keats?* I wondered what Alexander wanted to say about Greece. Perhaps if I asked what Greece did give him, we could begin to rebuild our friendship, which I feared was now in jeopardy.

"Alexander?" The great gray bell tower of the Basilica of Saint Paul's-without-the-Walls reared before us, above trees in Via Ostiense. The sudden thought that even the Apostle Paul had visited Greece—Athens, Thessaloniki, Corinth—made me say with feeling: "Listen to me. Believe me. I *am* eager to hear what you experienced in Greece. Alexander, for God's sake, I'm not that far away in my thoughts. I can believe . . . what you believe."

He turned and stared in my eyes. "Yes, I do trust you, Rupert, but it's just that one can't discuss such things with everyone."

"I'm not just anyone . . ."

"I know. I only was depressed by fear your mind no longer was open. Just because you're a man of the cloth, albeit an important one at that, Rupert, you must care and dare to hear of *other* realms of spiritual existence. Never fear new knowledge. Fear is serious, Rupert. You—you always had the most open mind of anyone I ever met. To lose that now will be your ruin. Do you hear what I'm saying? Answer me!"

"I do. I honestly do."

"Then we'll talk, but we must pay the chap first," And grinning in unequivocal friendship, Luxborough took a note from his wallet and told the driver to keep the change.

The cyclopean length of the white Basilica struck us, as did the army of *carabinieri* and *polizia*, the ambulances, the limousines, and the nuns rushing about. Suddenly we were caught in the excitement of the event, this being a very special Mass of the Holy Ghost which usually is celebrated only at the commencement of the Conclave which chooses the next pontiff.

His Holiness was officiating at this mass in memory of the brutal murder of a very high official of the Italian government who had been killed one year before by the Brigade. The recent spate of *brigatisti* terrorism in Italy had made the pope decide—against all warning—to hold this mass in a main church of Rome outside the Vatican, to tell the world that the Holy Catholic Church was taking a stand against the threat violence posed to all society. For this reason, security at the Basilica was the tightest I ever have seen. No matter what one's identity, police demanded tickets and searched people for weapons before anyone was allowed inside.

Saint Paul's was an auspicious choice for this mass. Not only was the tomb of one of Christ's Apostles beneath the High Holy Altar, but Paul himself had come to the fellowship of the Lord late in life. This message was being interpreted in Rome as meaning that even terrorists weren't so far removed from humanity as to be unable to be restored to it by repentance and by returning to Mother Church. The other message was that Paul had been a firm believer in law and order. This, too, was not taken lightly in Rome. Moreover, because of the pope's bravery and the import of a Mass of the Holy Ghost, the event was being televised all over Europe, not to mention North and South America, Asia, Africa, and Australia.

Having passed the security check, we entered the enormous Basilica through the north transept and were directed to our seats. The building cannot fail to impress a soul; one could not help gazing in awe at the splendor. Such a structure, with its eighty columns (twenty to a row), five naves, and its marvelous quadriporticus and garden of palms, has existed in various forms on the very same site since A.D. 390.

One felt invigorated just by being inside this very holy shrine, and I noticed immediately how impressed was Alexander, who was studying the classical severity of the granite Corinthian pillars and the long sweep of the flat, though gilded, ceiling.

Our seats were superb. Immediately to the left of the Holy Altar and not far above the steps leading into the Shrine of the Tomb of the Apostle, we were well placed. A dais with a throne was placed just before the stone railing overlooking the shrine; this was where His Holiness would officiate before going to the altar to celebrate the Mass. Behind the altar and beneath the apse's fabulous gold mosaic of Christ Enthroned, the Sistine Chapel Choir would momentarily be singing, and I must admit that I was beginning to feel as excited as a schoolboy. I knelt to pray.

15

Our seats were among those reserved for dignitaries and we watched as bishops and important guests of other denominations filed in. Quite a few introduced themselves to me. Many of them knew each other and some wondered aloud who I was. I met representatives of the Russian Orthodox, Eastern Orthodox, and various Protestant denominations as well as somebody from the World Council of Churches, and a number of people from the faiths of Judaism and Islam, all of whom expressed solidarity with the pope for taking such a strong stand against terrorism.

Each of the men I met appeared to have known and deeply missed the late Anglican Representative, and their condolences and wishes that I might draw inspiration from his example were moving and heartening. Alexander also was moved by the words of these august delegates and I was proud to introduce him to them.

The huge building was filling rapidly and the noise became a din of the world's languages. In the large central nave which terminated at the main portal could be seen many and various orders of sisters and brothers. The two side aisles were reserved for Romans; parishioners of the Basilica stood closest to the center, and the rest of Rome ranged along the walls. Even having to secure a ticket in advance did not deter the faithful who came from all over the region.

The excitement mounted in perceptible waves, and the throng of people flooding the Basilica was as a tide rolling toward its shore.

Just then, the choir of the Sistine Chapel entered from the sacristy, through the right transept. The inimitable perfection of the voices of the boys, leading the responses of the men, formed a harmony, which surged and receded, rose and fell.

The famous choir's impact on the faithful was immediate. The hubbub subsided noticeably. When I turned to Alexander, who was on my right, I saw that my friend was on his knees, his head in his hands, and was weeping.

There was definitely some *force* present within the Basilica which turned one's thoughts away from self toward contemplation of things higher. This intensification was frightening, as if the very air within the edifice was charged as much with the benevolence as with the wrath of God. The fear of God—this sublime joy—was as exciting as being on the seashore gazing toward the onrush of a storm behind the tide. It was all part of nature, and stirring to behold, yet one wondered just how such vast resources of divine energy ever could be controlled—and toward what virtuous goal?

Everybody I looked to, as if thinking the very same

62

question, was simultaneously gazing toward someone else, as if in search of the answer. And just at that moment, as I noticed gathered on either side of the chancel below the dais the bishops in purple on the left and the cardinals in crimson on the right (who had entered as my mind had been soaring with the choir), the choir stood up, the huge bronze doors opened, and the slow cadence of the pontifical procession began.

Wave after wave of energy kept pulsing throughout the great building. Golden light streamed down through the tinted windows, and augmented the glow on the thousands of faces. The pope had arrived, and hysteria was fighting for control of the crowd.

Each time that the Vicar of Christ turned to one side then the other, as the *sedia gestatoria* His Holiness was carried on swayed softly from left then to right, the throng applauded fervently and shouted '*Viva il papa—Viva!*,' and the choir which was singing "Christus Vincit" seemed to sing louder and more celestially all the time, until the whole length of the Basilica had been traversed. But it was the burst of flashbulbs from countless cameras recording the pope's majestic entrance which made the whole event seem so like a fantastic dream.

Being near the altar and so close to the Sistine Chapel choir is a memorable experience for anyone attending a mass celebrated by the Holy Father. I gazed at the kindly face of this deeply pious man, as he was being allowed to tread upon the carpet leading to the dais once the *sedia* had been taken away, and I tried to go back four centuries to the rupture between Canterbury and Rome, but it seemed an almost impossible intellectual feat in this setting. There I was, representative of seventy million Christians of the Anglican Communion, scheduled soon for an audience of the holy man before me, who now was being cheered wildly as he mounted the dais to his throne, and it suddenly seemed incomprehensible to me that Angli-

63

cans and Romans had any such *differences* at all, that one vast group of Christianity even needed to have a representative sent to conduct diplomacy with the other. That Unity must be worked for seemed so noble—yes—but that Christ's kingdom was at odds at all seemed so regrettably sad if not tragic!

The alternating currents of energy within the ornate walls now had centered on one solitary human being. The pope began the Mass of the Holy Ghost and said, *"Fratelli, per celebrare degnamente i santi misteri, riconosciamo i nostri peccati."*

This simple sentence, invoking us to acknowledge our sins, hit me so hard that even though I held the beautifully bound hundred-page booklet which allowed one to follow the Mass, and even though I did follow and recite and sing with the many who were present, for some reason my spirit felt so humbled that I can't even recall any particulars of the Mass until the actual blessing of the Host. It all seemed to soothe some wayward part of my soul so comfortingly that I let myself be transported away, borne by the angelic voices of the choir.

Cardinal Monsignani later said, while we were kidnapped, that he had been watching me, and that when he'd first met me I had had the look on my face of one lost, but inside the Basilica I appeared a man newly found. I only recall having returned slowly to normal consciousness as the assembly began to receive the Eucharist. The choir's singing of the "Canto di Communione" was so forceful, so harmonious, that many seated about me were reduced to tears.

It was just then that I was able to recall how stirring had been the Holy Father's sermon. His appeal for the continuance of our humanity, and his plea to the *brigatisti* and to other terrorists all over the world were for them not to murder this civilization which has been building slowly for so many thousands of years. His Holiness posited the *Good* of our culture, and his was a very emotional address, not at all mere sentences preached.

Many of the dignitaries were Catholic and were beginning to stand to partake of *la Cena del Signore*. It was then, particularly, that it struck me as brutal that history caused a split between Canterbury and Rome. At that moment of the Mass I needed so badly to go to the altar for Communion. But not I—no—not an *Anglican*. It couldn't be done. Why, the Archbishop of Canterbury's diplomat in Rome would be chastised for breaching the wall still dividing the world of Christ.

This restriction—not to be able to share in this event which my soul longed to do—seemed terribly unjust to me. It was at that moment that my friend Alexander pushed past me, in order to do the very thing I could not do.

Even if Alexander were truly pagan, I suddenly was glad that he, a confirmed Anglican, was doing what was impossible for me. Hardly anyone of rank within the Vatican would know him, and in my heart I was sure Cardinal Monsignani would not say one word against Alexander for taking the Communion, an Anglican taking Catholic Communion right from the hands of the pope. The cardinal would later confirm this to me, when we were held captive.

Luxborough's face was radiant when he returned, and I couldn't help wondering . . . just what did he believe? What he admitted to the world about his ideas . . . were they but a fraction of deeper beliefs retained inside? I couldn't wait to discuss this with him.

Soon thereafter the Pontifical Mass ended. Once again His Holiness was held aloft in the red-velvet, gold, and bejeweled *sedia*. The choir of the Sistine Chapel was exalting the Holy Ghost, whose presence was so very much felt, in the loveliest music heard so far. I stood awestruck at the sight, watching the right hand of the pontiff being

65

raised in benediction toward the left and toward the right, as his other hand gripped tightly a glittering crosier, as the mass of people kept cheering wildly, and as His Holiness at last vanished from sight.

I had witnessed one side of the papacy, that which is public and brings meaning and divine intervention to the worship of so many thousands. And soon, in just eight days' time, I would have the true honor of an audience of the Holy Father, to be witness to a very private side of the Church, in hopes of furthering a dialogue that sought to do good for all mankind.

But alas, only seven days later, Cardinal Monsignani and I were kidnapped. Crime dictated that my audience of the pope would not occur.

16

Lord Luxborough and I parted after the mass. He was engaged in another part of the city, but we took the *Metropolitano* together to the Colosseum where we said good night.

As my taxi rushed me round the Palatine to dine with Princess Aurora, the dozen huge bells in the gray tower of St. Paul's kept resounding the exultancy of the Eucharist in my mind. Also, I kept reflecting on the sight of His Holiness departing from the shrine in his convertible limousine, for some courageous reason not protected by bullet proof glass. He was standing upright so as to greet the huge throng outside the quadriporticus.

Everyone was certain the pope would leave with utmost protection, given that he had held a Mass against violence, but nothing shielded him except the invisible force of the Trinity, which had just been invoked in the Mass.

I was in a happy mood—jubilant even—when I

reached the palazzo at half past eight. Principessa Aurora had seen the Mass televised so she knew roughly when to expect me. I was ushered into her private apartments by a maternal maid wearing a dress of brown checks and an apron. She showed me through rooms which bore the least amount of change of all those in the palazzo; the silk on the walls and even the marble on the floors were faded to shades no longer close to the originals. The odor of the chambers was remarkable, like almonds being roasted, or sherry.

The dowager princess looked exhausted from her birthday party. She was taking a cigarette, smoking with an ivory holder a good foot long. She was watching television, so I apologized for keeping her waiting and we immediately moved from the small sitting room to dine in a *camera* next door.

She pointed to my seat at a very large, round, once white table. Immediately I was struck by a centerpiece of rare yellow orchids, on which I commented but got no response, as the princess obviously was more interested in the pope. She patted her dyed strawberry-blond hair, gave her cigarette holder to the butler, a short stout fellow with great black eyebrows, and allowed herself to be seated.

"Did you enjoy the Mass?" She began and brushed a sleeve of her black dress.

"Tremendously. It was a very moving experience."

"I'm so glad. I saw it all on television. It's been some time since I've seen His Holiness in person. My last audience was public—meaning for families of Roma Nera."

"When was that?"

"The fourteenth of January, 1967, in the Sala Clementina. I attended, but of course Guadagno has seen the pope quite often since—person to person that is. Also my sons-in-law. But I have not . . . for years."

I sensed a bone of contention had been found on the

princess's plate, so I avoided any direct question and commented on the exquisite *risotto funghi.* The butler beamed, exited, then returned suddenly to fiddle with his hands by the lowboy.

The astute princess knew I was curious, though, so answered without being asked: "My brother the cardinal obviously has given you his views on the current state of the Church, but I daresay he and I see things from vastly different vistas. His mind is a phenomenon—he jokes that nobody in the family has such intelligence as that wastrel grandson of mine, Ercole—but truly, Rupert, the family's strength is the cardinal himself. I only wish he hadn't such fondness for that *ragazzo.* Ercole will turn on him someday, and soon—just you wait and see."

After this diversionary diatribe, the princess returned to the Church. "Arcadio, being one of the shrewdest men in the Vatican, received all the brains of our father, who was terrifyingly gifted. The cardinal will outlive *me,* by the sheer fact of his intellect. *Io sono troppo mondana . . . per nostra esistenza."*

"I must say the cardinal is most respected in England." I did not comment on that last sentence.

"Are you being diplomatic, or do you mean Arcadio is respected by the Archbishop of Canterbury himself?" the princess queried, then smiled benignly. I was finding the lady highly amusing, as acute a critic as some not unnotorious English duchesses. "Oh don't mind me. I like you, Rupert. You're a beautifully healthy man to look at, and you can even be classed as intelligent. Not that I judge you solely because you're from the venerable See of Canterbury, but because I enjoyed watching you the first evening that we dined."

"Thank you, Principessa," I acknowledged while not cracking a smile.

"My *dîners à deux* are infamous in this insane city— you likely haven't heard, but they are. I prefer the solitary dinner guest. It's far more *intime.* Don't you agree?"

I agreed.

"Then we'll get along fine. This *risotto* is marvelous. I wonder what Geraldina put in it—saffron?"

"I think so," I said without thinking.

Back on the track, Principessa Aurora continued: "You, though, have such an enormous amount to do I don't see how you possibly can concentrate. Thank God it's summer and the Season is drawing to a close. Oh, our youngest daughter is having the christening of her newborn son next Sunday. The cardinal is officiating and of course your presence is requested. It's at the Collemandina villa in the region La Ciociaria east of Rome." She paused. "Most of this palazzo will be shut, but I shall leave you a maid who can do your cooking if you care to reside in Rome. The Anglican Centre closes soon anyway, for the summer, does it not?"

"That's right, but because I'm new here I feel I should leave it open through July, and take only August off. It might be of use to visitors this coming month."

"And your first papal audience is scheduled for next week?

"Monday."

"That should prove important. Are you nervous?"

"Yes, I should admit it."

"So was I the last time I saw him, but for a totally different reason. Shall I tell you?"

"Please," I stated as the *risotto* was being cleared and delicious-looking filets mignons with fresh peas were being served.

"Not everybody likes my attitude today, I daresay, especially my brother. But the reason I asked you to dine tonight was that I felt the sooner you know this the better, for you and for your work. You, being of noble blood, will understand this. Of course, you might scoff and go away saying, 'Well, she's only *become* a princess whereas her background really is bourgeois,' and that I don't deny.

But, I am mother to a major prince of Rome, two princesses, a marchesa, and a countess, so I do speak with authority, though behind my back little people do say I'm just a *nouvelle arrivée.*"

"My own mother was a singer."

"I know. I knew her well."

"You did?" I asked, wondering how much of Rome Mother didn't know.

"Louise sat right where you sit now. We dined *à deux.*"

This made me shiver and I began to listen to the princess in earnest.

"But back to the Vatican. I said I was nervous when I was last received by the pope. This was the last time Roma Nera was 'invited' to give our annual New Year's salutations to His Holiness, meaning to the papacy, an institution our families had literally created. This was not just an elitist group from Hong Kong; this was *il patriziato e la nobiltà romana* who called that Saturday. And I must say that I was nervous, and I am solely speaking for myself here, please note, only because I had many fears, for years, that we, as a valid part of Roman civilization, were slowly being pushed away from what . . . we . . . had . . . created!"

My eyes widened to saucers at the princess's emphasized words.

"This is no blanket statement, I might add, insofar as I'm a true Catholic myself and what the pope says about religion I take seriously. If he says 'Go to mass three times a day' I do it, but recently there has come about in the Vatican the notion that so many of the benefits to the papacy which were given with love and devotion, by the nobility, now are to be dispensed with—and I daresay dispensed with *overnight*! For, what is time to families who have seen the Vatican change and endure for centuries? Time is a trustworthy thing, but it began to strike me, after the Second Vatican Council, that time no longer is trusted. Time was one of the things on our, and on the Vatican's, side. We, and the papacy, had had so much of it, right from the days of Christ. It is *no* laughing matter—and nothing to take lightly—and I wish I could make my point known more strongly!"

"Have you thought of asking for a private audience?"

"Yes, and it would be granted. I've had quite a few. But the cardinal thinks it would not go down well, even though I receive the majority of the cardinals of the Curia, who dine here and who confide similar sentiments."

"But Cardinal Monsignani must feel closer to Roma Nera than does any other cardinal, given your family ties. Obviously he's far more predisposed than, say, foreign cardinals, or those with quasi-socialistic leanings."

"True. But *he* is the family's scion of the spirit, if you see what I mean. He feels the situation is under control. He's on the Secretariat for Christian Unity and Lord only knows what other posts, but he's also the sharpest 'investment whip' the Vatican's had since the war. He spends time in London, Paris, and New York, ostensibly discussing Unity but also gauging the world's stock exchanges. He feels the Church is 'his business'; should I intrude, though I am a dowager principessa of a major Roman house, he knows I'd certainly tell the pope what's on my mind, and I would! I do not in the least object to Vatican investment policy. I told you I'm far too mundane—mind you, if it weren't for Catholic funds, the world's markets would collapse overnight—but I do have what we shall call 'misgivings' about the way in which our class, the *nobiltà*, has been dealt with of late."

The princess glanced at the orchids. "To be brutally honest, the pope needs Black Rome as outlets for investing Vatican incomes, but Black Rome doesn't really need the pope. If this sounds like heresy, so be it. God will judge me for it. In all fairness, however, I must say that for centuries our old families have been the bulwark for the papacy and therefore of untold and great service, yet now we are being pushed aside, thanks to Americanization of

efficiency, a streamlined bureaucracy, and a democrati-
zation of structure which is in fact *not* democratic. The
Eternal City never has been a playground for liberty—
which is the sole reason it's remained eternal to this day!"

That certainly was an oration as Roman as Cicero. Yet the
princess also managed to finish her steak before I had
gotten through half of mine. I was too busy listening.

She continued: "It's ironic. Nobody can get rid of the
aristocracy. We endure here in Rome as nowhere else on
earth, and it doesn't matter one iota that we don't have
a king or queen. What could be better than a pope, someone spiritually so far above most of mankind? If the papacy
brought out a *discorso* saying that the Apostolic See hated
the nobility, still we would defend the pope to the death,
as we are good, practicing Catholics. Rome is strange. You
can't expect Unity *with* Rome until Rome is good and
ready. That's very frank but very true."

The butler came, readying the table for the *dolce.*

"This summer, it's best you make as little noise as
possible. Let the cardinals see what a *good* young man you
are. But do accept as many invitations as possible, not
only in this house—I shall introduce you to people—but
from people you will meet through your work in the Doria.
Do partake of as much of our social life as you can stomach.
Who knows how many more years it will last? Its grandeur
is hanging on for dear life. Do you realize that I've seen
ambassadors, sitting in the very chair you now occupy,
break down like silly girls and cry—one from the People's
Republic of China, even—because they get morbidly upset
when they are recalled from Rome. This city is the diplomat's dream. Where else do you find so *many* families
still living and entertaining in palaces the size and luxury
of those we have here? It's incredible, when one stops to
think of it. England doesn't even have the type of high
life still very much a part of Society as we know it in Rome!

I daresay it's like Saint Petersburg—before the Revolution."

The *dolce* came, an enticing ring of fresh strawberry *gelato* made at the palace and served with whipped cream. The butler was as attentive as an ancient patrician's slave.

While tasting the exquisite dessert I savored the words of the princess. The last time we had dined I noticed also that she did not speak during the final course. It must be her tactic—to let her words sink in.

As the plates were being cleared, the principessa stood up and began to speak as we walked toward her sitting room.

"Have you never thought of marrying—or have you taken vows?"

She caught me completely off guard, but I replied, "No, I mean, I've never taken vows of celibacy, because . . . I *would* like to marry." I hung my head as I said this, because privately, without telling anybody, I had made a vow of chastity on the day of my ordination, but my lack of control had broken it many times.

"Well." She sat to take a last cigarette, "Let us see what we can do about the situation this summer."

17

The next morning was Monday, and I walked to Palazzo Doria, arriving at my office before nine. Hardly had I a moment to think when my secretary, a short and very quiet middle-aged lady from Buckinghamshire, nervously came into my office and said a "very pushy" young chap was "poking about the library" and "says he knows you and has an appointment."

This irritated me as I couldn't imagine who it could be, so I asked her to come back with his name. Shortly, she returned and said, "Don Ercole Roseazzini." She apologized, having just realized I was lodging with his family.

Ercole entered, all muscles and sweat and literally exploding out of his dirty white corduroy trousers. I looked at him and stifled a laugh, as he sat and grunted, "You're not so much older than I, so don't pretend you know any more than I do."

Hardly "good morning." I asked him if that was all he'd come to say.

"Just seeing how you'd react." He broke into a grin and pulled at his groin, as if I should take that vulgarity as a sign of affection. "You like it here—in Rome?"

"I don't mind. It's rather hot."

"This's nothing. Just you wait."

I could hardly wait for him to leave, but was curious to hear what had prompted his call. He soon came right to the point.

"What do you think about my sister?"

"Serafina?"

"We have a mongoloid in the family, too. Haven't you heard?"

"That's not funny."

"It's no joke. She's my mother's youngest child. She's eight. Nobody ever sees her—nobody ever goes to see her—nobody except for *me!*"

I didn't know what to say, but he continued. "The family just forgets about her, like it forgets ninety-nine percent of Italy. One percent, that's important—all important—the upper crust of Rome. Even Florence is shit to my father."

"Why are you telling me this?"

"You're a priest, you're young. You should have *feelings.* If you're not just phony."

"Of course I have feelings."

"Then come with me and visit my little sister."

"But . . . I have an office. You . . . don't mean now?"

"Yes, now."

74

"Are you playing games with me, Ercole?" I demanded and stared him in the eye. He did not flinch, but looked like a cobra ready to strike.

"Then . . . you won't come."

"I'm busy. Can't you see?"

"Then what about Serafina? She cares for you, you know."

"Don't talk rubbish. What's Serafina got to do with this?"

"I'm through with her now, you know."

"No, I don't know, nor do I want to."

"But if you'd come with me to visit Angela, I would have given you Serafina."

"What?" The fellow was spouting nonsense.

Ercole stood and stopped the conversation as abruptly as he'd started it. He stated defiantly, "You're just like the rest of them—concerned only with yourself, with preserving the nightmare of this rotten society!"

I stood openmouthed for some time after he had left, wondering 'Why me?' What was the meaning, if any, behind his words of attack?

18

Ercole's visit bothered me no end and set the tone for the entire week. I couldn't get his words out of my mind; they were so similar to what I heard all too frequently in my South London parish. There, however, I had a basic understanding of the social problems involved. I was an easy target for the young people who often took their aggressions out on me. But the kids almost always would come back after a cooling-off period to apologize for the 'aggro,' and we'd be better friends for it. I always got on better with black teens, too. They saw me as a rebel, someone not afraid to leave the posh world of my father to see what life was like for the poor.

Ercole was a different case entirely. He couldn't be reacting against me because of disparate social backgrounds. The more I thought about the things he said to me, the more illogical he appeared. But, rudeness and shouting aside, was I the only one in the house with whom he felt he could talk?

I became more aggravated as the morning wore on. What was behind Ercole's words?

In the midst of celebrating the daily Communion in the Anglican Centre's chapel, I decided to tell the boy I would accompany him to visit the unfortunate Angela. I then said a prayer for both the little girl and Ercole, whom I felt I must get to know.

Of the handful of communicants at chapel, an elderly couple from the Anglican Church of Uganda were my guests for the midday meal. The gentleman was a retired vicar from colonial Africa, originally from Ontario. Rev. Addison's wife Ruth, a courageous and tough little woman from Kenya, was black, and she had telephoned me to say that she and her husband recently had moved to Rome and would like to meet me. Ruth had mentioned how dangerous life had been for Christians in Uganda, how they performed their mission as long and as faithfully as they could, so I felt they should be honored with interesting guests. I invited the director of the Roman Catholic Centro pro Unione, an Atonement friar I had not yet met, as well as Principessa Dulcinea and Lord Luxborough. They'd been kind enough to introduce me to their work, so I felt I should reciprocate. Luckily, neither was needed at Cinecittà that day.

Dulcinea and Alexander arrived at a quarter to one, just after Father Mauro, the director of the Centro. My cook Graziella, whom I inherited from the previous representative, was quite nervous, for no justifiable reason but simply because it was the first meal she had prepared and served for me. Her fears were groundless; she managed with the greatest success.

The princess looked ravishing in an orange silk dress, a 1920s jet-and-gold necklace, summer gloves, and black shoes and matching bag. The black accessories accented her high black coiffure, and I noticed how Ruth, in a splashy African print, kept staring at the princess throughout the meal but talked volubly so not to appear to be staring. Alexander, who wore a beige jacket and open-necked shirt, was showing off his tan, and both the reverend, a huge chap built like a bull, and the father, who was tall, with a hawklike visage, stared at my handsome blond friend, and talked equally volubly.

During the meal I was pleasantly surprised by Luxborough's pertinent comments about the Anglican Church. I hadn't intended that the conversation turn upon things ecclesiastic, but it did, and the two Catholics, Father Mauro and Principessa Roseazzini, provided a fair balance to a very weighty report on ghastly things that had happened in Uganda. The father was particularly moved and asked the Addisons to visit his Centro in the Piazza Navona so that they might consider giving a lecture in the autumn. I felt very pleased; my idea of bringing Catholic and Anglican together over lunch had proven constructive.

"Unity," I stated as we took coffee on the rooftop garden, "is as important to strive for at the one-to-one level as at the diplomatic echelon where formal statements are published between the Archbishop of Canterbury and the Bishop of Rome."

After chatting in the pergola on the roof, we retreated downstairs, away from the brutal sun. The Addisons and Father Mauro said their good-byes, thanking me for receiving them, and Alexander went to the Centre's library and browsed through our collection of books. Princess Dulcinea obviously had asked him to wait for her, as well as having requested a private conversation with me.

There had been something somber about the princess at lunch. This wasn't at all the Dulcinea I had seen before, with her family and with her "fans" at the studio. I couldn't decide if today's formality was just another quirk or if she actually was troubled. Being a good actress by any standard, she could speak her own mind. I refused to draw conclusions.

The princess sat stiffly in a blue armchair, which did not match her dress at all. This irritated her, so she stood. As Graziella passed through the room with the coffee cups, the princess turned her back on the woman, and I realized then that she must be particularly upset about something. She came right to the point though she looked at the wall and not at me.

"Were you visited by my son this morning?"

"Yes," I stated, surprised she knew.

"Ercole has no right to disturb you like this—you with so much to do here!" Dulcinea turned to face me squarely. "What did he say to you?"

"I really don't know. It was all so quick, so unexpected. I think . . . he chose to come . . ."

"Because he's up to no good, that's why! He did it to irritate me, his father, his grandmother, above all his sister. I'm staying on in Rome, but his father and my mother-in-law are just leaving for the country. Serafina's now ill, yet *he* comes to us this morning and . . . and starts yelling that he . . . he was going to the Doria to see what type of a man *you* were."

"What?" was all I could mumble.

The princess obviously was telling but a fraction of what was going on in her family. I really wasn't interested in probing, nor involving myself further in the domestic situation.

"I stayed to speak with you, but I know you should

78

be relaxing," she continued meekly and sat beside me on a sofa, "and . . . I apologize for my son's behavior . . . which is strange even to me lately . . . and which . . . neither I nor my . . . family can seem to understand though . . . we have tried and tried and *tried* with that boy. But for the past two years he's been drifting further away from us."

Principessa Dulcinea began to cry, lightly at first, then in sobs which she tried to stop. I put my hands on her shoulders to comfort her, but she pulled herself together and forced herself to regain composure. "Serafina now is ill . . . and I can't make sense out of her either. It's all too much. Thank God we've one who's not . . . Oduardo's such a *stable* boy it's . . . I know I'm babbling but I wish the cardinal were back. I need to . . . . This whole year's been *hell* for me. If only you knew."

"It's not been jolly for me, either," I sighed. "What is—what's the matter with Serafina?"

The princess gazed at me in a kind of horror. "We . . . we don't know. What did Ercole tell you?"

"Nothing about . . . he only . . . said something about Angela," and I said the little girl's name as if I could not hold it back.

"Oh," the princess whimpered. Then after a silence she stated, "I . . . see. So now you know. Angela's . . . *come si chiama?* . . ."

Again the noble lady started to weep. "It's Angela I believe why . . . why Ercole's turned against me but I . . . my child . . . my Angela I just can't live with her it's a sin a mortal sin I know and truly . . . gives me great pain but . . . she's not fit and she's . . . so better off where she is. . . . The sisters take such good care—"

"Please, you don't—"

"Did Ercole ask you to go see her? Is *that* what he did?"

"Yes," I admitted. "I would have if he—"

"No, he couldn't ask you decently, could he!"

79

"I was busy. I'm so sorry."

"You have a job to do, but does *he* understand what holding a job means to anyone?"

"I think I can break through to him, Dulcinea, we— he and I—are of the same background and perhaps I can tell, I mean talk to him better than—"

"Try. Go ahead . . . try. He's doomed, Rupert, doomed. I see it plainly. I'm his *mother* for God's sake, I see it with a mother's eyes. He'll end up killing himself soon—or somebody else, I just know it."

"Let me talk with him."

"He won't listen to a thing you say. The cardinal's convinced he's possessed. Monsignani saw it twelve months ago and I laughed—no—I flew in a rage and would have nothing to do with my husband's uncle for over two months. But then . . . I too, I, his own mother, Rupert, who was blind to such things out of my insane love for that boy (have you looked closely at that boy?—any mother would be a monster not to love a son who looks the way he does—and with such intelligence) I. . . . Two years ago his popularity in Rome was unbelievable! Nobody, ever, have I seen with Ercole's quickness . . . quickness which now has led him down a dark path of —"

"When did it begin?"

"When he went to *university!*" She spat out the last word as if it were filth. "There—there he met the slime of society—there he was influenced by the sorts we'd been able to keep away from him at home. They got him into politics!" she shouted, then smashed her fist into the cushion of the sofa.

She stood abruptly, to pace about the room. Never had I seen an angry Roman woman before, except in films and operas, and I must say the princess's outburst was shocking.

"*Politics*, that's what did it, all this agitation, this left wing, this radical, this seething revolution simmering right here in our midst at university after university in this sick country. They should shut all the universities of Italy. Ercole's assinine 'scholarly' friends turned him totally against the values of his ancestors. They made him hate even me, his own mother. Ercole blamed me, my class, my noble background for not caring at all about humanity. He said it showed most by my 'putting Angela away.' What idiocy! He became awful at table—so bad my husband forbade him to eat with us. This was a year ago, when the cardinal drew his own conclusions."

I suddenly saw my own dear mother, as this lady stood at the mantel wiping her eyes.

"He was still in the university then, but the cardinal said, 'Your boy's possessed.' What would *you* have done?"

She was staring at me, waiting for an answer.

"I . . . I flew into a rage and my husband banished the boy from our table. I still had *faith* in my son. It was only a year since he entered the university. I felt he'd come back, back to us with more love than before, if allowed to see the rest of Italy, what it was like, even if he did associate with . . . We shouldn't be so old-fashioned not to let him try for himself! But—the cardinal was right— within two months Ercole quit the university and since then he's been an enigma to us all. My husband's thrown the boy out of the house twice and threatened to have him cut off from all inheritance, not because he quit, for it's a relatively new thing that we of the aristocracy even *attend* the university at all, but Ercole hasn't shown a single sign of being interested in *anything* the family has to offer. Need I say, with our relations, something of interest could be found! *O Dio mio*—whatever it is we can't figure out. Ercole refuses to discuss with any of us what he does all day."

Just then Luxborough knocked and strode into the drawing room. The princess grabbed her bag and drew herself up, apologized for taking our time, then asked if we might accompany her to a restaurant that evening as her husband was in the country with his mother. Alexander asked for a rain check, as he was dining at Ostia, but I was free so accepted. My friends said good-bye shortly thereafter, and I resumed work on my correspondence, though I was rather shaken and found it difficult to accomplish what I needed to do.

19

Contrary to what I was told, Serafina hadn't left for the country but still was in Rome. When I returned to my rooms, I was surprised to hear her call down to me from the first-floor balcony overlooking my small garden courtyard.

"It's so hot," she said and moved a tanned arm across her wavy blond hair to push it from her eyes.

"Of course," I said, intrigued. "Come down here where it's cool."

Within minutes the charming beauty was in my sitting room. She certainly didn't look ill to me, though her mother had said she was. Seeing those long tanned legs protruding from tight blue-jean cutoffs, and her torso barely covered by a skimpy top, I found it hard to believe she'd ever been ill in her life. I offered something cool to drink, and she accepted *acqua minerale*.

Face to face with the girl, alone, I became a bit warm beneath the clerical collar, not to mention the beard. Stupidly, I asked, "Isn't your mother here?"

"I don't know," she replied and looked annoyed that I had mentioned another woman.

There was a long silence, made worse by the fact that the girl's legs caused my eyes to water. The shapely sight turned my thoughts to a jumble.

"Mother says Ercole came to see you this morning," said Serafina, breaking the silence.

"He's . . . very odd, your brother," I sighed, not wishing to repeat the dialogue which had been bothering me all day.

82

"Why do you say odd?"

"Do you think he's normal? He wanted me to leave my office and immediately accompany him to visit your— Angela. I would have, had he given more than a moment's notice." I drank my vodka and orange juice, frustrated now by the discussion with Serafina.

"I wish Angela were dead," the girl snapped, then paced the room just as her mother had done.

"Does Ercole wish Angela dead, too?"

"He's the only one who doesn't! He's the only one who visits Angela—that's why everyone hates him."

"Isn't it because he left university?"

"They rejoiced at that. Nobody liked the students he was friends with."

"Did you meet them?"

"Some were all right, others were too crazy, too po-litical. I'm not ninety—I understand the *ragazzi*—even if I don't believe all the rubbish that they say."

"I'm not ninety, either," I said seriously, stroking my beard and glaring at the girl.

"I know," she replied hesitantly. "I like you. I feel I can talk to you."

"Then talk to me."

"But you're a priest—and an *Anglican* priest which's worse! It's strange speaking with you, me dressed for the street and you looking like you crawled out of a confes-sional."

"What should I put on?"

"Don't you ever wear jeans? If you're not as old as you say"—she giggled like a schoolgirl—"put something *hip* on, maybe I'll talk to you then. Go on . . ."

I felt like grabbing her, dragging her to my bedroom, but fought the impulse away. If it were true, as the cardinal said, that Serafina still went out chaperoned, she likely would be a virgin. With that thought, I stripped and slid into a pair of faded jeans. Flinging on a casual shirt, I buttoned it only above the navel and rolled the sleeves

deliberately beneath the armpits. To be told to remove my
clericals made my change of clothes almost as liberating
as if I were standing nude in front of the titillating girl. I
strode back into the sitting room feeling randy.

"God," she cried. "It's not the same man!"

"Don't be a child," I chided, leaning against the mantel and staring at her.

"Are you coming . . . with us tonight?"

"With us? Who's us?"

"Mother and me, out to eat?"

"Where're you going?"

"Wear that. Don't be a boring priest—I'm sick of
priests, cardinals, archbishops. And she looked at me provocatively. "Come, a young *marchese*. You are one anyway,
aren't you?"

"You know I am because I told you."

"Then be yourself tonight. Don't act like a 'man of
God.' And I won't let Mother act like a movie star. And—
and me, I won't act like a young girl. I'll act . . . a mature
woman."

"You're funny," was all I could say as I went up to
her and kissed her hard on the mouth.

20

Serafina did not have tremendous willpower. She wanted
more time with me when I finished kissing her. She was
unable to force herself from me as spontaneously as she'd
come into my rooms. Yet even after she did leave me, it
was as if I'd just been with a ghost. I worried and wondered: how would I act the next time the vision appeared?

Kissing her delectable body, feeling the warmth of
her softness as I pressed deeply in the reaches of her flesh,
floods of responses drowned the priest but not the man
I'd been coaxing into being since leaving London for
Rome. Being so loose before and after my ordination had

caused me morbid introspection these two years. Wanting to love, wanting to make love, wanting to be loved were constant concerns to me. I know I speak for all young men who become priests when I say that sex isn't a thing one forgets just by trying to forget.

There's something so primal about Rome. The city's constantly at the point of orgasm. People won't like the metaphor, but her atmosphere is so supercharged that even those who come alone to Rome soon begin itching with lust to make love, to unloosen. Even the most puritan tourist discovers a longing for the inconsequential rendezvous, yearning for the pretty boy or girl standing there invitingly against the ancient stonework. In Rome love is everywhere and those who don't have it suddenly want it! You *see* this hunger, even in the eyes of the most venerated nun.

Rome has never allowed people to be pure. I came to Rome to propitiate some sin, yet found myself immersed in a city that glories in sin. Only God's fool comes to Rome expecting propitiation; the spirits of those many ruttish evils here proffer only what one prays to avoid!

I don't know what took hold of me . . . that first fervent kiss with Serafina. I became convinced at that moment that she was as in love with me as I with her. I said idiotic things to her, the first things that came to my mind, in order to steer clear of a silence that would force me to gaze at her wantonly again—whereupon I would lunge at her and bury myself within her luscious frame. Mad things I said to her! Did she listen to a word?

I confessed to her my fears, how I felt I failed as a priest in London, how I doubted my mission in Rome. She appeared to find it difficult to understand what I said, yet I continued to talk—that I might not be tempted to violate her body.

Only a priest can truly appreciate the curse of wearing the clerical collar. It is hard to maintain a proper perspective—dressed all in black and professionally wed to God—

as countless people unburden themselves on you. Oh, Christ! A priest needs confession, too, needs it more, perhaps, than the rest of mankind. And it isn't as if he has the need to gossip, to divulge the terrible secrets that he hears, but a priest does need release—certainly as much, if not more, than those to whom he listens.

I whispered many things to Serafina that Monday evening: bits about my family, my fear of losing our inheritance, of becoming the Marquess, of becoming the priest, of becoming the Representative to the pope.

I confessed I loved her and that I felt confused. She began to cry.

I changed the subject. What could one say? I spoke about the most fearsome thing I knew—hardly a proper thing to tell the girl to whom you've pledged your heart. I told her I felt cursed, truly cursed, in that love never had worked for me. Love always had been something negative, something urging union, something undulating uncompromisingly straight to death!

Serafina cringed at that word. She admitted that her brother seemed so close to death now. She felt powerless to protect him, to guide him. They'd been close—too close—but Ercole was gone now, and so far from help.

I wouldn't listen to her speech about Ercole. I hated him—did not want to hear anything about the stupid boy who seemed so vain, so spiritually lost, perhaps more lost than myself. Later I forgave him, and repented as I knew he badly needed help. For now, however, I was reluctant to intervene. Getting close to Ercole would alienate me from his sister.

Damn the thought of death! Despite the girl seated before me and despite my conscience or what little remained with me, I remained powerless against its hold on me. I had to speak about it.

Serafina tossed blond strands from her eyes and

gazed at me as if I were out of my mind. I told her, "I need *redemption*. Only someone like you can give it to me."

"Do you hear what you're asking me?" she shouted. "What in God's name are you saying?"

"I need to confess. I feel the Devil inside me. Something horrible kicked me into the priesthood. I shoved myself to the Church, against my own, and my family's, better judgments. It's fiendish, this call of the so-called divine!"

"Are you running away from something?"

A voice from deep within me answered, "I pray not— that I may be running, if at all, *to* something higher."

"What higher?" Serafina demanded.

"It loses if put in personal terms, but it loses if kept inside. Everything sounds so false. People run away in droves."

"What do you mean!" she shouted.

"To say I'm going toward Christ."

"Christ—oh God—you all say the same stupid thing. Can't you priests, you idiots, ever speak to human beings without using the tired words Jesus or Christ or—"

"Let me explain, Serafina."

"If you do explain, Rupert, will it be expelling some strange thing only inside you and not something higher, not something relative to all mankind?"

"Can't I say what's on my mind?" I glared across the glass coffee table at the girl and wondered, Why do I love her?

We tried to smile yet could not. We tried to frown yet could not. We reached out our right hands. Hers was not long enough. The horrid table was a wall between us.

Then her rigidity broke like an egg. She sighed and smiled shyly, and urged me to speak. I did. I needed to talk to her about death, to rid myself of its terrible weight.

"I confess ... I fear I'll never marry—that though I

badly want to, I'll never father a child. No son . . . no one to carry on my name."

Serafina stared, this time with comprehension. There were tears in her eyes.

"I long so much to marry, to be a father."

She turned her head away.

"All the relationships I've had to date—those that meant something to me, anyway—have come to a bad end."

"How do you know?" Serafina challenged. "Can't you just accept death as it comes? It's there for us all—who's to say we cause it?"

"Five years ago I had a fiancée—her name was Vivienne—who drowned herself in the sea off Cornwall. I loved her very, very much. It hurts. . . . You even remind me of her. Yes, you do. No, please don't shy away from me now! Don't, for the love of God, think I feel for you simply because you remind me of her or. . . . Believe me, that's not it at all. But Vivienne *died*. Why?"

I started to weep, though I stammered on about this woman of my past, whose image was with me still. The vision of Vivienne was always murky, like the sea where she disappeared, thick with decomposing plants and rotting fish. "We . . . we had a child but he died. Vivienne couldn't stand the strain . . . was tormented by his death, blamed herself. And I . . . all my love could not keep her alive."

"Please, Rupert, you don't have to tell me any more. I feel I understand, I really do."

"Our child, this extension of our flesh and our souls, lived until just before his birth. Vivienne had been so happy once. She was everything I hoped to find in a lover, but I think . . . I think for her I was a sort of shelter against change. I know now that she was another, a different person from the one I thought I knew—and that I loved her too much. She was a woman meant for better than me, Serafina. So . . . she left me, left me for a quick end in a cold sea—and I fled to the Church. Now you see why I am so afraid, why death..."

Serafina refused to let me continue. "It's all right," she murmured and came and put her arms about me. "Don't talk now. You and I, we both feel it. There's nothing more for you to say now, Rupert." And she paused and looked tenderly at me. "I love you...I do. Just be calm...be calm."

21

After initial intimacy, after expectancy becomes reality, feelings one imagined find themselves weighed against those that actually transpired. Consequently, both Serafina and I seemed to react away from each other later Monday evening when we accompanied her mother to dinner.

Serafina, in an austere, antiquated brown dress, looked even less attractive by draping over her shoulders a garish, man's sweater two decades old and smelling of mothballs. I found this entertaining, much to her secret enjoyment. Outwardly, she showed warmth to me by complaining of an upset stomach, though she ate like a horse.

Principessa Dulcinea looked the contrary. She dressed to kill the staff of the Osteria dei Liberti, who knew her. For some foolhardy reason she was wearing real jewels, which caused a sensation as we made our entrance through the three gardens of the lively "countryside" restaurant in the old Appian Way.

The princess didn't telephone in advance; thus, her arrival in a peach satin dress and sparkling gold-chain and pink-coral necklace with matching bracelets on both arms caused the waiters much concern as they followed us between the tables. Even amidst tropically lush foliage, the charming establishment was "not chic," the principessa whispered. "I come here only because the staff dotes on me. They love my film friends."

They also loved calling her *principessa*. The word worked wonders to clear an unkempt couple who were taking far too long with their *dolce*. By this time the foliage was parting in the first two gardens so that the third could be spied upon. There was a pained look on Serafina's face, but I found the whole scene hilarious and couldn't stop snickering.

Amusement ceased before we had a chance to see the menu; a gregarious fifteen-year-old came up and asked for Dulcinea's autograph. This shocked me into realizing that the woman at our table truly was enough of a film star to be recognized by *la gente*. I'd never been "out" with the princess before, yet felt stupid I hadn't understood what a star she must be. It reminded me of many experiences with my mother in London.

The boy, wonderstruck and bashfully brash in asking Dulcinea for her signature, caused Serafina to turn away in disgust. Eyes watering, the boy thanked the princess too profusely for being *gentilissima*. Serafina frowned as her mother held out her gorgeous hand to the boy. He bowed and kissed it obsequiously, then ran to the table of his blushing father who had urged the lad on in the first place.

Duty performed, the principessa took her menu as if nothing had occurred. I was amazed at her grace and glad I'd gone against Serafina's urging that I wear jeans. The comfortable light green suit seemed more appropriate for the evening.

Perhaps I was falling in love as much with Serafina as with the opportunity for continued society of her mother? I chose *tagliatelli alla Poppea* on this thought. The name Poppea caught my mood; she, the infamous mistress of Nero. I was pleased when both women ordered the same.

This romantic nighttime garden in the ancient Appian Way placed the three of us closer to the evenings of Nero than we would have been had we dined in Rome. The narrow ancient lane, which millions had traversed southward from the Seven Hills since the time of the emperors, was very much alive today. Its parallel mud walls stood firm and forbidding against the warp of centuries.

With two marvels before me, even the *pasta Poppea* conjured notions of physical love. My legs kept brushing against Serafina's. The night was warm, the conversation brilliant, and the eyes in the candlelight alive.

"Look, a firefly," Serafina cried with delight, a child again. The tiny bug settled on a nearby bay leaf. "It's the only one about."

The solitary insect blinked with regularity, then took its leave. I reached to where the firefly had been, picked a leaf from the bay tree, and brushed it against my lips. The aroma, so sweet in the moist evening air, was intoxicating. I gave the pungent leaf to Serafina, who put it to her mouth and bit it, then tossed it backward over her hair. Her mother watched all this with startled amusement. At that instant I believe Princess Roseazzini realized that her daughter and I were in love.

This thought made us all stop. The lighthearted, typically Roman gossip of the women ceased. We found ourselves isolated in muteness within the nocturnal garden. All ears, it seemed, strained our way.

I was taken aback that Serafina chose to break the silence by announcing: "My cousin Sabina is having a party two nights from now. Would you like to come? It's her *ballo*, and if you come you must dress formally, *not* like a Trappist monk."

That innocuous phrase turned the garden into a gaggle. Waiters suddenly appeared from nowhere. Peace, or the timelessness felt a few seconds before, now seemed painful to us. The multitude of voices was reassuring.

During the quiet, beneath the table, I'd been squeezing Serafina's legs tightly between my own, so tightly I felt I'd burst with the strain.

Principessa Dulcinea countered her daughter's invitation by saying: "Everybody's told you how wicked we are, how we lock up Serafina after dinner, how we only send her out 'into the world' with an armed escort. Well, it's not true, *cara*, is it?" Mother poked daughter playfully, as the cardinal's words of warning flashed in my mind. "The cardinal," she continued, reading my thoughts, "likes everyone to believe his family refuses to exist in this century, preferring that we persist in the more wicked ones of days gone by."

Serafina rebutted this defiantly: "It's true. Every girl my age has already had her coming out! But I sit at home and play piano, play piano, play—"

"You choose to play piano. We never chain you to it," the princess said forcefully.

"I'm sick of piano. When can I have my coming out?"

"In your condition, dear, I wouldn't recommend a party at all."

That phrase jarred my thoughts. It sounded like a warning, but I pushed that idea from my mind. Whatever was going on between mother and daughter—or whatever was the problem with the girl's health—was none of my business.

"I'm fine. . . . I . . . I just need plenty of rest," Serafina said hesitantly, as I gazed at her intently for some indication of illness.

"Then go with your uncle to Tunisia. You know he does absolutely *niente* there, how the last time you were there you said you died of boredom. Well, it would be *perfetto* for you."

"After the christening, then I'll think about it."

"That means you've a week to think to your heart's content. I shall expect 'yes or no' by Sunday midnight. Is

92

that understood? Tunisia—or your father and I shall make *other* arrangements."

The whole thing sounded personal, so I fidgeted with my bread in the upper-class Italian fashion, trying to break pieces off it with my left hand only, a manual trick I had not yet mastered.

Seeing my discomfort, and noticing that everyone in the restaurant was staring, the princess changed the subject to one she thought less tedious. "What did you do, Rupert," and she glared at the eavesdroppers, "after I left you this morning? Did you say mass?"

Such a juxtaposition of sentences made all the tongues wag doubly hard, and I laughed at the lady's wit. Serafina pouted.

"I worked on *Dialogue*, our Centre's newsletter. I only say mass at noon, by the way. You should come."

"We're Catholic," Dulcinea said apologetically.

"What's that matter? I'll come, Rupert, and even take Communion," said Serafina defiantly.

"If you do, take your sinful brother. *He* needs divine intervention more than you and I together. Seriously, Rupert, on Monday you take your letters of accreditation to the pope, but when you and the pontiff are face to face, what will you push for? Has the Archbishop of Canterbury given you specific instructions?"

The princess asked this loudly, provocatively, in Italian, so the whole restaurant would hear. She did this just to tease me, since we'd spoken of this concern just two days before.

I answered: "His Holiness and I likely shall exchange greetings, and then discuss the wording of proposed Agreed Statements between the Anglican Communion and the Church of Rome."

"Which means you *won't* say mass together. You think I'm joking, Rupert, but I'm curious about diplomats, that's all. You're such a secretive lot."

93

"Most of the work for Unity between the two Churches occurs in committee. By the time I or anybody else, such as the Archbishop of Canterbury, meet the Holy Father, almost everything has been said in advance, so a meeting is mainly a formality."

"I love formality," the princess sarcastically declaimed and stared an obtrusive old woman in the eye to turn her away. "It cuts the ice. But back in London, at that parish you had, was it a slum?"

"Somewhat."

"Did you despise your work?"

"I daresay it was a strain. This post I now have is more—"

"Your style, I know," and Dulcinea took out a compact and did her face. "But Rupert, England is an *atheistic* place, really. Didn't you feel—"

"I was always near collapse. It's far more exhausting than . . . I didn't realize being a parish priest takes all one's energy away. Working with juvenile delinquents, helping pupils with problems at school, visiting the sick, calling on the elderly, doing administration, correspondence, planning, budgeting, banking, meetings meetings meetings, with just the occasional flash of insight into God. So *little* time for meditation on the forces of the Lord, for whom, supposedly, one's working."

"Don't look for insights in Rome," Serafina warned.

"It's just as difficult for priests in Italy today. Social pressures here are tremendous," the mother added with conviction, flinging her compact in her bag.

"*Punto*," the daughter acknowledged. "But was that all, Rupert?"

"The list's endless. London's no paradise. Two times per week . . . telephone the undertaker, arrange for funerals; the Parochial Church Council; Electoral Roll of the parish; the poor; urgent requests for help; the dying; unwed mothers; the insane; the occasional call to be the

diocesan exorcist, I mean, to *call* the diocesan exorcist;
Bible study groups; preparing sermons; matins, Communion, evensong."

"How did you cope?" Serafina asked mildly.

"I didn't. You live 'over the shop.' Everyone demands
you always be at service. People use you for social show,
invite you to the most dreadful events. You're just a bu-
reaucrat in a huge organization. You've only one day off
per week—never enough time to unwind. Worse, you
must be nice to everyone."

"I'd find that last one the killer," the princess stated
and asked for a peach to finish off her meal. I took a
banana, and split it with Serafina. "I *hate* being nice to
everybody."

"Plus some priests are 'called' to God. Others are
called to 'save the world'; they really should be social
workers. Both somehow land inside the Church, which
produces not a few tensions. The Church in England—not
just the Church *of* England—has uncountable tensions.
Far too many churches exist where few should be—and
fewer where most are needed. Priests are rottenly paid.
Though they get free housing, it's hard to struggle by. No
wonder many of them fall in love with each other, instead
of fathering a family which costs too much money."

The principessa gazed at me with feigned shock.

"Thousands of abandoned churches in Britain are falling to vandalism or rot, but efforts to convert them to
dwellings, let's say, often are frustrated. One's not allowed
to live in a consecrated edifice, even if it's redundant. It's
such rubbish. Consecration makes the vibrations better to
live with."

"Much of it must be due to apathy," the princess said
correctly.

"And in Britain, we've the recurrent philosophical
line, dating from the Reformation, 'every man his own
priest.' "

"Your job wasn't *all* disheartening, Rupert," Serafina said kindly. "You did something good or the archbishop wouldn't have sent you here."

I paused and thought. "Great joy to be felt everywhere is that small numbers mean greater sincerity of worshippers. I did feel this in London. The fact exists that Church Unity isn't just a stupid phrase. It's something happening, and now. This is a result of the Holy Spirit, and it gives one strength to continue. I just wonder for myself if I ever was meant to have become a priest in the first place."

22

The next morning—Tuesday—I got up feeling groggy. Having tossed and turned all night, disturbed by very crude dreams of chases and serpents and falling through space, I was awakened by a telephone call from the cardinal's aged valet who said His Eminence was arriving from Palermo that morning but was flying to Florence later that evening and would return Wednesday afternoon. Therefore, could I dine with His Eminence Thursday evening at eight? Thursday I was free, so accepted.

Then, I got another surprise. My grandfather's sister's husband's sister (it always took me ages to figure out the relationship), Lady Winifred, whom we all called aunt, had just arrived in Rome with my brother and two of my sisters. Without any planning and without having let me in on the secret, Aunt Winifred had decided to whisk the three off to Greece. She was taking them to meet Mother's side of the family after all these years.

"But that's marvelous," I said. I suddenly felt very sad that I couldn't go with them. "The children will love it!"

"They had better," coughed Aunt Winifred. "I'm on

96

my last leg. Do you hear this dreadful frog? I'm dying, I tell you, the croup's killing me."

"When can I see you?"

"You can't. I'm in bed. But I'm sending the three children to your palace for lunch. Cancel everything."

"Of course—but today I'm free."

"Fancy that." And Her Ladyship coughed up a lung.

"You're not joking with me, are you? Are you honestly here in Rome? You're *really* going to Mother's family?"

After more hacking, Aunt Winifred revived herself sufficiently to say: "Take them someplace quaint, not expensive. They're spoilt enough at home . . . and everyone will spoil them in Athens." Lady Winifred, a duke's daughter, was very rich and had taken a maternal interest in our family since my parents' deaths. She had installed herself in the east wing of our home.

I replied: "I'll bring them back to your hotel. Where *are* you, by the way?"

"They'll tell you. I'm dying, Rupert." And again she coughed a fit. "This trip's mainly for me. See you."

Having been roused, I made my own breakfast. The cook supplied by the dowager princess quickly let it be known that she was available only for the two main meals.

Thinking of Aunt Winifred, Amy, Louise, and Nicholas, I set out at half past eight toward the Capitoline and the ancient Forum. The huge black swallows of Rome kept twisting and soaring above the pillars and the ivy.

Happy at the prospect of seeing my family, I was inspired by the walk. After passing on the right the great arch of Septimius Severus and the brown brick Curia, from which the present senate of cardinals directly takes its name, I turned left at the Mamertine Prison where both Saints Peter and Paul were incarcerated and walked up the abandoned lane Clivo Argentario.

There always was the same gaudily garbed woman

feeding a snarling pride of cats, a scraggly lot which rubbed skinny frames against her with raucous indiscretion. Seeing my collar, she always would curtsy, in a sarcastic and archaic manner, then tell the cats that I was "to be avoided."

This morning in particular I certainly did feel like being avoided and avoiding everyone. Aunt Winifred must be up to something. How long would my family be in town? I knew so little. God, I'd love to be going. . . .

Crossing the Piazza Venezia, a terrible traffic intersection, was almost my last act as I dodged Lancias and Lotuses while snatches of dialogue from the evening before coursed through my head. Much more than an Anglican priest's duties had been discussed. And there was much that hadn't been discussed—as the pained look on Serafina's passionate face kept telling me.

We had ended the evening by talking about Ercole. Serafina had confided to us that she had spoken with him after he barged in on me, that he said he didn't really want me to go see Angela but that he only was "testing me."

"Testing for what?" I asked.

"Who knows. Does it matter? You've far too much to worry about than to trouble yourself with a teen-ager needing electroshock therapy," Principessa Dulcinea said retributively.

"Mama, for God's sake, he's not an animal!" Serafina intervened.

"He's certainly not *housebroken* then. I do believe, Serafina, he needs psychoanalytical help. What else can we do? You surely can't control him, and you, *cara*, are the sole one he seems to take a fancy to."

Serafina blushed and turned away.

"What does he talk to you about?" I wondered.

The girl turned her head, so her mother answered for her: "Politics! He's a walking Marx machine. Propaganda. Rubbish. He knows nothing else anymore."

"It's difficult to believe," I said.

98

"Tell me. My friends call me mad. Nobody—not a single friend of mine in Rome—is willing to believe such a radical being lives in Palazzo Roseazzini. They say 'She's making the whole thing up' or 'He'll grow out of it' or 'All he needs is a good girl.' Good girl—why he's so good-looking he always was invited to the best parties till a year ago. If he didn't have a chance to find a 'good girl' then, he must have been blind or *queer*! He stopped completely— a year ago he stopped associating with everyone. All his childhood friends, all his countless cousins up and down this whole Italian peninsula—why he gave them all a very rude gesture and said, 'Screw them all.' *That's* Ercole—in a nutshell."

Thank God, Dulcinea's last outburst occurred in the car, as it would surely have meant scandal in the restaurant. Serafina just stared out her window without seeing anything as we drove back toward the Palatine. The princess mumbled a bit more to herself and shook her elegant head sadly.

23

Having completed my office routine early, I waited impatiently for the arrival of Nicholas, Amy, and Louise. I was in the hallway when Graziella let them in, and my little brother was the first to make a dash for me. Then Amy and Louise were embracing me warmly. From then on, it would be difficult to say precisely what happened, so happy was I to see my three favorites from home.

On the way to the restaurant, we traded family gossip and they filled me in on the latest. But as we just had one afternoon together before Lady Winifred shuttled the three to Mother's ancestral land, I didn't want to ruin their brief stay in Rome wasting time on matters we were all too familiar with; feelings were mutual, so by the time we'd wound our way through the narrow streets behind Palazzo Doria, we had ceased talking about the family altogether.

I took them to a marvelous *trattoria* in Via del Gesu called Da Ezio. Its outdoor café, shaded by umbrellas, sits in a pocket *piazzina* big enough for only one lorry. The three buildings walling it in are sooty and downright ugly only to the unobservant eye. They all liked the place immensely, to my delight. To the pleasure of us all, the *bruto tempo* was cooling, the sky now overcast with gray clouds. In a first-floor window, a lone canary chanted melodiously throughout the meal.

"God—isn't Nicholas getting big?" I asked in amazement. Already he was pushing six feet, though he hadn't yet shaved. His wavy hair was brown, and now he was parting it in the middle and brushing it back behind his ears, which stuck out like Grandfather's. It was good to see him beginning to take pride in his appearance. A lady's man, it was plain.

"Big and still as stupid as ever," Amy added.

"Oh, he is not," Louise retorted.

Amy was getting to look so much like Mother it was eerie. The trip, I presumed, had been arranged by Aunt Winifred on Amy's behalf—to get her out of England and away from her recurrent depressions. Amy and I looked quite alike with dark hair and penetrating dark eyes. Thank God there wasn't a sign of depression from Amy today. The Greeks would adore her.

Louise, on the other hand, looked much like Father. A true Broxbourne, she was an impeccable English beauty, with perfectly straight hair a shade beyond blond. Her eyes were dark like ours, though—and she confessed that many young lads had taken a fancy to her of late. She was the equestrian of the family, in training for Olympic competition.

As soon as we ordered, Amy raised a toast "to the Archbishop of Canterbury." She said she and Nicholas called at Canterbury Cathedral last Sunday. That certainly brought back memories. "Plus, I've been studying about you," she said. "I didn't know there were so many connections between Canterbury and Rome."

"It's plain to any fool," Nicholas butted in, having studied too. "Reconciliation's *unavoidable*."

We laughed at his choice of word, but he carried the ball further. "When was it, 597 or something, Pope Gregory the First sent Augustine to Canterbury from a monastery in Rome—which one, Louise?"

Louise pondered, "Uh . . . San Andrea's, wasn't it?"

"You've all studied," I said, amazed.

"Of course," Nicholas returned.

"To Canterbury," Louise concluded the toast, "*and* Rome. It was a big trip thirteen centuries ago."

"To Aethelberht, King of Kent," I added.

"Aethelberht . . . didn't he have a Christian wife?" asked Amy.

"The King of Paris's daughter," Nicholas added.

"Nicholas remembers everything," Louise declared and patted him lightly on the head.

"Poor Augustine only lived eight more years but never shirked his work . . . founding abbeys, converting heathens . . ." Amy was bubbling.

"Canterbury still has the oldest church continuously used in England—the same one Aethelberht was baptized in," Nicholas declaimed.

"Bravo," Amy punctuated.

"Saint Martin's," I added, hard to keep the pace of the discussion. Like all our family sessions, this was a blend of gravity and jest.

"Cantiacorum, Durovernum, Cantwarabyrig—what silly names Canterbury had," Nicholas stated. "To silly names." And he raised a toast to which we all drank. I had never seen my brother guzzle so much wine. It must be Eton.

"Why don't we drink to Rome or Athens?" Amy laughed and pointed to the caged canary. "I never understood about canons. What do *they* do?"

Louise looked at me apologetically, then pointed to the wine. "Amy never knows when to quit—always asking silly questions."

"How else do you learn. It's not every day we get to talk to our *fascinating* brother," Amy said to me, but glared at Nicholas.

"Canons are to cathedrals," I replied, "as curates are to churches, as deans of cathedrals are to vicars."

"How algebraic. No wonder all the Anglicans are joining Rome. It sounds as if Rome's less complicated," Amy retorted.

"Then there're residentiary as opposed to honorary canons . . ." I continued.

"Didn't canons take off where monks left over . . . I mean take over where monks left off . . . at Henry the Eighth's dissolution?" Nicholas asked Louise, then spilled wine on his shirt.

"How do you know?" Louise replied. "By the way, Rupert, your one year in London—technically you were a curate though acting as a vicar. Doesn't one need three years . . ."

"Called serving one's title," I said.

"Three years before becoming . . ." she continued.

"An incumbent, or a vicar, or a rector, they all mean the same but they aren't beneath the same boss I was. Anglican dioceses are subdivided into rural deaneries, you see, and my boss was a rural dean."

"Who's his boss?" Amy asked.

"An archdeacon," I said.

"And his?" she persisted.

"A bishop."

Amy sighed and poured more wine. "*You,* I'm sorry to say, aren't following canon law," Amy said triumphantly, "since you wear mustaches!"

"He also has holes in his socks, he dances, he takes walks without clericals and, God roast his randy soul, he doesn't wear a nightcap," Nicholas added.

"My ears, Rupert, you sinner," Amy whined, rather bibulously.

"Who told you these things?" Louise asked Nicholas belligerently. "Technically," she added, "Rupert's safe, since he wears a *full* beard. Mustaches by themselves are verboten."

"Why?" demanded Amy.

"They used to think wearing mustaches meant a lad must be a rake," I answered, pulling mine wantonly.

"Mustaches meant vicars were too hairy to save souls," Nicholas guffawed.

"Oh, shut up!" retorted Amy. "By the way, now that there's a priest for lunch, let's talk about animals."

"Here she goes. She grew up baptized but now she believes in Buddha," Nicholas snorted and chugged more wine.

"I'm *convinced* animals have souls—better than yours." Amy poked Nicholas's chest savagely. "But what's the official version, from Canterbury?"

"Pets may have representations in the eternal beyond . . ." I began.

"But da Church say animals ain't got no soul," Nicholas completed in quite a good Soul accent. Something else from Eton?

"Stupid—*people* don't have soul. One only finds idiotic animals . . . after they've been under the influence of idiotic human beings. Furthermore, I don't care what you three believe, or preach. I firmly believe even plants have souls," Amy declared.

"So there," Nicholas said sarcastically.

"What's all this rubbish about souls?" Louise asked. "It's not just the soul that's saved so to speak. Aren't Christians supposed to believe that the *body* gets carried away too?"

103

"Your body always gets carried away," Nicholas said hilariously.

Louise blushed crimson. "Oh, you always mock me, but I'm being serious for a change!"

"Man from his birth is prone to sin," Amy said, then added, "that's the official view."

"And the unofficial?" Nicholas queried.

"Blasphemous acts are often closer to the religious than the so-called divine," Louise concluded.

"Would a saint masturbate?" Nicholas asked while the three of us gagged on our wine. "God, what's wrong with asking?"

"Well, research a book on it. You'd have an international best seller," Amy chided.

"I'll call it *Holy Wankers*," Nicholas decided.

"Oh, Nicholas!" We three disapproved loudly and in unison.

"Seriously, I don't think it's sinful," Nicholas pleaded.

"You don't think anything's sinful," chuckled Amy. "Have you ever made confession?"

"Have you?" Nicholas returned.

"Never," Amy admitted.

"Me neither," offered Louise. "How does it feel, Rupert, hearing such . . . such intimate things all the time?"

"Kinky," I answered, rather one for the wine myself.

"Sometimes I wonder—do you, Rupert?—about what happens to priests, at Judgment?" Amy reflected and sighed. The way she said that changed the whole tone of the conversation. "For years you go on hearing the pitiful, the depraved, the lost, the lonely. You hear them and feel for them and absolve them of their sins, which somehow by the Holy Spirit you retain inside. But what happens to all those retentions at Judgment?"

"Where *is* heaven in the first place?" Nicholas demanded and jerked the conversation back to earth.

"After Judgment, our own sins and those retained within us likely vanish into the Great Forgotten," I stated.

"Where in hell's that?" Nicholas wanted to know. "Doesn't anybody ever ask *pertinent* questions at divinity school?"

"Yes, but . . ." I started.

"Yes, but . . . nobody knows precisely, nobody mortal that is," Louise reflected, then added, "We can fabricate that heaven or the Holy Ghost are found in the fourth dimension . . ."

"Free from space and time?" Nicholas asked.

"But," Louise continued, "it's not ours to know what existence is . . . on the other side of death."

"On the other side of life," Amy stated softly, philosophically. "Christianity might offer something, but it keeps too much to its repository of secrets. I could believe . . . but doubts always gnaw me. For one, I can't accept that the Holy Spirit is *male*! That thought I find insane and irrational."

"Well, it's dogma," Louise added.

"Damn dogma! What good do dogmatics do?" Amy asked. "The day will come soon when we must admit that the universe is more than just the limited order set up through someone called Christ, when people from this planet set foot on another one with life, with totally different though just as valid religious truths as those known here."

"Likely truer truths," Nicholas said.

"Since the myriad of beliefs and ideas on this earth doesn't prove one single thing," Amy finished, and downed her drink too.

"Amy," Louise stated seriously yet kindly, "the Lord never stops revealing his ways to the world."

"If He keeps on like He's done, haphazardly since Christ's horrid Crucifixion (though the atrocities and run of savage events 'in the name of the Lord' supposedly are signs that 'God is revealing Himself' like some flasher in Regent's Park), then woe to humanity. Let the earth become nothing but a bomb shelter, useless, one hundred

105

percent useless against the Bomb. Reveal Himself He might, but how soon for mankind who might, sooner than He thinks, find something in outer space more peaceable, more credible in which to believe. Rupert, your Lord Jehovah, wrathful conception of Christians and Jews, is running out of time!"

Amy grabbed an apple from the fruit bowl held by the waiter, then tossed it high in the air, as if it were the earth hurtling through space. But Louise threw a long arm up and caught it, then held the apple aloft.

"Amy," Louise said, "your apple was created by God . . . of nothing. Of nothing . . . God set the universe's processes in motion by his love. He so loved life, He wanted life to share in his creativity which allows processes to develop naturally. So to life, to humanity in particular, the gift free-will He gave," and gave back the apple to Amy. "Then, because free will strayed, God gave his only Son . . . in sacrifice for mankind's evil. Why—because of *love* for humanity. Don't you see this, Amy? Isn't it a moving testament of love of unspeakable pureness?"

Amy took a juicy bite of the apple, chomped and chomped, and did not reply. The words and the apple were nourishment enough. I could tell by the look in her eye, though, that she had simply chosen not to speak— though she had plenty left to say.

"If your God,"—Amy pointed to Louise after an embarrassingly long silence—"and your God"—she pointed to me—"and their God lodged in Saint Peter's"—and she pointed out to all of Rome—"were so loving—and if He does save everyone by having crucified his Son, then He therefore destroyed free will at the conclusion of the Crucifixion—so what're we worrying about? But, if He doesn't save everyone, if He isn't universalist, then He isn't sharing his love with all the universe, and what you're spouting is just a pack of lies at worst, or silly old wives' tales at best."

106

24

It's never ceased to amaze me what brilliant thoughts can issue forth from the most ordinary minds . . . prodded by a bit of alcohol. Not that anybody in the Broxbourne family needed cajoling. My father always blamed our hortatory natures on our mother. "She's just a barbarian . . . Dionysiac!" he used to snarl. But it was precisely the Dionysiac part of her great Greek soul that attracted him to her.

At half past two, well along the road to total Dionysian abandon, I suddenly noted the time. "Good grief, I forgot all about it." Then I felt depressed. We'd soon be parting.

"Forgot what?" Nicholas wondered. He'd forgotten everything.

"I'll have to meet you after my appointment." I didn't say I was needed at Cinecittà as they'd be upset they couldn't go.

"When's that?" Amy wondered.

"Three till five or so," I answered.

"But, we're leaving for Athens at five," Louise said sadly. "They better have good horses there to ride!"

"You should've stayed home then," Nicholas muttered. "All she's done is bitch about leaving her bloody nag."

"I forgot my appointment . . ." I said and shook my head. "You'll have to apologize to Aunt Winifred for me."

Having showed my brother and sisters to the large square named Largo Argentina, I hailed a taxi for them. Wishing them a safe journey, I sadly parted from them and watched them waving till the traffic hid them from sight. If Mother had only lived . . . to be in Athens with them. If Father were alive, too . . . oh God, *why* couldn't we all be there together? Choking back tears, I flagged my own cab and sat back as it rushed to the film city.

I arrived at the studio at three, and hoped that this was the last that *Moctezuma* needed from me. Having arrived alone and in clericals, I was refused entry by the guard, so I dropped the names of author Lord Luxborough (*niente*), director Bochmann (*niente*), and lastly Principessa Roseazzini, which did mean something to the pistol-hugging thug who telephoned for someone to fetch me.

An outrageous female with almost no hair—what little she had was pink—and dressed in a baggy silver-lamé jumpsuit over her shot-putter's frame, eventually arrived on a Harley and said: "You late." We hurried to the building for the film.

The stooge led me to Makeup and then groomed me for the scene to be shot: "For you—priest of Conquest Spain—this is your great moment for glory," she said, apologizing since the director was busy. "This priest you play . . . he's mad like Cortés. It's you and Cortés the camera sees. The whole Spanish army stands behind you two this time. All Christian Spain follows this cross you hold because *you* start the crazy march across the sacred causeway. You go to the Aztec city in the middle of Mexico Lake."

"Why me?"

"*You* hold the cross. *You* the man are the word of the Lord . . . in real life, no?"

"Don't remind me."

"For a priest . . . you're not so stupid. Here, I give you my card. Call me because you need some *redemption*. I like too much the way your beards curl, Father!"

The silver-lamé demon vanished as quickly as she had zoomed me to Makeup. Her card showed two dice with the words Snake Eyes and her telephone number. I tore the card up.

Soon another stranger stormed in. "Bochmann's calling

you—hurry!" This one, a skinny boy who could not speak English, led me through a maze of flats and equally flat staring faces, one of which handed me the same gilt cross I'd held before. The atmosphere in the studio was eerie.

As I bore the cross behind the urchin, suddenly great arc lights swiveled and veered past me. They did so once again, after circling dizzily past a huge crowd of helmeted men. Polished headpieces glistened, then vanished. A thousand men, illumined for a second, had been moving as one mass from left to right. I now could hardly see a thing as the two arcs were trained on me.

"*Vorsicht*, Priest," the heavy German voice of the director boomed in apology from a derrick which was swerving toward me from above. Both arcs flashed up to meet him. "Just testing. *Ja—jetzt richtig*. Stay where you are."

I could hardly see, let alone move. The mob of conquistadors certainly was audible, though invisible. Hundreds of heavy feet were tramping across the studio floor to get behind me and Cortés, who suddenly loomed beside me big as Goliath. The conqueror was one of those body builders so popular in Italian films of the fifties. Cortés slammed me on the back so hard I wanted to hit him, but thought better of it when I noted his size.

"Ready?" he asked in Italian.

I looked at him again and wondered "Ready for what?" For some reason, an orchestra suddenly blared from loudspeakers everywhere to get us in a conquering mood. It was the Mormon Tabernacle Choir's rendition of "Onward Christian Soldiers," a morbid hymn I had always detested.

"*Nein, du Arsh-Loch,*" the German screamed at his sound man, as the great beams again flashed at Cortés and me. "Not that garbage song but 'Christus Vincit' by the Sistine Chapel Choir!"

"Good God," I said aloud. "They're blaspheming the Vatican's music! I can't act in this."

109

Cortés shot me a dirty look, then made a fist and flexed his left biceps beneath my nose. I thought, Jesus save me, it'll all be over soon.

"I want you soldiers," Bochmann continued, "to think like popes, not like marching manic-depressives! I want *meaning* in those feet—goose steps—like this." And he showed us, as the lights did a quick flip to Bochmann in his cherry picker. "Got it? To the music of the Sistine Chapel Choir. You're going to cross this causeway"—and he pointed to a blank grimy floor—"not to decimate a country but to save a civilization's wayward souls. Do it for Christ! You're Christians. Across this causeway, in this sickening city, sits evil, sits sin, sits the Devil himself . . ."

We were forced to march, as "Christus Vincit" began to guide our steps. I didn't like any of it, the atmosphere truly was bloodthirsty. I did begin to feel like a Spaniard, though no ancient Mexico was looming ahead, no sacred causeway was stretching across water.

But—"and one TWO THREE FOUR . . . and one TWO THREE FOUR," the singsong beat shouted by the German above us prodded us on, as we plodded like monsters toward conquest.

The heaviness of the cross, the interminable length of the studio, the lights glaring in our faces and the sacrilegious playing of holy music were making us sweat, making our expressions appear more and more brutal. I was a priest of this Christ—but what in God's name was I doing in this macabre celluloid fantasy?

After what seemed an eternity of marching, the hoarse German voice seemed in frightfully perfect "sync" with the angelic Latin of the Sistine Chapel Choir. Our boot sounds became one with our heartbeats. I was all but having visions: step pyramids were rising up beyond me; acrid water was waving on both sides of me.

The cross—it seemed not only to carry itself forward,

110

but it also tugged along the masculine terror behind me, the thousands of brawny soldiers.

Suddenly it got to me: *Why were we doing this!*

My mind, lanced as if by conquistadors, couldn't help screaming out, "STOP!"

"Cut—*perfect*—miraculous—a miracle—a miracle!" The director was jumping in his high box like a kid at Christmas. Christian soldiers of Renaissance Spain were pounding me on the back—for some wicked and gamey reason. And before I knew it, I was being kissed fervently by Princess Dulcinea, then by Alexander, then by Gerhard Bochmann, then by more and more people, all of whom suddenly appeared from nowhere.

25

I returned to the palazzo feeling giddy. Luxborough had produced champagne which he, Bochmann, the princess, and many others and I drank after shooting the scene. In the middle of the chatter, Dulcinea requested I dine with Serafina, as she herself would be elsewhere and the prince was at Castello Roseazzini on the coast. Alexander also invited me to dine the next day, and I couldn't help thinking they all were cracked, being so congratulatory, but they kept saying: "You should've seen your face—what a satanic expression! It'll make the film." So be it, but I doubted it.

Dulcinea dropped me off in Via di San Teodoro and continued to her destination. I straggled to my apartments, then nipped into my courtyard for a snooze on a slab stolen from some ruin, likely the Forum. It must have been a dreamless two hours later that I woke thinking a spider was on my face—but was startled that Serafina was dangling a powder puff onto my nose from a string and a bamboo pole.

"Get up," she coaxed. "Don't you want to eat?" and she giggled. "I'll meet you at the stairs."

Without freshening, I staggered past the foliage and through my rooms to the hall where Serafina, in a loud dress—white with huge lavender flowers—threw her arms round me and gave me a heartening kiss.

"Serafina?" came a gruff male shout down the staircase. "Hurry up, it's getting cold."

"Who cares?" she whispered and bit my ear.

"Someone will see us," I teased.

"Let them," she taunted in return and led me up the marble *scala*.

Entering the third floor, we were greeted by Ercole, who held open the door. He was barechested and barefooted, and hadn't shaved in days. He was wearing soiled red trousers which looked like bloomers. "It's cold," he snarled and led us to the dining room.

Each meal in Italy is an adventure. I hadn't expected Ercole at this one, and didn't know what to say. I didn't care to talk to him, so forced him to say the first word, which was not till midway through the *pastasciutta*. "Serafina's in love, you know."

I feigned astonishment, "With whom?"

"With me." And he lewdly grinned at his sister. "You can take her body, Rupert, but I'll always own her soul."

"Don't speak so coarsely before this young lady," I said firmly and stared him in the eye.

"Maybe she'll grow out of it . . . now that she's intimate with a priest," Ercole said, finished his pasta, then folded his arms behind the curls of his head in order to show us his hairy armpits. "You come from Canterbury, don't you?"

"Why ask foolish questions?" Serafina retorted.

"I forgot. In Italy . . . no, in Roma Nera . . . nobody

112

asks personal questions. God forbid someone dare ask, 'Well what, dear Serafina, are you doing this afternoon?' The whole of so-called Society is so spoilt we never know what we're doing, ever. We just flit through existence, being waited on, having servants like this bastard"—and Ercole grabbed the groin of the handsome youth from Sicily who was serving cold cuts of roast beef and french beans—"and destesting anybody who works for a living. Work—ugh—*sporca cosa*." Then Ercole winked at the Sicilian and fondled his own groin. "But aw-aw-aw . . . I'm being nasty. One never must be outré at table—good show—tut-tut. Do tell me about Canterbury."

"Why should I," I replied, "when you've likely never been there?"

"He has," Serafina said as painfully as if her last tooth had just been extracted.

"I adored it." And Ercole grimaced mock-demurely. "Where else on earth could one find pieces of Aaron's Rod, bits of the very clay from which Adam was made, and the right arm of his dear Lordship, the knight Saint George?"

"That was mediaeval Canterbury," I answered.

"Canterbury Tales of the world . . . unite," Ercole said idiotically and laughed. I couldn't tell if he was being witty in his own perverse way, or loathsome, or was maybe just high on some drug.

"Do you hate me, Ercole?" I asked abruptly.

"God no," he despaired almost genuinely. "I think you'd make a brother-in-law . . . if only you'd become a Catholic layman. We couldn't have an Anglican priest in the family, could we?"

Serafina spoke up: "Ercole, let it be. If you don't like Rupert, why don't you be a man and say so."

"Why don't we *pretend* . . . like everybody else does . . . pretend our way through life? Like him here, Anglicans will pretend to love Catholics after the two Churches kiss each other sweetly and bye-bye go all those

113

unspeakable crimes and all those nightmares of so many centuries."

"Why talk of it!" Serafina snapped.

"It's Rupert's job . . . Why can't we talk about his job at table? Would you prefer we gossip our way to the apricots? Serafina, dear, did you know Roast Beef looks *lovely* on this plate, but he doesn't go at all with French Beans— she's far too chic—she owns seventeen palazzi—he only rents a tiny dirty room in a working-class neighborhood which *we* never never never see."

"Must you always talk politics!" she shouted. "I'm sick to death of your ranting about what you say is evil. If you hate our world so much, our class that's weaned and pampered and tolerated your presence so graciously, then go into the world and get yourself a job—that's right—a job to change what seems so heartless! Help people—don't just complain—go out and help those you feel such empathy for."

"And you?" Ercole calmly asked.

"Me? I'm a pianist and I'm working damned hard to get somewhere, to make something of myself so I just won't sit about and sponge off people or bitch about them till the day I die."

"Being a concert pianist . . . how does that help people?" enquired Ercole seriously.

"Much," declared Serafina, "much. I know two ways in this life to help humanity: one, directly by aiding those less fortunate; the other, by artistic creativity. The first helps the body, the second helps the soul. You—incessantly analyzing life as only being something political— you are ever and only concerned with the first, with the body."

"Once the world changes the body, then it can change the soul," he replied.

"Wrong! Never can the two separate. Body *and* soul," the girl said vehemently, "both and together. You know how we can help this sick world: let fifty percent of hu-

114

manity help the body, rid poverty, restore decency; but let the other fifty percent create the conditions of beauty, of contemplation, of inspiration *into which* the first fifty percent can go."

What a declaration, so succinctly put, and from the lips of this often reticent girl. I sat with my mouth open, and found it impossible to finish my meal.

26

Ercole soured the meal and Serafina's disposition. Because he wouldn't leave us alone, I left shortly thereafter. Serafina complained of cramps, obviously depressed after her inspired outburst. I admit being let down that she didn't even offer to walk me to the door, but had asked the servant to do so.

After I kissed her hand, she gripped her stomach and rushed to sit down. As I was leaving, I expected to hear shouting behind me, but heard nothing. What a pair, I thought, and wondered just what type of a being Ercole really was. Strange—he didn't mention a thing about his taunting visit to me the day before. Nor did he say a word about Angela.

I decided to shrug off what resentment I harbored against Ercole by telling myself to accept his rancor, and her cramps, as indicative of their behavior. I could hardly say I knew them. Who was I to judge?

Once in my rooms, though, I mulled over the day's events, and began contrasting my sisters with Serafina Roseazzini. At least all three were alike in their search for a decent way to live in this day and age. I wondered how Amy and Serafina would get along?

That Serafina had such a mad brother, no small impediment to our love with his testing of me, only gave me more impetus to carry on, to see where the affair would lead. Already it had led the girl to express a theory of society as profound as any I had ever heard.

The more I thought of Serafina's words, the more practical and sane they sounded. Perhaps all women felt likewise. Fifty percent to aid, fifty to create . . .

I suddenly ached to hold the girl, to make love to her, to tell her I loved her.

Rome was so overwhelming that it struck me later that evening that I should go on a religious retreat. The many abbeys in the environs of the Holy City had proven beneficial to the contemplative and the troubled for centuries. There were books I wanted to read, and much thinking to do, both all but impossible with Rome's social life distracting me.

Yes, this idea seemed proper, and timely. I needed peace of mind for planning the autumn's work, but more so to rejuvenate my prayer life, which had been slumbering of late.

Did Serafina ever feel like this?

The thought of her made me even more miserable.

Should I even be falling in love at this crucial time of my life?

But love . . . is the Lord . . .

It had all been too much, too quickly. In six short days I should be meeting His Holiness the Pope.

That thought sobered me considerably. I decided that tomorrow morning I would find somewhere for an ascetic retreat the weekend after my private audience at Castel Gandolfo.

27

Before my secretary could contact a monastery Wednesday morning, Serafina's brother called. At nine o'clock I certainly didn't expect him, and his arrival was so close after mine that I suspected he had followed me. Maybe my avoiding the "cat woman" in the Clivo had caused the bad luck, but that idea seemed mad. The cardinal's superstition and the pervasive eeriness of the Roseazzini household was rubbing off on me. Not that I came from a stable home myself.

There was Ercole in my office, all smiles and cheer. My secretary closed the door on us. "Thought I'd say hello," he stated and fondled his manhood in the lackluster Italian manner.

"Oh," I replied.

"Busy?"

"Just trying to wake up."

"Sleepy?"

"Did you come here for a reason?"

"I can't really say I hate you," he said and yawned. "You know . . . Serafina thinks she loves you."

Was he playing another game or speaking frankly? I said nothing.

"She's immature," he continued, "and very brilliant. We haven't agreed on things for years. Her mind is shut to everything I say. We communicate in other ways."

"Can't you communicate with your brother?" I asked. "He seems a decent chap."

"We hate each other. He's my father's friend. Serafina's my mother's. I live alone—I've most in common with our sister they sent away."

Sadness in his voice was new. Or was it feigned? I felt he was reaching out to me, searching for someone

117

with whom to communicate. Was this thought naïve? I wanted to trust the boy, but could not. I asked: "What is it, Ercole? Why . . . why are you here? Please tell me . . . what's on your mind?"

"I don't trust you!" he snapped.

This didn't surprise me. "I don't trust you, either."

"So we're even."

"So . . . we admit it. Let's talk openly. I feel you need a friend. Is Serafina your only friend?"

"She's her mother's. I have . . . many. The family doesn't like them. I live a life apart."

"How do you know the family—"

"Father's said so many times. He says, 'Your cousins and children of *our* friends are more than enough to give you an army of associates of all shades and persuasions.' But I hate them all and they hate me, so *basta così*—let live and die. They will . . . sooner than they think."

"I know how you feel," I said seriously. "My own family and people of my class . . . I often find boring enough to kill. But that's life—that's families—that's friends. Often the best people are those one comes across by chance—the odd encounter—like you and me. It wasn't planned, it just happened."

"Serafina's ill. It's my fault. I upset her so," he grimaced, dodging my tactic which wasn't to his liking.

"What's her problem?" I asked.

"Nerves? Who knows."

"Your mother wants to send her to Tunisia."

"Mother'd like to fly her off to Pluto. Now everything either of us does is considered filthy."

"Why?"

"Ask the principessa," he said derisively. Then he stared off, looking truly demonic, and spoke more to the window than to me. "If you want Serafina's soul . . . even *that* can be arranged."

"What?" I asked incredulously.

"If you want her, I'll let you have her."

118

What rapport we just established was shattered. I reacted sharply. "Are you playing the pimp? I forbid you to come here anymore—to speak such trash! Is that all, Ercole?"

"Next time will you call the *polizia*?" he whispered, as if he weren't in the room. I felt he was listening to someone else's voice.

"Ercole, what's wrong?" I said, suddenly feeling compassion for his pitifulness. "Why come to me? Why say these things?"

"You're a priest." His reply was barely audible.

"So? Your own uncle's a cardinal. For God's sake, Ercole, you've one of the most spiritual men of the whole Catholic Church beneath your own roof. Your uncle's a *good* man, Ercole. I beg you, go to him, speak your mind. You used to, didn't you?"

The boy refused to answer, lost in thought.

"Your uncle, Ercole—"

"Has committed unforgivable crimes against the people!" he blurted like a gun going off. "He's turned my family against me. He's not content to represent the odious ways of Holy Church and her finances; he's also misrepresenting me."

"He loves you, Ercole, he told me. You—of all his family—you, Ercole, he says, are the brightest the family's ever produced."

"He would say that. But—do you know why?"

"Why?" I demanded.

"Two years ago . . . I still was at school, not at Rome University. We've a place by the sea, a *castello*, and . . . we had a family there as . . . guarding it when we weren't in residence, a Sicilian family like the boy we have now. The family was good, but no—not to my father or uncle. They had four kids, the oldest my age, a boy and three small girls—no—Riccardo was a year younger. Understand, they were there ten years. Riccardo and my brother and sister and I, we always were together, when we were at

119

the sea. But two years ago my mother had a birthday party for the cardinal, in the courtyard, and the maid, Riccardo's mother, and his caretaker father were helping. But more help was needed. So, without asking Riccardo, who never did such a thing in his life, my mother went to Rome on my father's orders and bought a butler's uniform for Riccardo to wear. In other words they suddenly were changing my friend from a child to a servant, a *slave*, without his knowing what was happening. I had a fit. Neither Serafina nor I could believe it. We'd all played together, but suddenly our friend was taken from us, *utilized*, like some lackey of ancient Rome just because he was an extra body in the castle."

It started to come together in my mind. "So what happened?"

"I told him, 'Don't you dare wear that damned jacket or wait on them like they expect you to!' Riccardo's father was proud, thickheaded like me. He'd often confided in me, 'Never will I let my son become a servant,' though he himself hadn't been so lucky. All my life, for some reason, servants have trusted me. I've always felt closer to them than to my own class."

"Then?"

"There was the showdown, of course. The cardinal got blue in the face. My father even hit me, for 'impertinence of talking revolution with the staff'—'it's not done'—'it's never been done in our family'—'how dare you put ideas in their heads.' "

I chose my words with care. "Italy still does feel rather feudal."

"The principessa saw the seriousness of the situation and tried to save it, but my father wouldn't bend. He said: '*I'm Prince*, and my word will be followed by all! Italy's fault today isn't her system . . . it's her fathers; nobody has backbone anymore; all Italians are sheep longing for a shepherd; nobody's got guts to lead the flock.' Et cetera, et cetera. 'Riccardo *will* become a butler or his whole family will be turned out cold.' "

"And?"

"The whole family was turned out cold."

"My God."

"They were forced to return to Sicily—to nothing. Serafina and I gave them all the money we had in the bank."

"And Oduardo—what did he do in the midst of all this?"

"Stupid Oduardo stayed blank as ever. I begged him for money, but his answer was, 'What do you want it for—an LP record?' "

I shook my head.

"With the *castello* in chaos, the nearby village soon knew what *il signor principe* had done. Its local council being Communist, not much sympathy for the castle came from the residents. My father had a barrage of defenses ready in case his action was disputed."

"Was it?"

"You must be joking. This is Italy, not England. The cardinal's birthday party was canceled, though, much to my father's disgust. Since then, in the Roseazzini household I'm persona non grata. They all think it's fun blaming my 'unpopularity' not on this fiasco, about which nobody speaks, but on my 'being possessed by the Devil,' or 'feeling outrage at Angela's incarceration,' or 'falling into evil company at university,' or other assinine excuses. None of them ever will admit that my feelings didn't just spring fully formed from my skull two years ago; they've been slowly developing since I was a boy. My views—considered so radical—were radical at age ten, had anyone in the family cared to talk to me sincerely instead of gossiping or trading *bon mots*."

On that happy note Ercole rose. "I'm going. Perhaps we'll see each other ten days from now."

"Are you going on a trip?"

"Not really—just somewhere in the country. *Ciao*," he said and left.

Somewhere in the country—that reminded me to or-

121

ganize the retreat. I called my secretary and broached the subject with her. If anyone would know, Vera Wainwright would. The quiet lady had worked five years for the Anglican Centre, and it was she who took charge after my predecessor's death. Without hesitation, Vera did know of a monastery. I left her to telephone, and promised to check with her after lunch.

28

After midday Eucharist I hopped a number 64 bus to the Tiber, then turned off Corso Vittorio Emanuele into Via dei Banchi Nuovi. Finding the Pietrolomini residence, I passed the *portière*, then ascended by lift to the third floor to dine with Luxborough.

He was lounging on the sofa, in the same salon where we had had tea. He wasn't reading or doing anything constructive. His head was thrown back and he was staring at the ceiling beams. He muttered hello without turning to me.

"You look a sight," I commented and sat opposite him. He appeared morose. His white shirt was open.

"Headache," he said. "Working on a new book, did I tell you? Mornings I write. They don't shoot the sodding film before lunch. The cinema crowd here . . . God, can you bear them? They drive me batty."

"My few times at Cinecittà have left me dizzy."

"You were super though, smashing in fact!"

"Don't be absurd."

"I know, it'll ruin our appetites. Hungry?" Alexander asked.

"Starving. How's your big-breasted cook doing?"

"Wouldn't you like to know?"

At that moment the cook opened the double doors

122

to the *sala di pranza*. Prettier this time, her manly shoulders seemed less formidable and her bushy orange hair was caught in a net. She also was smiling, a vast amelioration.

"The grin's for you, not me," Luxborough said, buttoning his shirt. "You pierced her soul last Sunday."

I winked at the girl, but she frowned and vanished into the pantry.

"Wait till you see what she cooked for you," he said slyly.

A marvelous *pasta di calamari*, delicious octopus in a delicate white sauce, arrived. "She trudged all the way to Campo di Fiori just to get it fresh this morning."

"The Campo's just around the corner. I'm not that much of a tourist," I told him, then complimented the cook in Italian. The girl giggled, then disappeared.

"It's definitely her soul you control," the fellow continued.

"Speaking of which, old boot, sorry to wax rotten but I must comment on something you mentioned Sunday. You said—"

Before I could finish he read my mind, "I said . . . you and I were *deviates*, because we have a stupid compunction to translate our spirits' transgressions."

"But what do you mean by that?"

"Artists do it creatively, priests spiritually."

I winced. "Don't be so bloody facile. Priests can be more creative than poets. You deal with words and priests with human beings."

"How fulfilling," Alexander said sarcastically.

"No, listen. Do you know Serafina Roseazzini?"

"Of course, you idiot. The one built like—"

"It happens the girl's got a brain," I laughed.

"No."

The cook entered with more pasta, to make the second round.

"This one's only got half a brain. That's all she needs," Luxborough declaimed and nodded her way.

"Listen," and I tried to encapsulate Serafina's philosphical theory.

Alexander sneered: "She could quote theory from the phone directory and you'd pull your beard and say 'goo-goo.' All you care about, Broxbourne, is theory leading straight to her. . . ."

"Don't be a twit."

"Propose to her. Whisk her away."

"She hasn't 'come out' yet."

"Better move quick then," he laughed.

I was getting nowhere on this tack so I tried another gambit. "You also said Sunday . . . poetically you draw inspiration from ancient Greece and—"

"Nothing new, is it?"

"And embrace the pagan pantheon, but why on earth did you take *Christian* Communion at the papal mass?"

"I don't know," he replied blandly.

"Do you believe in it?"

"No. I was carried away. I get that way sometimes . . . end up doing the silliest things I'd never dream of doing in pensive moments."

"Do you regret taking Communion?"

"Regret it? Hell, no. Did me no harm, a bit of biscuit."

"How can you do such a thing of import if you say you've *seen* gods of ancient Greece? You're mad!"

"Not all the gods, old bean. Anyhow, I can do such a thing simply by doing it."

I shouted, "Aren't you hypocritical."

This didn't faze him in the least. "No," he said calmly. "It's not that one can avoid Christianity in Rome. It's rather moving . . . to see how it inspires so many people. I must admit, though, that I have *not* been inspired by things Christian. I daresay they've agitated me into contemplation."

"Just like your mother!" I exclaimed. Lady Celeste was known to have no Christian sentiments whatsoever.

"I'll let you in on a secret. Even though things Christian, or Judeo-Christian for that matter, agitate me into thinking, such thinking invariably leads back (the logic leads back) to things ancient Greek. Sorry, that's just how my poor brain functions."

I chewed that with the delicious chicken, yet felt that even though we were approaching something profound, nothing Alexander had told me was extraordinary, so I asked: "Luxborough, are you making it up? Did you truly see a god of ancient Greece?" I was dying to laugh, but forced myself not to.

The fellow closed his eyes tightly and was silent for some time. Then, with his eyes shut he uttered:

> So that the Sun may next day rise,
> And not go coursing wild the Skies,
> Anew Orphéos be born, BE BORN!,
> To honor the World with Song!

"What's that?" I asked, moved.

"What I wrote . . . having visited Delphi. I should like to live there . . . forever. You've never been?"

"Not even to Athens. Nowhere in Greece I'm ashamed to say."

"But your mother's Greek!"

"I know. Strange . . . Mother never took us. I've a whole set of relatives I've never seen."

"But that's insane."

"Mother forgot them all, but then took them by surprise two years before she died and did a huge concert tour in her homeland."

"Why the hell didn't you go?"

"Like a fool, I pretended I was busy, too busy reading about God at Cambridge. I regret it now—to the core of my being. Mother sang all the Greek songs she knew as a girl. It was the high point of her career. Her people loved her . . . forgave her everything. She went during Orthodox Easter when the feeling of the Risen Christ is so powerful

125

in Greece. Her people rose with her . . . she gave them so much strength. She even sang one evening, she said, in the ancient amphitheater of Epidavros."

"And you didn't go? Are you crazy?" Alexander paused. "By the way, you know Hefferon, my best-mate who just won the World Championship in the 1500-meters—we were at Christ Church together? I've decided I'm sending him to Greece next year. He'll have his doctorate in classics and he deserves a trip."

"He'll like that," I said, then admitted finally, "yesterday . . . Aunt Winifred was here. She passed through with Nicholas, Amy, and Louise. She's taking them to meet our family . . . our other half . . . in Greece."

"And you're not going?"

"How can I?"

"Go in August. Bloody hell, Broxbourne, you alarm me. It's your *family*, you know."

"I promised Serafina I'd take her to Kent."

"Rupert, are you afraid of the part of you that's Greek? You are, aren't you? You're afraid that when you see Greece, it will rip the Christian mask right off your face!"

I couldn't answer. He had touched something true within my soul.

Alexander took a long sip of wine. "Rupert, you're half Greek. You've more Hellenic lore inside you than you'll ever know. I'd give anything to have what your blood has. Ah God—both our educations filled our vapid brains with mythic glory since the first day we could read. Have you forgotten it all, Rupert?"

"No," I admitted weakly, seeing my mother in my mind.

"You've been brainwashed by clerical strictures which—"

"Which give me *structure* for my life, just as your being able to say, 'I'm an author,' gives you. At least, being a priest is something, Alexander! Even if its tenets contradict your own, even if it agitates you for ages, even if it never inspires a single couplet from you."

"But your priesthood . . . is it something phenomenal to you, or something innate? It's no joke, Rupert. Don't you fear roasting in hell, if beliefs you posit *aren't* really those which you believe?"

"What about you, writing line after line, composing things you state by artistic license as truth for mankind . . . yet after having written them you glare at the page with horror and say, 'That's not right,' though you've allowed them to slide into print. Don't *you* fear fate's retribution?"

"So, both of us are phonies, eh?"

"Likely," I heard myself reply.

> Yet the Poet, fated to state such ravings
> For all *men—this being his loftiest goal—*
> Alongside Death must likewise stroll.

"Same poem?" I asked.

"Same poem," he replied sadly. "And you, the priest, must listen to such ravings. You must invoke the spirit of the universe . . . to beckon its mysterious labor."

"Alexander, without your wanting the Christian Holy Ghost whom you spurn, you still can't help but invoke its mysterious labor, and somehow this odd factor of creation settles in your brain unbeseeched, and causes you to write things of beauty."

"Perhaps this Christian Holy Ghost is really what makes me turn to the lost things of beauty of the pagan past?"

"Perhaps. Who understands the ways of God?"

"Or . . . who understands the gods?"

29

Back at the office, I went over what my friend had said. Lunch had ended on a positive note. I confessed to Luxborough how much I needed a period of serious meditation, and he said he desired the same.

Having mentioned that I wished to go on retreat, he told me: "Forget a bloody monastery where nobody knows you. You'll only be an intruder." He suggested we rent a car and go to his host's house, Casino Ticchio, near Naples two weeks from now. Count Pietrolomini had left him the keys.

Alexander needed a long weekend to write in peace, so he called for the cook and asked if she'd mind a trip south. She agreed and we asked her to telephone the *contadino* of the villa to ready the place for our arrival.

This suited us perfectly. It would allow for a bit of sightseeing on the way. I certainly wasn't in the mood for isolation with people I didn't know. When I told this to my secretary, though, she didn't take to the idea at all. Vera felt I *needed* asylum in a monastery!

That afternoon the Secretariat for Promoting Christian Unity telephoned from the Vatican to confirm the wording of a mutual agreement which had not yet been made public. We chatted informally about the ordination of women, a hot issue to say the least. It wasn't a cardinal with whom I spoke but a *monsignore* I hadn't met. He arranged my visit to their offices in Via del Erba on Tuesday, after my official reception by *Sua Santità*.

I left work immediately thereafter to rest before the party at Villa Ferrucci that evening. The event for Serafina's seventeen-year-old cousin Sabina, a very popular *principessina*

I was told, was bound to be one of the biggest of the Season.

At six Prince Guadagno's Sicilian footman delivered a note from Serafina. She ordered me not to wear clericals, and insisted I must be in formal evening wear. As I pulled my suit from the closet, I had to laugh at the rest of the note. Serafina had found our residence, Dexter Mote, in a book of English manor houses and asked if I might take her to visit it this summer. I replied on her letter, "In August—when the office is closed," then signed it with the word "Love."

Shortly thereafter the telephone rang. Serafina's voice was jubilant: "Really? Can you invite me formally? Papa will accept, I know he will. Oh, I'm so excited—I've not been to England before. If you don't invite me, they'll pack me off to Tunisia."

"What's wrong with your health anyway?" I finally inquired after debating whether or not I ought to ask her.

But the question didn't faze her. She replied chipperly: "You know—girl problems. Nerves and all. I'm better though, I think it's all in my head." She changed the subject and told me to pick her up at eight. "Wait till you see what I'm wearing. You won't believe it."

I didn't! Serafina came through double doors into a frescoed anteroom with a medieval feel to it, where I was waiting. I very nearly dropped my drink. She walked directly to me and offered her hand, which I kissed over her gloves. She looked spectacular.

What gloves, what an outfit! Her mania for clothes from the fifties had been indulged once again. I gawked at her and asked, "Did you find this in a secondhand shop, too?"

"Valentino did it for me," she retorted, insulted. "Don't you like it?"

I loved it—the dangerously high blood-red spiked

129

heels, the blood-red opera gloves which came within inches of her shoulders, the blood-red sequined turban banded in white pearls, and the enormous ruby earrings and matching necklace which must have been worth a fortune.

"Heirlooms?" I asked.

"Heirlooms. I don't care if the whole Brigade attacks the villa tonight. I'm going in style and wearing *jewels!*"

Her dress almost outdid the rubies. It was skin tight and strapless, exposing the back and barely cupping the breasts. The gown, of pearl white sequins, had a great blood-red stripe from right breast to left calf. The skirt was slashed, being longer on the left than on the right. It was incredibly daring.

"Do all girls dress like this in Rome?" I asked stupidly.

"None of them. I'm the only one. You watch—they'll all be in dresses to their toenails. But they're used to me now. At first I caused a scandal—I wore blue-black silk, slit to the buttocks and sheer, for a girl friend's debut. Her fussy mother was horrified, but I blew her kissy-kissy and got away with it! Now they just shrug their shoulders and say: 'Well, she *is* Dulcinea's daughter. What do you expect with a *star* in the family?' We Roseazzini are a very bold lot. We get away with things other families cannot. Don't ask me why. Are you ready?"

I gave her my arm. She pulled a long crimson cigarette holder from her bosom and handed me a small oblong lighter of onyx, mother-of-pearl, and gold. I lit her cigarette, and we descended three flights to the palace courtyard, where a giant footman I'd never seen before opened the door of an enormous white 1959 Cadillac.

30

Villa Ferrucci is classified as a middle-sized Roman estate. This means it appears colossal to most observers, but in fact it is not as grandiose as some. After saying a few words about the place as our chauffeur drove into Via di San Teodoro, Serafina asked: "I heard Ercole barged in on you again. What for this time?"

While I recapitulated the story her brother told me about his antagonism toward his family and class, Serafina couldn't stop laughing, though it occurred to me that she, too, found the story sad. "He changes it every time I hear it."

"But then—it's true? He did intervene over the servants?"

"Do you really want to know?"

I nodded.

"Intervene's hardly the word. Intercourse is more like it."

"What?"

"The truth is that Ercole was caught"—and she hesitated over the phrasing—"caught sodomizing Riccardo's younger sister. Yes—I know—but he was caught by Riccardo who beat him up, though Riccardo's hardly as strong."

"Ercole said Riccardo was his good friend."

"Rubbish! They hated each other—because of Riccardo's sister Mina. She was thirteen but looked twenty-five. *Siciliana*, you know."

"Why . . . would even that cause a whole family to be told—"

"Another of Ercole's lies. He never tells the truth, Rupert, you must understand that. One, he's a male nymphomaniac. Two, he was . . . having it with that girl all

summer. Day and night. She got pregnant. Oh, it's a mess.
Her father was a good worker but missed Sicily, so he
used this as an excuse and threatened my father—yes he
did just that—threatened us because my father's son got
his little girl pregnant. So, my father, who's exceptionally
kindhearted, agreed to give a sum of money and even had
the girl . . . I mean Mina was enabled to have an abortion."

I sighed and squeezed Serafina's hand, seeing how
distasteful the admission was. She smiled and whispered:
"I feel so close to you . . . . I . . . it's so good to be able
to speak about these things but because you're a priest it
makes it . . . makes it easier for me because I know it's
probably nothing you haven't heard. Do you understand?"

"Don't think like that," I whispered in her ear. "I'm
a human being who happens to have become a priest."

We crossed the Tiber and drove along Via Aurelia Antica
toward Monti di Creta, where the villa of Serafina's father's
sister, Principessa Licia Ferrucci, was receiving her five
hundred guests.

I must say, nothing in England ever prepared me for
what I took part in that night. One could hardly dismiss
the sight of three hundred beautiful women in gowns and
jewels, but Serafina kept saying "The whole thing's silly."
However, I know she was daydreaming of having her own
coming-out party.

As we turned off the Aurelia Antica and drove
through the main gate, we saw dozens of cars before us.
Serafina's excitement increased by the second. "I wasn't
going . . . till I met you," she confided and snuggled close.
"Wait till you see this place. Sabina's done wonders."

Wonders, indeed. The late-eighteenth-century villa
itself was a wonder, with its great classical-revival mansion
looming at the end of an avenue of palms and eight-meter
mounds of white and pink oleander.

"Oh, but this is nothing. The party is behind the

house. We get out here." And she pointed ahead to where the limousines were stopping. "We go up the stairs to the main house and greet the Ferrucci with Sabina, then we go through the house to the terrace overlooking the sunken garden, which will be lit with hundreds of torches. Next we cross the garden. Sabina's had a huge tent from the Renascimento placed on the opposite terrace in front of the *pavillon*. You'll see—just wait."

The beige-columned Ferrucci home truly was a picture of luxury, and the long line of gorgeous guests, family, and friends enhanced it no end as they wove up the graceful S-shaped ramp to the villa proper. Everyone gawked at Serafina, I must say, and she caused a sensation as we stepped out of the huge white automobile with the great fins.

From there on until we reached the tent and the tables and the drinks—the whole experience really was exceptional. Even Serafina commented upon it, as we stepped onto the villa's back portico which afforded an unforgettable view of the sunken garden. The formally clipped hedges were a riot of pinks and purples. And to the right, the garden gave onto a spectacular panorama of all of the city. "*Guarda . . . tutta Roma*," Serafina said, delighted.

"I adore this place!" she said as we descended to the garden which suddenly seemed more water than plants; fountains began bubbling and splashing wherever one happened to look. The whole scene was so sublimely illumined by torches and small plates of *lampade*—wax lamps used in the palazzi of Rome—that it all seemed like a dream.

I thanked God for the lovely woman by my side. But subconsciously I was apprehensive, for Sabina upset Serafina when we greeted her by saying that Ercole had come after all, "wearing dirty jeans and a filthy work-shirt."

"I pray we don't see him," Serafina stated to her cousin, then greeted her relatives with a worried look.

133

As we paused at the center of the *giardino*, by a remarkable fountain of sea nymphs cavorting for the attention of Poseidon, Serafina introduced me to scores of beautiful women and handsome men. Then she led me up to the tent, where a large group was assembling. The sides of the blue-and-white-striped shelter had been rolled up, to allow a view of the garden. A band was playing mood music from the thirties, with piano, brass, and violins.

Sabina's relatives were so numerous that only the immediate family's seating had been arranged in advance. With five hundred guests, this was undoubtedly wise, but Serafina decided to find a table immediately and chose one with people she did not know.

Not long thereafter the buzzing in the tent suddenly stopped, and everyone rushed to the terrace to watch the entrance of the family. "Not everyone in Rome does things in this old-fashioned flamboyant manner," Serafina said. Obviously, Principe Orazio Ferrucci intended that this evening for his eldest daughter be one that nobody in Rome would ever forget.

Leading the procession from the main villa through the sunken garden was Cardinal Monsignani, who was escorted by two exceptionally handsome blond fifteen-year-old twins who served as *portatori di ceri* or acolytes and carried sizeable gold candlesticks. They were from his titular church in south Rome, and they alone caused a sensation, though in no way upstaged the cardinal, whose cross and ring, both encrusted with diamonds, glittered clear across the garden.

Behind them came the Dowager Principessa Aurora Roseazzini, who was actually being carried on a litter! Even her granddaughter didn't know the doyenne was entering *à l'égyptienne*. The crowd was truly astonished. I managed to catch Princess Dulcinea's eye from afar and noticed that her mouth was agape. Serafina simply said, "Gram's been a bit tired. This garden . . . it's so frightfully long."

As the paternal grandparents were deceased, the next to come were Sabina's brothers Agostino and Cesare, fourteen and thirteen, and then their sister Galeazza, aged eleven. They were followed by their mother, Princess Licia, who was escorted by her brother Averardo, the sole bachelor of the Roseazzini house. Each small group of the family had been preceded by a lavender-liveried servant holding a golden candelabra.

Four servants illuminated the way of Prince Ferrucci and his daughter Principessina Sabina. The prince was in the formal attire of the Knights of Malta, and his daughter was gowned in white silk. A small diadem of diamonds and tremendous pearls graced her head and matching diamonds and pearls adorned her neck and arms. Everyone watched speechlessly as she ascended the terrace steps from the sunken garden on the arm of her father. Then suddenly, the whole party burst into ecstatic applause for the beauty of the event.

The cardinal, Princess Aurora, and Sabina's brothers, sister, and mother were standing on the dais within the great tent. The crowd followed as Prince Orazio led his daughter inside to the table of honor.

Liveried servants and candle bearers stood in position by their candles, set on pedestals throughout the night. Then, the band began to play melodies that were undeniably romantic.

When the family was seated, the cardinal stood to praise his niece and to welcome the guests on behalf of the house. Then he said a short benediction, after which the serving of the meal commenced.

Everyone talked about the "entrance" at length. Serafina, accepted as an authority because she was a member of the family, announced to our table of eight that the melodramatic parade really was staged as a *buffo*.

"The prince—my uncle—wanted to begin the evening on a light note. It was his idea to walk theatrically from the house through the garden. But wait till you see the finale. It's extravagant enough for a patron saint south of Naples! Of course this whole party is rather bizarre. But Sabina loves crazy ideas. She's got the most outrageous sense of humor that I know."

Everyone stared at Serafina's gown, probably wondering how any cousin of hers could be more outrageous.

There were three French couples at our table, one of whom was amusing indeed. The Duke de Chevrônne's son and his wife had brought with them two couples from Paris; they all knew Sabina's father, who was a friend of the absent duke's. The de Chevrônnes were very chic, both involved in haute couture, and remarked that they would love to have Serafina model for them in Paris.

Even though we were at a formal dinner and Serafina really should have spoken to everyone, she was more intent on asking me about England, which obviously was now a primary concern of hers. The Parisians eavesdropped while Serafina queried me about my family's estate in Kent. Soon the whole table was involved in a discussion of the continuance of nobility, of country houses, of our whole way of life in Europe.

"Rome has a splendor that surpasses that of Paris before the Revolution—I mean, look at this party, this setting, this phenomenal formal garden at our feet. These *servants*!" Jacques-Donatien de Chevrônne was incredulous.

"Oh, Uncle Orazio borrowed them from the rest of the family—they're not all his," Serafina said to everyone's amazement. "The others are hired." Then, seeing the table's astonishment, she asked me: "Don't you live like this in England? I mean—with a formal royal court and all those supporting families?"

"It's quieter," I told her. "Much quieter."

"We certainly don't broadcast our events. I mean, the only people in Rome who know about tonight are *Nera*, plus . . . our designers."

136

"If designers in Rome are half as bitchy as those in Paris, the entire Eternal City knows about Fête Ferrucci, I'll bet you," dared Monique de Chevrônne, a stunning black-haired beauty. "Mmm, this smoked salmon is *délicieux*."

"Rupert, is it true Arabs are buying all the manors in Britain?" queried Jacques-Donatien.

"Some have even become *lords* of the manor, formally. At least if Yanks come and settle, they speak somewhat the same language," I declared.

"That's disputable," one of the other Frenchmen said.

"Are manor-holders still addressed as squire?" Monique asked snidely.

"Sometimes—if they're not titled. It depends on the locals—if they feel someone comports himself squirely," I said and laughed. "Lords of the manor, though, own half the village greens of the country, and much 'common land.' "

"What's everyone in England going to do? Your taxes are the laughingstock of Europe. They're abominable! You won't have a country house left if they all go the way of Mentmore," de Chevrônne remarked.

"What's Mentmore?" Serafina demanded.

"A huge Rothschild house that had to be sold for taxes," I stated. "It's put the fear of God into everyone. Well, what can we do? If the Department of the Environment takes a grand home, the family goes and there go its innate traditions. Even the visiting public senses the loss, and attendance goes down."

"Do you know Woburn?" Monique asked.

"Yes, but not all families have such assets or estates to start with. My family certainly hasn't. Those with less are the most hard hit."

"You can always hold concerts on your property, or open a golf course, shops, swimming"—de Chevrônne paused—"or . . . a zoo."

"Oh Jacques! Hordes of ghastly tourists tramping all

over one's home, turning it into a sickening carnival. The problem with England is its insane taxes—the West's worst. Correct your tax structure, and you'll save the fabric of society, its old traditions and its new demands," Monique declared with conviction.

I commented, "You certainly seem to know your—"

"My degree's in economics. I handle our business and my husband creates the designs," said Monique. "My thesis was on the British tax situation. It's disgusting, yet it's so simple to resolve. You must pass a law to allow one's overhead for the upkeep of an old estate to be written off your income taxes. It's the only way to save the houses— and Britain certainly has houses worth saving—and not just as idiot boxes for queues of gawking sightseers."

"Woburn gets a million visitors a year. I don't see how they cope," I said.

"Look at Italy. Taxes aren't low, but still, families flourish. A life-style such as this"—and Monique waved a sapphire toward the garden and the guests—"can continue, though it too is fighting for survival, need we say."

"It depresses me, the British situation," I admitted.

"Are you the head of your house? You're titled, aren't you?" inquired Monique.

"Yes."

"Then go to the House of Lords and lobby with Commons. Change the situation. Don't just sit and cry 'the estate's falling in, the estate's falling in.' *Do* something about it! Just as the French Revolution sacked our beautiful châteaux, so your fiendish tax structure is sacking your great country estates." Monique beamed, and finished off her glass of champagne.

The table fell silent, and we all looked about at the ladies and the jewels and the beauty, and wondered how much longer such a life-style can persist. The servants were just lowering the sides of the tent. The *secondo* was being brought with a different beverage. The band was finishing

138

a rendition of "Smoke Gets in Your Eyes," and a trio of country musicians was entering to enliven the mood with gay songs of the *provincia di Roma*.

Serafina looked longingly at me and smiled, then squeezed my hand beneath the table. But I was lost in thought, mulling over Monique de Chevrônne's words.

31

The banquet having concluded with a *gelato* of fresh peaches, various gentlemen of the family stood and raised toasts to lovely Sabina. Suddenly, Serafina pressed my hand and said, "I'll be right back." She stood from the table, walked across the large dance floor to the table of honor, then bent across it to say something to her cousin. Sabina nodded.

The whole table, and then the five hundred guests, began to cheer. Serafina walked to the band's dais. From the piano she grabbed a microphone, then turned to address the crowd. She looked ravishing, and her voice was firm and warm. There was not a sound in the tent.

"Please forgive me if I'm doing what's not normally done. But I'm doing it for Sabina. She's my cousin—I've known her all my life. I really love her. I want everything to be perfect for her—and I want her to know that we're not afraid to say . . . we feel for her tonight!"

There was deafening applause. She continued, "With your permission, I would like to play something for Sabina now, something which I hope puts in music what I sense that we all feel."

The applause continued. Serafina put the microphone on the ledge of the piano and sat. Slowly she began to play as well as to sing a moving love song, which she had written herself. It was beautiful, melodious, and melancholy. But it also was tinged with the hope of happiness

139

and I noted that it moved many people to tears. Such a spontaneous and loving gesture was so unexpected, so unquestionably a message from the heart, that no one doubted its genuineness.

The applause for Serafina's kind song was so loud, so invigorating, that she ran across the floor to hug her cousin who was standing to embrace her. The two girls remained together with their hands held tight as the cheering continued. Then, Serafina deftly stood back, and bowed graciously to Sabina, who bowed with consummate elegance to the whole assembly.

It was an incredibly stirring moment. Prince Ferrucci motioned to the band, which immediately began to play a popular waltz. The ball had begun. The transition occurred so smoothly that I saw many young men wipe their eyes. They were looking on the young ladies with hope, while they followed the majestic Prince and his daughter. The two had begun to dance.

Serafina again was seated near me. Her performance so moved me I couldn't help but grab her hand as the men at our table stood. Then, I kissed it. Not at all surprised, the gentlemen followed suit, as did others at nearby tables. Serafina, however, had eyes only for her uncle and cousin.

The music continued long into the night and we danced and danced with the crowd. Then, sometime before midnight, Serafina led me out to the terrace. We strolled past many couples who were gazing at the half moon. With her hand in mine we walked down the stone stairs that were lined with sphinxes brought from Egypt.

We began wandering through the sunken garden whose fragrance was so intoxicating this humid night. The music from the party grew fainter. The notes were losing touch, obscured by the splashing of ubiquitous fountains.

We passed the place where the nymphs were cavorting

with Poseidon, and Serafina guided me along a pebbled orange path. We were moving toward the magnificent view of Rome. I put my arm around her as tightly as I could. As we walked along in sensate silence, an occasional night bird let out a shrill cry.

Ahead, a stone balustrade was backed by a mass of white roses, a ghostly wall in the moonlight. The green of the planting appeared dark blue. Directly before us was an archway with a wrought-iron gate. Suddenly Serafina produced a key from her bosom and laughed. "I came this morning. Sabina gave me the key. I wanted to show you the English garden . . . just the two of us . . . alone."

My heart quickened. I grabbed the girl even tighter and kissed her hard. But she pulled away to ram the key in the lock, and opened the creaking gate. We hurried inside and shut it again.

The path we entered was covered by a trellis heavy with roses. The potent aroma from the profusion of pink blossoms was an aphrodisiac. My insides tingling, I threw both arms around Serafina and began kissing her face.

Our desire nearly caused us to fall, but Serafina forced me on, to go down, down the slope of Monti di Creta, down beneath the roses, down and well out of sight of the crowds partying above us.

As we descended, our arms linked, the roses above us gave way to holly, and the air became *fresca* and damp. The sudden coolness renewed my ardor, like water being splashed on one's face just after having made love.

"We've arrived!" she announced and broke free from my hold, then ran into a diamond-shaped enclosure. "Isn't it magic? It's the English garden."

I was entranced. The spot so captured an indescribable Englishness that I instantly became nostalgic. It was the five thick oaks that so impressed me. Two flanked the entrance and there stood one in each of the three other corners.

141

Yet the *walls* of the garden . . . they were what brought back the memories. Four walls, tall as a man, old mossy brick, deep rusty red, an occasional orange, some almost black. Each wall had three Gothic arches and each of these contained a bench, above which a niche displayed a severe Tudor animal on its haunches, each one a mythic Queen's Beast. Behind and above the walls were holly hedges, twice as high. The oaks and the hedges contained the small garden so well that it felt like its own little world, one of perfect peace.

Serafina led me to the right on the gravel path, to the farthest point of the diamond. Before the oak, she lit a wax *lampada* which she said she "nicked" from the party that morning. Its yellow illumination was helpful. So little moonlight penetrated the hedges and the oaks.

I greatly appreciated the garden's design. The outer rim of the diamond was a walkway. It hemmed in a lower level of the same shape, which one reached by four brick steps placed at each of the four corners. The inner level sloped toward a pool. Between the four staircases, sloping trapezoids were planted with pansies and bordered by a tiny hedge of rue. The large end of each trapezoid formed a wall against the upper level and served as a planter for pinks.

"This is my favorite place in all of Rome!" Serafina confided like a child. She snuggled close. "I come here every time I visit this house—night or day. Isn't the fountain fabulous?"

Indeed it was. A white marble unicorn stood near a beautiful medieval maiden who was holding a vase of water. The unicorn was bent on one knee, and was drinking, its solitary horn forever dipped into the liquid.

"Only at such a moment as this," I heard myself saying, "is the unicorn vulnerable to be caught—when its horn is submerged in the water."

"It's such a sad myth," Serafina whispered, and

sighed deeply. She then tossed a pebble into the pool, which was shaped like a Maltese cross. "My uncle's ancestor, who built this garden, was a famous Knight of Malta. He fought with the British at Trafalgar."

"Come," I said, and led Serafina down the small steps to the fountain. We embraced and silently gazed about us. Two pear trees fanned out between the three Gothic arches of each of the four brick walls. A small bed of marigolds spread at the foot of each pear tree.

Serafina dropped another stone to the water and looked sadly at the unicorn. "She has the beast chained—did you notice?"

I looked. Round its neck was a collar and a chain, which climbed up the marble maiden's leg to one of her hands on the vase. I held Serafina's face in my hands. "Only a virgin, they say, is capable of capturing a unicorn."

"I know," Serafina said faintly. She buried her face in my chest. "Oh Rupert, I want to tell you so many things."

"There's time . . . thank God we have time," I whispered.

"I love you."

"I love you, too!"

The garden seemed to spin as the echo of our words was swallowed in the dripping of the fountain.

"*What's that?*" Serafina suddenly shouted and pulled close, then apart in fright. "Did you hear that?"

"What?" I only heard the fountain and our heartbeats.

"God, there's something *in* here."

"Here—the garden?"

"Yes, the garden!" snarled a gruff male voice whose owner dropped out of an oak by the entrance.

143

32

"My God! Ercole! You bastard, you pig! *Porca miseria*—I'll kill you for this!" and Serafina lunged up the steps to the spot where her brother had dropped from the tree. "I'll kill you! How dare you do this to me? Spying on me—like a filthy swine."

Before Ercole could recover his balance from the fall, his sister was on him, pelting him on the head with her fists. "You stinking bastard . . ."

"Get off—get away," he shouted more like a scream of fright, surprising for a boy supposedly so powerful. They stood apart and glowered at each other.

"How'd you get your filthy body up that tree? Oh, I know, you bastard, we used to play here. Right? We played here and that's the only tree we could climb from the other side of the hedge. What've you been doing—sitting in that damned tree all night—knowing I always come here—right? Watching my every move? Well, Ercole, did you get your thrill for the evening? Did Ercole get his kicks? What were you doing in that tree all this time—playing with yourself?"

I had rushed to stand beside her in case her brother attacked her. Instead of reacting angrily in a fist-flinging rage as I expected, Ercole began to laugh demoniacally. Then, almost reduced to tears of selfish hilarity, he asked his sister strangely, "And now—for the key—if the *principessina* doesn't mind—the key—so her slovenly *principino* can leave?" Again he laughed so evilly.

"Ugh," Serafina shuddered and flung the key at his feet. "Get it and go. Get out of here. You're done for now, Ercole. I won't let you get away with this—ever. You might have thought you owned me until now, but open your eyes tonight and see how I've become a *woman*!

144

"With him?" asked Ercole, laughing.

"With me," I answered and started after him.

"No, don't. Just let him go. Ercole—go away now—go—go home," she said as if he were four years old. "Go home—go to bed and leave me in peace."

Ercole laughed derisively, then turned and ran up the path. "And leave the gate open!" Serafina shouted.

"Both you and your hot lover will pay for this insult. I only . . . only wanted to be the first to congratulate you . . . but never now . . . now I know you both hate me."

"Oh, *Ercole!*" Serafina screamed shrilly, as the ghostly form of her brother disappeared within the shadows of the trellis.

At the instant Serafina let out her agonized wail, the first blast of the party's fireworks exploded and flashed a wicked red glow which shocked our strained vision in the dark enclosure. I held Serafina tight, by the two oaks of the entrance. She was shaking so I didn't dare speak.

"He haunts me so . . . you've no idea. I wish he were dead. I tell you, Rupert, I've often plotted how to kill him!"

Soon a machine-gun repartee of white starry bursts blasted the night. I said for consolation: "Come, we must get out of here. The fireworks at least . . ."

"I don't care, he's ruined my evening," she said. The woman within her finally gave way to the girl, and she let herself cry. "Ruined it."

"Come along."

"And . . . though . . . in his own sick way—and I know my poor brother's sick, Rupert, which is why I've bent over backward to cope with him when everyone else has abandoned him—but in Ercole's own way . . . which is a child's way . . . I don't think he was in that tree to be harmful. He was only making a joke, a kid's joke. Like a little boy he's . . . he's jealous of you, Rupert . . . since I'm really the only one he's got."

I squeezed Serafina tight and kissed her, so as not to let

her speak through her tears, so as not to have to hear any more of what already was too strange. We were beneath the roses now, and soon were pushing open the iron gate.

Serafina dried her eyes, as the fireworks glowed green like tremendous flowers of primal deities of Alba Longa. Then she shoved the big key back down between her breasts and we stepped into the formal garden, whilst not one single couple out of the many knew or cared what drama just had occurred a few short meters away.

All eyes were directed skyward. Stars blinked and colored smoke hung in the air between blasts, which continued for some time. The crowd kept shouting *"Bravo!"* as each display outdid the last, as the party was drawing to a close.

Then, the last series of explosions was so spectacular—yellow flowers with diamond white bombs, red trailers, blue stars, then golden comets going off in hundreds of directions—that all the rooftops of Rome far below were set alight. The crowd kept cheering and clapping. Even Serafina couldn't help expressing true delight, as I kept staring in her eyes. Then I led her out of the villa and into the night.

33

I felt wretched the next day. Distressing dreams of England and of the party had plagued my sleep. The ride back to Palazzo Roseazzini had been upsetting also. Serafina had "taken ill" suddenly, so she said, with "cramps." I was convinced that her brother's appearance was the cause.

The weird relationship between the two defied comprehension, but try as I did, I could not stop thinking about it. It was all the more troublesome in that Serafina let Ercole come between us; she refused to let me kiss her in the car on the way home.

The more I thought about it, the more my worry increased. By the time dawn had broken, I had accepted Cardinal Monsignani's judgment that Ercole must be possessed. What else could explain such erratic, such deviant behavior? Plus, Ercole was certainly a good liar. He'd told me he was leaving for the country, yet appeared at a family affair in Rome, dropping like a snake from a tree!

Feeling somewhat better after my long siesta, I readied myself for dinner with the cardinal. It was to be formal, and we would talk business. I hoped business would occupy us, for I was anxious to avoid any discussion of my involvement with his niece.

Tactfully, His Eminence made not one allusion to his family; it was as if I had never met any of them nor was living in their house. I began to wonder if he might be displeased with me. I was quite sure he had seen me without my clericals at the villa. Perhaps his businesslike manner indicated dissatisfaction with my behavior.

I couldn't help recalling Friday's dinner in the same room, but nothing looked as I recalled it. The chairs were changed. Both looked more like mediaeval thrones than those when I had dined with Princess Aurora. Even His Eminence looked different. Wearing a black cassock with black buttons, he displayed no cross about his neck nor even a ring. His black eyes seemed smaller, deeper set. He appeared shorter, more corpulent. His nose looked bigger and his face thinner. I was much disoriented by these changes. Were they all in my mind?

Conversation began dramatically. "What do you think, Milord Broxbourne, of the pope's being infallible?" His Eminence asked dryly. My eyes widened. I felt a bit ill. It was just such a question I feared having to answer when the archbishop had told me of the job.

"It . . ." I swallowed. "It definitely has caused concern with Christians, no matter what their denomination," I said with reticence, glancing at the butler whom I also did not recognize. He was middle-aged and, as I looked at him, stuck up his nose and left the room.

The silence was agony for me, so I continued, "Most people don't even realize that only two declarations from the Holy See have been stated as infallible."

That brought a response from the cardinal. "Correct. The 1870 Infallibility Pronouncement itself, and the 1950 *Munificentissimus Deus* when the Assumption of the Blessed Virgin was formally decreed to be dogma of the Faith."

"Mention of infallibility engenders problems, for the world can readily accept Rome's primacy, as opposed to her infallibility," I said, responding more emphatically to the curried *risotto* than to the conversation.

"*Assistentia divina* gives *immunitatis ab errore*. Speaking ex cathedra, His Holiness not only does not err, but moreover a priori he cannot. The Protestant tradition of your Anglican Church—that is, that part of it which protested against the *infallibilitas* of Rome—of course is no small factor to overcome for Unity."

What was the cardinal trying to tell me? He continued, "This same *assistentia*, I'm convinced, has been laboring unfailingly to effect Unity for the last one hundred years, in spite of history, in spite of bastions of mortal and I daresay idiotic defense."

I sighed with relief. Those last two words took the tang out of the overly spiced rice. I quenched my thirst with cold white wine.

"Since 1896," His Eminence went on with a slight smile, "I can see six moves which history or plain hard work have contributed toward Ecumenism. Two of these nobody considers, but I do."

"What are they?" I asked with interest.

"The first is the 1896 Denunciation of Anglicanism itself, which may have done more to help Unity than hinder it. Saying the Anglican Church forever was a rebel made Anglicans and Catholics look to how similar, and how unrebellious, the Sister Church of the Anglican Communion really was."

"Fascinating."

"This soul-searching carried on till the second move, which was history, World War One. That brutal event told everyone in no uncertain terms that certain factors of European culture had to be defended, as well as being factors of Christianity which united and kept Europe civilized—or tried to at least—in the face of industrialization. The so-called War to End All Wars caused the introspection which led to the third move."

At this point the butler returned with more rice, of which I took a generous helping as the taste was suddenly very much to my liking. The cardinal refused another helping and waved his left hand fussily and continued.

"The third, of course, is Malines, with which your grandfather was involved. The world was still so set politically as to prevent agreements of the type we now enact. Though the discussions at Malines were important, nothing happened. History again interrupted with the fourth move—World War Two—whose cataclysm led to such spiritual reevaluation in the forties as you, my young friend, can't imagine. But one development of consequence was the founding of the World Council of Churches in 1948, the fifth move."

"Rome didn't look kindly on this at first, did she?"

"Sometimes God's ways are even withheld from Rome." His Eminence answered enigmatically and chuckled. "The World Council . . . Holy Church has come to respect and deeply love. Its work has been of the greatest import, and likely led to the intellectual climate at the end of the fifties which made the sixth move—Vatican II of course—necessary. In the early Sixties, though, many of us in the Curia didn't see Vatican II as necessary till after it concluded. Again, the mystery of the Holy Ghost."

Plates were replaced for the *secondo*. I hesitated, as His Eminence looked eager to say more. I took my pork chop and vegetables in silence.

"The Lord certainly is enigmatic," Cardinal Monsignani stated and pondered the profundity of his words. "It only struck me lately, but when Pope John moved to override a certain draft proposal at the Vatican Council, the Holy Father was doing more for Ecumenism than any other act in recent time."

"What draft was this?" I asked, unafraid in my ignorance.

"*De Duplici Fonte Revelationis*—which, just as throughout Roman history, the Curia, of which I am a part and which wrote the draft, promoted both Scripture and tradition as the two fountainheads for today's religious life."

"By tradition—the draft meant Rome's own?" I queried.

"Precisely. Rome's own. The *acatholici* at Vatican II were horrified. When this occurred I hardly could comprehend the non-Roman forces which made them detest the document so. My views since have widened, due to continuing ecumenical discussions."

"Which, Canterbury prays, soon shall lead to Anglican Orders being declared valid," I stated as a reminder of a very major point. "It always struck the British as strange that even though the East and West did have such a schism, albeit older than the Reformation, Eastern Orders never were declared invalid by Rome."

I let that one sink in, then continued: "We have seen three important joint documents published lately by Rome and Canterbury, yet these statements simply are agreements. There do exist some crucial issues, such as recognizing Anglican Orders, toward which Rome now must give the sign."

Since His Eminence did not ask "What sign," I went on. "This is easily effected by two steps. The first is by decree, which would allow Partial Communion between

Catholic and Anglican, meaning that parishioners can receive the Eucharist at each other's altar, but the priest can
only celebrate within his own domain. This situation exists
between the Churches of England and of Sweden. One
decree . . . is all that this would require."

The cardinal uttered something I did not catch, so I
persisted. "The second step would be Full Communion,
which would take longer, as contrary to the first step
where the Church of England still would exist, let us say
that by the second the Church *in* England would have to
be established. This could take fifty years to effect diocesan
reorganization, et cetera. Moreover, problems with the
Crown would have to be worked out, which of course
would place this on a higher level of international diplomacy than it now is. At present, for example, I am in
contact with my embassy but function independently from
it."

"Your monarch as supreme governor of your established Church does pose problems," Cardinal Monsignani
answered, obviously pondering something left unsaid.
"Serious Anglicans," he continued as the butler cleared
the table, "are concerned . . . which of their traditions
would survive in a united Church."

I did not know how to take this, so said nothing. The
man continued: " 'Union will have to be advanced by truth,
by love and by prayer.' So said His Holiness, my good
man, to the council members of the Anglican Centre where
you work. Please, allow me this opportunity, on behalf
of the Secretariat for Promoting Christian Unity, to praise
your Centre, and also your superior the Bishop Secretary
General of the Anglican Consultative Council, whom I
have met there."

I took three Regina Claudia plums, and felt enormously
content. The meal had not gone badly. His Eminence was
adding informally, "As for your *udienza* on Monday, we
shall be at Castelangelina of course on Sunday, but I'm

leaving that afternoon for Verona, whereas you will be requested to stay. Do let me lend you my chauffeur, who knows the road and will drive you to Castel Gandolfo. Is that suitable?"

"Yes—yes indeed. Thank you so very much!"

"And you have your *invito* to show as your pass? The security's strict, you realize."

"Yes, I've received it."

"*Buonissimo*," said the cardinal amicably, then added coldly before we left the table, "According to many in Rome, one cannot forget that Anglicanism is not in the true apostolic succession, that it did reject papal authority, that it did go ahead and found its own universal communion and, for centuries in comparison to other denominations, it did stand as the most anti-Rome of them all."

34

We retired to the cardinal's library to share a toast of *grappa*. "To Ecumenism," His Eminence said, then begged my leave. He had documents to read and a letter to write. I was thankful that my involvement with Serafina had not been mentioned.

Only an hour had passed. It was just nine o'clock but I was quite fatigued, yet didn't want to sleep so went to sit in my garden.

Seated on the stone bench by the fountain, the erotic sound of water plopping in the pool and the sight of the tumescent satyr jumbled what thoughts of Unity I brought downstairs. I undid my collar and unbuttoned the black shirt in a fit. Suddenly overcome by my hypocrisy, I threw the collar in the pool, then laughed aloud hilariously!

Just as I was leaning back on the bench, laughing still, something landed on my chest with a thud. I was startled to see that it was a stiff white bra.

"It's from the fifties—isn't it a scream—almost as hard as your collar," Serafina shouted in jest. "Fling it in the water with yours!"

I did just that. Then I signaled her to be quiet, to come to my room. But she shook her head, so I said, "Then I'll come up and get you."

"Ssshhh . . . not so loud," she reprimanded and hung her forearms over the balcony's railing.

"Aren't you cold?" I asked, both meanings intended. She was wearing a canary yellow sleeveless blouse.

"Me?" She stood and playfully fluffed her hair.

"Yes, you. What about your—"

"Bra? *Gia usato*—secondhand. Atrocious, isn't it? All padding, and stiff!"

"Get down here this minute. I can't bear this."

"I'm chilly. Change your funeral uniform and I'll throw on a bit more."

"A bit more off."

"You're so vulgar. How'd you ever get to be a priest?"

"I'm a lamb compared to some of those horny buggers."

"Stop!"

"You love it."

"Meet me at the *portière*. And take those things out to dry. I bought that bra to *wear*."

"Like I bought my collar."

"We'll go to a *caffè*, all right? It's so early—and I'm so bored."

"Come here then."

"Stop it. Meet me at the door. *Ciao*."

"*Ciao*," I said, my blood racing.

For fifteen minutes I waited impatiently at the gate, wondering what she'd be dressed in this time. I heard her feet before I saw her, clomping along the west colonnade. Then she turned into the south colonnade where I was standing. God—she had done it again! I held to that same opinion as she ran to embrace me.

153

Her hair was pulled back into a pony tail secured with girlish barrettes which were decorated with blue plastic swans. Electric-purple pedal pushers revealed a few inches of shapely legs, but my eye was stopped short by yellow bobby sox and chartreuse spike heels. This chaotic assemblage of colors was topped by a blisteringly hot-pink blouse. Serafina had turned the collar up and rolled its sleeves to her armpits. Her lips and eyelids were painted white. It was stunning somehow, but on someone else it easily could have been dismissed as ridiculous.

"Trying out for the team?" was all I could manage as I stared at her handbag, a deflated American basketball with handles.

"Care for gum?" she asked and blew a big bubble as I tried to kiss her. "Not here—the porter's looking," she joked and pulled away. The porter opened the great black door.

"Do you have some place in particular . . . where you wish to exhibit yourself?" I asked, taking her hand and a piece of bubble gum.

"It's from Brooklyn—chews like a dream," she said, and we both blew bubbles in the faces of oncoming tourists, Germans no doubt. "Let's just walk and see where we get."

Where we got I hardly recall. Serafina walked me miles through nocturnal Rome. I do remember dashing down the steps to the Trevi Fountain where she had me throw in all my change!

The Trevi has long been a favorite subject of filmmakers and it was this thought that suddenly caused Serafina to remember a message from her mother to me. "Your presence is requested," she declared, "at Cinecittà tomorrow afternoon . . . for one last, one final, scene for *Moctezuma*."

That night I learned more about Rome than I ever had before. Serafina chatted about this and that as we passed shop after palazzo after piazza. Her erudition was remarkable. Needless to say, it was a pleasure just being in her company—eye-catching as it was.

Like her uncle the cardinal, however, she really said nothing that was even slightly personal nor uttered one word about the family. I didn't ask any questions about them. It seemed more appropriate to end the evening at the Caffè Canova, staring at the people in the Piazza del Popolo and gossiping about the latest fads in London.

35

Next morning, my secretary took off early, complaining, "It's Friday—there's simply *nothing* to do—and it's too bleeding hot." Where she went I haven't the foggiest.

Then Principessa Dulcinea telephoned, but would not come to lunch. "I'm just too lazy to leave the house." When I asked for Serafina, her mother had "no idea where she's hiding." Just before hanging up, Dulcinea asked me to meet her at half past two outside Palazzo Doria in Piazza Grazioli. "I'll pick you up with the Cadillac—if it'll fit!"

Friday morning brought one trouble after another. Dozens of "scholars" of sorts visited the Centre's library, and I was left to cope with their queries, none of which were answerable. This wouldn't have been arduous had one question been interesting. Thank God no one stayed past quarter to noon. As no one was there, I didn't say Communion. But I felt guilty for deciding against it, and retired to dine in solitude.

If you haven't gathered . . . I'd been praying less and less these past days. My spirituality was at an impasse— blocked by an interior monologue which kept thwarting direct or even indirect communion with God. It's vapid to say the fault was too much socializing. Such preoccupation can be enriching if one adheres rigorously to a schedule of prayer. But I was about ready to admit, though, that I didn't even know how to pray.

This thought kept nagging me like a monotonous refrain, like some stupid pop song, when into Piazza Grazioli drove Dulcinea in the ludicrous 1959 Cadillac. Ludicrous or not, it distracted me and I was more than happy to discover that it was air-conditioned. I let myself sink into its cuddly plushness like a child put to bed by its mother.

Once again, my noble driver seemed too depleted for conversation. It was the start of Rome's wicked summer heat. Both of us just grunted the whole way to Cinecittà.

"You can take this oil burner tomorrow," the princess did finally say as we pulled up to the studio and stopped, "since Serafina needs a day at the sea. It's her grandmother's idea. You drive, don't you?"

An endless queue of strangely painted faces greeted us as we entered the building. Aztec slave girls were being led from one set to another by the same Amazon in silver lamé I'd seen before. "Snake Eyes," I heard myself saying as she passed and pinched me hard on the behind.

"You not call," she muttered savagely and shook her head. She vanished round a flat with her female slaves.

I fumbled my way to Makeup. Dulcinea had disappeared. Nobody came for me, and the makeup girl was insipid, so I tried to find my way back but got lost. No one seemed capable of conversation either. All Rome seemed totally spent. I was getting increasingly irate and sweaty in my efforts to get directions when suddenly I was accosted by Snake Eyes who slapped my hand and said, "You late!"

"I don't care," I retorted. "Where am I supposed to be? What am I doing today?"

"We go to Bochmann." I followed her patch of pink hair.

We'd gone about halfway when Alexander suddenly darted from behind a gigantic sculpture of the plumed serpent god, Quetzalcoatl, and muttered: "Can't speak now—I'm off to Capri this weekend—phone me Monday—Dulcinea spoke about the Ferrucci affair—you with that belle of the ball—proposed to her yet?"

Then before he vanished, and before I could answer, he startled me by saying: "Wait till you see who's playing Moctezuma. Do you remember Paul De Soto? I introduced you two three years ago."

"No."

"I did too. My classics master at Westminster, my drama coach for the Latin play? He was only twenty-eight the year I went up to Oxford. You know—he quit teaching ten years ago—to star in—"

"Oh, him...from that West End hit? He went to New York with it, didn't he?"

"Then to Hollywood. The film made millions. He's been in California seven years now. Big box office. But I lured him back. Guess how?"

"God knows."

"You won't believe it, but he told me once he was descended from the conquistador De Soto's family."

"Who?"

"The Spaniard who discovered the Mississippi!"

"You're joking."

"So I sold it to him, saying he could exonerate his bloodthirsty ancestors by playing Moctezuma."

"He bought that?"

"Bought it? He even went to Acapulco to get a proper Mexican tan!"

I stood staring at Quetzalcoatl, then shook my head. I was curious how De Soto would look as Moctezuma.

"Come," continued Snake Eyes tugging me along. "You late."

Suddenly we were hearing tinkly music. Very odd, from

157

some other planet it sounded. Then we turned and came upon a lagoon—a huge water-set which was in fact a collapsible pool. It was so stunning I gasped.

This was the emperor's *chimapas*, his famous floating gardens, one of the most exotic pleasure haunts ever devised by man, now just a memory from the grandeur that once was Mexico.

"If this is what technicians' tricks can do for a set, imagine what the real gardens looked like?" I remarked to Snake Eyes, but she was gone.

The most fantastic thing about this scene was that I was to be in it! It had all but escaped me that in Alexander's novel there was a chapter wherein the conquistadors' priest tries to convert Moctezuma to Christianity. The priest actually rubs a cross of water on the heathen's brow. But the priest (who is being drawn on a floating isle with the royal party, Cortés, and chosen Spaniards, including the bawd the princess was playing) suffers the shock of having doubts about his faith.

This happens, the book explains, because the Spaniard becomes more and more hypnotized by the incredibility of Aztec culture. His heightened spirituality becomes ever more receptive to the pagan subtleties all around him. While he arrived in Mexico loathing anything pagan, this Spaniard becomes so overwhelmed by ancient Mexico City that he keeps being seduced by its charms. Pulled so strongly, the hapless priest reacts against the Aztec enticements more brutally each time. It is this man of God who urges that Cortés give Moctezuma up to death. This Spanish priest is driven to conclude that nothing but death is proper for such an alien monarch, for such a being who dares to flaunt the Devil so riotously in the face of Jesus Christ!

Bochmann carefully explained this to us. Our group of fifty or so included the Aztec king, and his court and their attendants, all of whom wore the most eerie feathered costumes I had seen to date. Everyone reclined on sofas of gold. This truly was paradise, an island literally built *to float*.

Two golden water craft shaped like sea serpents, bobbed ahead in the pool. They were tied to the isle and manned by slaves. The "serpents" were to pull the fabulous barge slowly as the scene was being enacted. It was to be shot "at night," lit by torches of silver and turquoise and shaped like iguanas with flames leaping out of great gaping mouths.

Parrots, cockatoos, flamingoes, and rare live birds of spectacular plumage were shepherded onto the craft to amuse us on this island that floated in the night. The birds began to screech wildly; the combination of weird jungle noises and shrieks caused a great deal of excitement.

I had to pace back and forth, to go from Cortés humped on one sofa to Moctezuma who sprawled on the opposite. The Aztec king was stark naked but for a codpiece of beaten gold inlaid with jade. He was wearing a headdress of feathers and gems to defy description. He was muscular and long and kept fondling his thighs to bewitch the Spanish, to drive them into a frenzy with Mexican native taboos.

Cortés's bawd was the first to succumb. Suddenly she was throwing herself at the monarch's feet, then kissing them, then sucking on them ferociously, running her tongue sloppily over his gem-adorned toes. She had to be dragged back by Spaniards in glistening iron helmets. She was deranged and half mad for sex with this ruler, and Moctezuma could plainly have cared less. Though I watched this take place, I could hardly believe that the woman so possessed was Princess Dulcinea Roseazzini!

The magic of the night was the possessor. Raw lust was unloosed, then repulsed, and I had to keep pacing from Moctezuma to Cortés, back and forth, back and forth.

It did all strike me as loathsome, yet I began to personify my role. The isle continued to move through the

159

most phenomenal nocturnal garden, and night birds continued to bleat out in heat.

Suddenly I felt the ecstatic push to rush to the side of the island, as it glided over beds of crimson water lilies, to prostrate myself, to cry out to Christ, to cup water into my hands, to bless it urgently, to race back to the sensuous, now *totally* nude form of Moctezuma.

The king of the Aztecs was being oiled by a host of frenzied boy slaves, whose hands missed no part of his regal frame, whose hands pushed hard to hasten the maximum of pleasure.

I prayed aloud as Cortés simply laughed. I bellowed for divine intervention. Then, with my hands I grabbed the tumescent king's head—my wet left hand on his jaw, my right hand tracing the cross in his brow—and I baptized the Aztec to the wails of those all round us.

Cortés stood up and sighed. "Now . . . Moctezuma is just like us . . . another soul lost in this world's tribulation."

36

Dowager Principessa Aurora had spent the last few days away from Rome, but she did return to the capital for our Friday dinner. As I entered her private apartments at eight o'clock, the same maternal maid beamed. She told me how much the princess was looking forward to our appointment, then showed me to the sitting room where Aurora was taking her cigarette.

As I entered, she pushed the button of her remote-control to turn the television off, then received my greeting from her armchair. She took a long puff from her ivory holder, then commenced a discussion.

"Tomorrow I have a favor to ask of you. Could you

accompany Serafina to Circeo, to call on an elderly couple who live in one of my houses? I'm letting them have some wine. Serafina said you could spent the day at the sea."

"Certainly," I said, eager to get out of Rome and be alone with the girl.

"You'll leave at nine tomorrow morning, with that white Sherman tank Serafina adores. She says you drive, so it's settled."

The principessa stood carefully and slowly walked to her dining room. We passed her stout butler who held the door. He smiled warmly this time, then hastened to hold his mistress's chair, whence he raced to the kitchen for the *primo.*

"I do hope memory doesn't fail me this evening," the dowager stated after being seated at the round table. "There are a number of things I mean to say to you. But first, did you enjoy our granddaughter's ball?"

"Very much."

"Other than Ercole's taking you and his sister by surprise," she stated rancorously. "I have decided that I no longer shall admit him to my presence, not that he'll be heartbroken."

A peasant-style pasta was served, with a sauce of olive oil, black olives, parsley, and heavily spiced with chopped red peppers.

"Seeing him drop from that tree . . . *is* something I won't ever forget," I admitted.

"Now do you believe us? The boy's *possessed*! We plan to have him exorcized." The princess said that last sentence dryly, without a hint of remorse. She drank some wine.

"Where is he now?" I asked.

"Who knows? He will bring shame to this house. He'll go criminal before he goes straight. If the cardinal would spend more time on his nephew's soul than on the toll of stock markets, perhaps the boy could be saved. The cardinal's always mumbling about Antichrist of late, but

161

if His Eminence would open his eyes, he'd see there *is* a fiend beneath his own roof. Ercole's heading for ruin—suicide, likely. What can be done? Rid him of some evil spirit? That's like pulling some rotten old tooth."

Needless to say, the discussion was not conducive to digestion. Plus, the pasta was far too spicy for my taste. I tried to change the subject. "Whose idea was it to have you carried on a litter at the ball?"

"Didn't you find it amusing?" She glared but cracked a smile. "It was Sabina's. I thought, why not? Give Rome something to gossip about, that's why I did it. The whole party was a bit *rétro*—not a drop of social realism, which we see too much of today. I'm so sick of reality. Why not a bit of fantasy now and then? People think they can't afford it now. How stupid! Everybody—especially the nobility today—is scared to death of being the least bit adventurous. Everybody is boring lately. Perhaps some people *are* scared of these terrorists? I couldn't care less, the world's always been terrifying."

She took a sip of water.

"I had to lecture Sabina's father for one whole meal, just like this one, to convince that reticent prince that people wouldn't laugh him out of Latium if he did have fireworks for his daughter's party. 'Fireworks are déclassé,' he said. Bah—people are even scared of showing off anymore. I'm all for showing off—a little's extremely good for the . . ."

"Digestion," I said.

"Precisely," Aurora concurred. "This pasta's frightful. Do you like it?"

"It is . . . a bit hot," I admitted.

"So is what I'm next going to say," she added, as if the pasta had been planned as a cue for her next line. "Last Sunday I spoke my mind about the too rapid changes in the Vatican of late. Well, I'm not through with the Holy See, but I do have some opinions which might strike you tonight as contradictory to what I said before. We spoke about the *patriziato*, Black Rome and its relationship to the pope, and I'm sure I sounded as if I were the great bastion of the *nobiltà*. Tonight I wish to tell you things I don't like about the *nobiltà*."

The dowager princess smiled wickedly. She waited for the platter of salmon patties to be brought to her, then took one plus a drop of spinach soufflé. She smirked at her plate, then continued.

"Everybody had a fit—privately of course—when the *Motu Proprio* was published which abolished eighteen ancient traditions from the Vatican in one fell swoop. That's right—eighteen old stand-bys suddenly went bye-bye, eighteen traditions no longer were a part of the pope's court, or half the court known as the Pontifical Chapel— the other half of court being the Pontifical Family, you know. Some of the abolitions, such as the Secret Chaplains and the Secret Clerks, nobody truly missed. But marvelous links with yesterday, such as the Prince Assistants, the Mace Bearers, the Custodian of the Sacred Triple Crowns, were done away with. Imagine the uproar in England if such venerable anachronisms suddenly were deemed useless? But no, not in Rome. No. We fought no changes. Everybody shrugged, and said the pope's word's *absolute*. So be it. But, my dear, there are channels for dissent, yet we chose not to use them. So here we sit, a handful of 'great families' who once had power and true control, and who are now slowly being shoved aside—and who say nothing! We're rotting away in our extravagant palazzi, continuing this *dolce vita* when the rest of the country and the rest of the world thinks Italy's over and done for. It's absurd."

She paused, took more spinach, then went on.

"Show me *one* young noble Roman boy or girl who doesn't want to leave Rome today. They would give anything to live permanently in London, Paris or more *au point*, New York. Rome has nothing of interest for the young, save legends, languor, lies. Look at Ercole. He's a prime example of what Rome does to children today. Rome has changed irremediably these past ten years. No longer is she the spiritual center of Christendom. She's just another piece of flotsam in the whirlpool of world events. And what's our so-called nobility doing to rectify the situation? What's noble . . . about this class of people, this class you've found yourself involved in? Good God, these very names so glamorous, so renowned, once *knew* how to rule, to do so so that Roma was adhered to. Now what do we do—*nulla!*"

Was the princess moving onto thin ice—veering toward fascism? But she was exceptionally quick, and read my mind.

"No. Not for a moment do I mean that our class should rally round a Duce, as in that period we no longer admire. But I do wish that of all the princes, marquesses, dukes, and what not here one would come out and show some public strength."

"Hasn't the time passed for that sort of thing?" I asked hesitantly.

"Who says so? That's what *they* all say! Nobody's got backbone; everyone's given up before anyone's even tried. My stupid grandson Ercole could have become a leader— had not some sick thing crawled inside him and died."

"What can any man do? Do you mean for him to go into politics?" I queried.

"Why not? Better yet, the quickest way to show influence is to publish in newspapers and air opinions on TV. What happens in Italy, in the Parliament, is so far from reality anyhow that everyone sees it as a joke. Our silly life of parties and villas and gossip is one type of irreality today, but the irreality of politics in this country is quite another."

"Then why should a prince . . . soil himself in it?"

"Because princes are involved with it, like it or not, though always at the top, always above the dirt-level intrigues. They sit on boards, they invest, they wield power with position, but it's done quietly, as if by a class of male ghosts."

"Isn't that the key to the continuance of the class—its invisibility to the masses?"

"That may be—a few years more—but to continue any longer will require this class to find a voice, not one unseen like the Holy Ghost of God, but one known and listened to by all the class and also by the masses. To be perfectly brutal, it doesn't seem we're getting any aid for this from the aforementioned Holy Ghost, if the changes in the pattern of things inside the Vatican are any clues at all. Perhaps, at long last, the nobility of Rome is being punished, its death knell being sounded by the pope, because our class so often did bleed this city dry as we comported ourselves and flaunted ourselves in such incommensurate, incomparable extravagance."

Part Two

Preface

It's now the end of February. As I sit in the den of my ancestral home Dexter Mote, I'm looking ahead to the spring when Serafina Roseazzini will become my wife. In a few months I shall be taking my seat in the House of Lords. I wish to speak about the execrable tax situation in Britain.

The future does not seem bleak. But I must admit I dread writing the second half of this book. Our kidnapping and captivity by the Brigade must now be reconstructed.

As you read this, a lot of your preconceived notions about terrorists will be shattered, as were mine. I'm not saying I came close to understanding them, though I was their hostage and therefore was privy to their depravity. You must read this as a testament of one who will try to report what he saw and heard. Our six weeks beneath the ground were nightmares. His Eminence Cardinal Arcadio Monsignani and I only kept our sanity by the grace of God.

169

The cardinal's family have assured me that they have faith in my discretion. Before beginning this book two months ago on New Year's Day, I was visited by Prince Guadagno Roseazzini. He gave me a note of confidence signed by members of his house whom I have had to describe herein. Conflicting opinions within a family, as well as within a social class or milieu, are always more entertaining when they are not recognizable as one's own.

Due to the tragedy that this book describes, Prince Guadagno told me he would rather I attempted it, than should some outsider. For reasons of their own, his family wish this story to be told, though certain Roman friends and acquaintances, both ecclesiastic and lay, have voiced the sternest disapproval.

I pray, therefore, that you the reader may acknowledge that the quite detailed portrayal of events in Part I is valid, since it bears so heavily on the incarceration described in Part II.

Broxbourne
Dexter Mote
Nr Canterbury
Kent

1

The cardinal and I were being driven east out of Rome on Sunday, July the third. The time was nine forty-five in the morning. We were expected about ten at Villa Collemandina, which lies fifteen kilometers northeast of Palestrina, above the small village of San Vito Romano. I can't tell you what the villa is like—I never did see it—but it lies to the northwest of the village and five kilometers up Monti Prenestini.

I honestly have no idea where we were when the ambush occurred. The cardinal was pensive, reading important papers his secretary had given him the night before. As I did not wish to disturb him, I said nothing, looked at the lovely scenery, and began to daydream about the day before with Serafina, which we had spent on Monte Circeo. . . .

The *casa colonica* of stone we visited was cared for by an elderly couple, originally from Tuscany, whom Princess

Aurora had known all her life. They fed us good, basic Tuscan food. After we had unloaded the car of supplies for them, Serafina led me up rocky paths from the inland eastern side of the mountain which was made so famous by Homer.

At last, after a good bit of exercise and foolery, we arrived at the summit and its view of the sea. Gazing across the Mediterranean, in the shade of a rise, Serafina revealed herself totally to me. I laid bare my soul to her. The heat made us giddy. The climb put fire in our veins. Roasting rocks and bushes of herbs aroused us, aroused us all over again. We were mad for each other's satisfaction. If others were present on the heights of the temptress of Ulysses, if pigs who once were men were rutting right by our naked feet, if Circe herself were pressing her hands on our bodies keeping us entwined—we saw nothing but each other's ecstatic happiness, saw love in each other's eyes.

I was thinking of nothing but Serafina when the first shot rang out. The first bullet hit the chauffeur and the Fiat crashed. There was not a farmhouse in sight. We had just passed a fork in the road. The car, I think, was going slightly uphill, to the right. I saw olive trees, stone walls, brambles. People—terrorists—how many I have no idea— *five?*—were on us immediately. It was all so well planned, so sudden.

The cardinal was stuttering. I felt faint from the impact. Other shots—*two?*—made sure the chauffeur was dead. The shots were muffled—silencers on the rifles. We were called out—no, pulled out—of the van by men wearing black masks. His Eminence fell on his knees to pray and was roughly yanked up. We were told we wouldn't be hurt if we complied. Then our eyes were covered by black rags. We were gagged. Quickly we were thrown into a van or something—God knows what—and were en route to our place of captivity.

172

Our hands were tied in the van. Our fear was enormous yet neither of us panicked. It all seemed too unreal. For some reason I didn't think they'd kill us—or kill us *then*.

We rode for about an hour, during which time I kept trying to block out the murder of the chauffeur. So quick, so accurately done. The precision terrified me. I kept dwelling on the vision of Serafina, yet recall an instinctual reaction to think about my family, my parents, though both were dead. That they were dead was no consolation.

By the time we got to our destination, my mind was a mess. I was thoroughly undone, my thoughts maggots in a seething beast's brain. Who were our captors? What did they want from us? It couldn't be *me*—few knew me in Rome. It must be for Cardinal Monsignani. That the terrorists even *knew* where the cardinal would be at such an hour on Sunday upset me greatly. Someone knowing the cardinal well must have . . .

I couldn't cope with analyzing and began seeing my home in Kent, flashes of Canterbury, hearing English to block out the raucous *italiano*. Who was pulling us from the van? Where *are* we? I wanted to shout but couldn't; the gag prevented it.

Canterbury—why was Canterbury in my mind, flashing like a Piccadilly neon sign? That's it—I was telling the cardinal when he and I left the palace this morning how I'd walked from London to Canterbury, on the old Pilgrim's Way, after my father died. I got no further than this. Monsignani was distracted, as soon as he got in the Fiat he set to work.

We were thrust from the heat outdoors into a frigid house, whereupon we were tugged by one, prodded by another, so we'd go down some stairs. It was getting colder, damper—some basement I thought. What a place to die—I recollect trying to say. Midway down the stairs there was an argument. I don't know. Suddenly our eyes were uncovered, but there wasn't much light anyway. We were told to keep moving, keep going *down*. We went down for what seemed minutes, then found ourselves in a cavern. His Eminence and I stared at each other, our eyes saying what our mouths could not express.

2

Directly before us was a metal table. Sitting at it was a man with a scraggly beard. Perhaps thirty, a bit bald, he looked tough as an ox.

"Well," he said, "you arrived." Then he looked at me and stated, "We don't really want you, but we'll keep you now that we got you."

He was fair, barrel-chested, and wore a blue work shirt and soiled blue work trousers. There was a pistol on the table. He began to brandish it. "All right," he said to those who brought us to our prison. "Go now. Thank you for the good job."

Another man, in his early twenties, tall, wiry, with curly black close-cropped hair, entered from the far side of the room and didn't say a word. He had a rifle over his shoulder, a military weapon. He took it off, put the butt on the linoleum floor, held it by the barrel. He glared at us.

"Finally got our cardinal," the man at the desk stated, as he leaned back and crossed his arms. "Monsignani— you have committed crime after crime against the people. You will be tried—sentenced—and maybe you'll survive— *if* the Vatican complies with our demands." Then he motioned from the other to us. "Beppe, put them in. Take the gags off. Give them handcuffs now, so I can watch."

His Eminence was freed first, his arms loosed from behind his back to swing forward for the cuffs. I was treated to the same.

"Over here." The leader stood and moved from his

174

chair. "You, Monsignani—sit here. Not you, priest. Stay put—you're not necessary. Monsignani, sit down."

The cardinal sat. The leader reached over his shoulder to grab a very old amber cross set in gold filigree and held by a traditional braided chain of gold thread and red silk. "What's this?" the man queried derisively and pulled the holy object from the Prince of the Church. "Hmmm—we can hock it," he stated smugly and tossed the chain at the feet of the younger *brigatista*. The brute didn't flinch, and let the cross flop on the dirty floor.

We were still gagged. I noticed tears welling in the cardinal's eyes. He looked as if he were praying.

"Stay here!" the leader brayed and came toward us, bent down to pick up a camera from the linoleum and said, "No, this one's for the press—let's have a great big Curia smile."

Cardinal Monsignani did not glance up, so the leader shouted, "Look, *Eminence*, face me or this bullet goes right in your brain."

The leader was aiming the Instamatic as his sidekick pointed the rifle. My fright must have shown. The cardinal looked at me, realized I wanted him to go along with the stupid demand, and stared straight ahead at the leader, who flashed the photo, then held the camera and waited for it to develop automatically. Soon the print ejected. The fellow grunted as if to say "Not bad."

"All right—take them away. Remove the gags and cuffs. Let them talk. Feed them. I don't want to see their faces till tomorrow."

The rectangular room was carved from living rock. The walls were wet. The air was rancid. Everything about the site was disagreeable. I scanned the chamber expecting to see weapons, equipment, pamphlets, radios—but there was nothing save the metal desk, the chair, the camera, the glaring fluorescent lamp hanging by two wires from the rock.

To the leader's right and behind him was a round

archway leading to where we were held captive. The place was so macabre, I began a Hail Mary as we were forced through the smelly corridor down to a room lit by one bare bulb. The lean character with the gun took no time in ungagging and uncuffing me, then forced me in the room with his rifle. He removed the rag from the cardinal's mouth, unlocked the cuffs, and pushed him in with me. A barred iron door closed with a clang. That was it. We were held hostage.

The glaring bulb illuminated two cots, flimsy iron frames with skinny mattresses, one sheet, and two blankets each. No pillows. We both sat down. There was nothing else in the small room. We both exhaled deeply. I felt like weeping, shouting, *doing* something, but my mouth hurt too much from the rag. The cardinal's did, too. Neither of us really knew what to say.

How many minutes went by I don't remember. Our fear was no small deterrent to conversation. When His Eminence did speak it was with total humility. He apologized for the state we now were in. "The captors obviously were after me."

A meal was served sometime later. A *pastasciutta*, oil and Parmesan, one tomato apiece, an opened tin of tuna. Beppe brought it, shoved it beneath the iron gate. I felt like vomiting, my stomach was so jumpy. We both ate unbearably slowly, to pass as much time as possible. Halfway through the meal Beppe rolled a half-corked bottle of red wine, half empty, into our cell and said: "Keep your glasses. Put everything else out the door. Don't hide your knives or you'll find them in your guts."

Hours passed. Another meal was shoved inside. I wondered aloud to His Eminence where the kitchen would be. "Who knows," he replied. We talked slowly, as if we never had spoken to one another before, as if we were enemies forced into reconciliation. We didn't voice the majority of our thoughts. Both of us wondered at the irony of our situation—an Anglican and a Catholic locked together . . . in a nightmarish situation of *Unity*!

We talked about where we were, imagining which part of Rome, or perhaps not Rome, we were in. I sensed we were somewhere farther away. The cardinal thought we were near the capital, quite near, a villa on the edge.

That first day—it was Sunday—the horror of the event kept us apart. The barrier between us as human beings, from such vastly different backgrounds, loomed between our beds which acted as our chairs. I don't remember much of what we spoke about. It was only necessary to pass time. I thought about asking the cardinal if we should pray together after the evening meal. But the cruel visage of Beppe loomed before us. "Go to sleep," he grumbled. "The light's going out." He turned to go up the hall and shouted, "Five minutes, then it's dark."

I felt ill. The occurrence seemed the most dreadful at that moment. Bestial capture, imprisonment, charges of "crimes against the people," then the eerie avoidance of us by our two captors (were more upstairs?) now seemed impossible to cope with in the thought of sudden darkness.

The mere idea of what to do with our clothes, of stripping off one's religious uniform in front of a total stranger, no doubt bothered the cardinal as much as it did me. There wasn't even a spot to lay our clothes on! His Eminence was handsomely dressed, to say the least, and I'm sure he never had to toss his costly vestments on his bed like a fool, nor crawl in the same bed to sleep. I said to him, "But what else can we do?"

"Use your clothes for a pillow. Who'll see us anyway but these animals?"

"Out with the light!" Beppe shouted. We were plunged into murky blackness.

3

I had nightmares that night, and for most nights thereafter. So did the cardinal. With no window to let the light
of day shine in, we were woken rudely by the naked light
bulb next morning at ten. Beppe was saying: "Hold your
glass near the gate. Get up. Have coffee."

We staggered out of our beds, setting the pattern for
many days to come, and held our glasses as coffee was
dumped inside. Beppe poured coffee with his right and
hot sugared milk with his left, and with such dexterity
that I felt he must have been a waiter once, a job that
turned him off work forever and that turned him toward
the activity of the Brigade.

I wasn't thinking right. The cardinal was looking different again, his corpulence now pure fat. I felt sorry I
thought this way, but I did. Mornings never were easy for
me, but to wake up after heinous dreams to a reality even
more gruesome was hardly conducive to pleasant thought.
I'm sure I looked disgusting to His Eminence, too: young
and tall and strong, not to mention bearded, which did
not endear me to him.

There we were, two workers for Christ, on prison
beds, in our underwear. Sipping coffee, wondering . . . what
next? Perhaps they'd kill us today.

We were still sipping our coffee when the leader from
the night before marched down the dim hall looking even
less jovial than we did. Pistol in his right hand, he said:
"Today the photo goes out, and with it our first communiqué. It reads"—and from his pocket he pulled a piece
of paper—" 'The Brigade claims total responsibility for yesterday's kidnapping of Cardinal Monsignani and the Reverend Broxbourne.' " Then he stared at me. "We know
your shitting name—think we're stupid, do you?"

178

"No," I replied.

"It goes on: 'They're being held in a people's jail, and will be tried by a People's Inquisition.' " Then he added, "It's really just you, Arcadio. You we'll deal with. But we say both of you in this first communiqué . . . for reasons of our own." He laughed evilly. "That's the public message. The private one to the pope is for the pope to come out publicly and urge the Italian government to release the *brigatisti* being held as political prisoners, and secondly, for the Vatican to give alms . . . to us . . . for your safe release."

The balding, sandy-brown haired leader was laughing. He looked at us like a monkey gripping the bars of a cage. The cardinal began praying aloud. This amused our captor even more.

"Too many have said lately that the strategy of the Proletarian Revolution of this country is only to attack the State. But they're fools if they believe government and capitalist leaders of industry, and journalists who salivate about these maniacs, are the Brigade's sole target. The Church thinks she's the most efficient organ in the carcass of *cultura italiana.* Just because she functions doesn't mean she can't be removed. The Church's an appendix—vestigial—unnecessary. Yes, we began our strategy by attacking Industry, then the State . . . and now . . . the Church. It's taken the Revolution quite some time to prepare for this latest maneuver. It's not that we didn't think of you saints in Mother Church before today. Damned entertaining you fools are. But truly—the Vatican controls the Italian economy anyway. You should have known we'd get round to you cardinals. You are *the hinges*—that's what your pompous name means." He turned to go and said, "Industrialists, journalists, politicians . . . they're boring compared to you bastards."

"Naïve . . . you're so very naïve," His Eminence stated vigorously.

"Then—teach us, Arcadio, teach us all you know.

That's why you're here. So get used to the idea!" Pointing his pistol at us, he added, "By the way, my name is Iacopo. Right, Arcadio? Right, Rupert?"

He turned and left. The cardinal sighed deeply. "I thought about this last night. Here we are, just two human beings, as I said that first day we met, but now . . . just alone and afraid. It's assinine to keep addressing each other as if we were lackeys at court. Call me Arcadio, please, Rupert?"

The tenderness in the old man's voice brought tears to my eyes. I reached out to hold his hand. Then the cardinal broke down and wept.

4

From what we had read in the papers about the Brigade, our captivity was no different than others. The organization of our *rapimento* had been faultless, and everybody began saying they thought that Germans were involved! Evidently the police were totally ignorant of our hiding place.

The small number of *brigatisti* present proved the commonly held opinion that the Brigade's structure is horizontal. I believe we were right to assume that Iacopo was the head of the cell in charge of our imprisonment and that he was in touch with others in the national organization, but it was very likely his aide Beppe was not. Given Iacopo's age, it was possible he could have been one of the group's founders. The cardinal mumbled as he composed himself Monday morning that Iacopo more likely was an agent of the Devil. The cardinal's theory, outlandish as it may sound, began to seem as plausible to me as any other, looking at conditions objectively.

Monday, the fourth of July, the day of my scheduled audience with His Holiness at Castel Gandolfo, the world press was reacting to our kidnapping. The pope, taking matters directly into his hands, called a secret meeting of those cardinals of the Curia able to return to Rome on such short notice. He had received the private communiqué issued by the Brigade.

All of this, of course, was unknown to us. For us, Monday introduced the horror of interrogation. Immediately after the midday meal—the same unappetizing fare as before—both Beppe and Iacopo arrived at our cell armed. The former stood outside with his rifle pointed at me. Iacopo entered and told His Eminence to move his bed flush against the wall opposite the door, so that our beds now formed an upside-down L.

"Both of you—get on Arcadio's bed."

I got up and sat beside the cardinal. Iacopo leaned against the wall next to Beppe's rifle barrel which poked through the bars of the door and said flatly: "It's time for an *inquisition*."

The way he said that word was terrifying.

"Now, the Church in Italy never has been a light-hearted matter," the revolutionary began. "To simplify matters I want you, Arcadio, to answer a few questions. You see, it's important for the people to know where the Vatican's money is going. It's the best-kept secret in all of Italy, if not the world."

"It's plain. We pay priests, run convents, run schools, pay for centers, for newspapers, for staff, for upkeep of Church property."

"Arcadio, you're not answering the question!" Iacopo's voice was ruthless. "What happens to the Vatican's *excess* income—all those sums available *after* you pay for the overhead of the empire you control?"

"There is very little excess. This the Church acknowledges with all honesty," declared His Eminence with conviction.

"You're lying," snarled the leader. "Lying! You don't expect the people to swallow that, do you?"

181

"People—what people?" retorted the cardinal, his courage mounting. I found his bravery astounding.

"*The* people!"

"The Church, the Holy Catholic Church, is far closer to whatever people you mean than your Brigade ever will be. Who ministers to their needs, both bodily and spiritual? Do you?"

"Enough, you silly fucker. Tell me—you're one of the chief economic experts in Europe—tell me about the activities of the Vatican's Administration of the Patrimony of the Apostolic See. You, along with the Cardinal Secretary of State and others, are on the committee which runs this key factor of Vatican finance. You're involved with its *Extraordinary* dealings, meaning the old Special Administration which was altered in 1968. These dealings began in 1929, didn't they, when Mussolini paid off the pope by giving him one billion five hundred fifty million lira to get him to sign the Concordat? These dealings have always been the *most* secret of them all. Where does this powerful economic force, this Extraordinary office of the Patrimony, get its huge sums? What do you do once you get them?"

The cardinal appeared placid in his silence.

"Tell me," screamed the *brigatista*.

Still the cardinal did not speak.

"Won't speak—will you?" And the leader clomped to the bed on which we sat, spit in the cardinal's face, and grabbed the cardinal's red *berretta*—his skullcap—unzipped his trousers, and urinated on it as we turned our heads away. The smell of piss was nauseating inside the dank cell. Into the steaming puddle at our feet the rebel threw the sopping piece of cloth, then stomped on it. He turned and left us in silence.

182

5

We suspected that the brutal Iacopo might resume the inquisition at any time, but in fact they left us alone the rest of the day. Nonetheless, our tension mounted. Such psychological scare tactics obviously were not planned.

We were fed as usual. Next morning we awoke to the sight of Beppe's gaunt face. He shouted at us to get out of bed. Again—my memory deserts me—I can't recollect how we got through the day, what we spoke of, but conversation was minimal.

Strange, neither the cardinal nor I mentioned saying mass together (we did have wine and bread), but I rationalized this reticence as a security measure against the possibility of provoking more appearances by our captors or separation from each other. The sight of the mostly silent Prince of the Church on the bed next to mine undeniably was reassuring. I now can't imagine being incarcerated there without the benefit of his calming spirituality, which pacified the dreary cubicle in spite of the urine on the floor and the *berretta* still there in it.

Next morning, Tuesday the fifth of July, things changed. With the coffee came the scraggly-bearded Iacopo, his face gray like granite. I wondered . . . did he ever surface, ever see the sun? I wondered where he ate, slept—upstairs? In the building we entered after being pulled from the van? I wondered . . . did anybody see us enter?

Doubtful.

Iacopo entered. We both had to sit on the cardinal's bed. He sat on mine. That made my guts knot.

"Guess who's interested in your whereabouts, Rupert?" he asked unpleasantly.

"Everybody, I'm sure," Cardinal Monsignani snapped.

"Shut up, you. Rupert—it seems your friend the Archbishop of—"

"He's my *boss*," I declared.

"Whatever the hell he is, he's begging for your release—praying for your soul."

I said nothing.

"Note—he's not praying for *our* souls." The leader guffawed. I later learned while recuperating at Castel Gandolfo that the pope had spoken by telephone directly to Lambeth Palace on Sunday, immediately after being told of our kidnapping, to assure His Grace that everything possible would be done to get us released quickly. The Archbishop of Canterbury issued a statement to the press two days later, after waiting for the Brigade to issue their first communiqué on Monday. Lambeth's statement emphasized that both the cardinal and I were "servants of the people of Christ's kingdom and were two workers attempting to effect Unity among Christians the world over."

As Iacopo read those words derisively, I was heartened even as my soul recoiled from the way the revolutionary was profaning the Lord's name. Cardinal Monsignani crossed himself in the name of *"il Padre, il Filio, e il Santo Spirito."* The man of the Brigade stared at us as if we were scum, then stated with bullet speed: "But to return to the inquisition."

"Why must you use that word?" posed the cardinal forcefully.

"Why did the Church use that word? Why did the Church torture so many helpless men and women of the working class for so-called sins we never committed?"

Iacopo glared at us, as if we two possibly could atone for the whole history of Christianity.

"I want you, Arcadio, to see if you know how to answer today. You're also a committee member of the Institute for Religious Works, vulgarly called the Bank. I want you to tell me where the Vatican's Bank invests its

184

colossal amounts of money, what shares you hold in major Italian corporations. Tell me!"

"Why do economic affairs so plague you?" His Eminence questioned quietly.

"Don't play stupid. The *Bank*—with its oh so selective clientele and power—what shares does it hold?"

"Any information on business transactions out of your realm would not help the cause of social justice which you espouse. Tell me, Iacopo, what is it your Brigade really wants?"

Iacopo seemed not to comprehend one word. "The Bank—you idiot—the Bank."

"What about the Bank?"

"You'll suffer for this, *Cardinal*!"

His Eminence just shook his head. Again, the leader bounded to us like a beast and shouted: "I should piss on both of you pieces of shit—but I value myself too highly! Give me that ring." He pointed to the cardinal's right hand with his shotgun and barked: "That's the one. That's right. Let's have it quick."

Without a murmur Monsignani slipped the precious amethyst off his fourth finger and held it out. The villain grabbed it as if he never had touched a jewel in his life. He grunted as he prodded it onto a thick finger. Knowing the ring had been a gift of the Holy Father, I felt the pain of his having to part with it. The cardinal said nothing, for hours.

The next morning—Wednesday—we were told by Beppe that the pope had issued a public plea for our release. He added that Iacopo was negotiating privately with the Vatican "on your behalf."

Neither of us was reassured by this declaration. The only good thing about the day was that Iacopo did not once pay us a visit, likely a ruse of his demented mind.

6

During those first four days of captivity I must confess to thinking little of any human beings but the cardinal and myself. Perhaps this was instinctual, I don't know.

Thursday at the "coffee call" I suddenly remembered having dreamed of Serafina in the English garden of her uncle's Roman villa. This recollection unloosed guilt at my selfish preoccupations.

After all that time alone with Arcadio Monsignani, I now urgently wanted to speak to him, and in a sense hoped to confess to him.

His Eminence, on the contrary, roused most uncommunicatively. I almost gave up hope of talking to him at all as he snapped at me while sipping his coffee. But he soon apologized warmly. The tone of his voice told me that he, too, needed to let loose pent-up thoughts. I think the most oppressive thing was the dearth of sunlight.

I mentioned this, making a stab at the darkness, and it did the trick. We spent the whole of Thursday talking. I felt purged by the end of that day.

For some strange reason, we even had a laugh or two together, professing faith and ourselves in God's hands. Moreover we professed faith in the same God, the same rites, the same ways to commune with Him. That day taught us both a lot, and we broke into a fit of hilarity— catharsis of anxiety—late that afternoon. We realized it took a kidnapping to get Anglican and Catholic to live together peacefully, in a true state of unity, albeit jailed in the same foul cell.

"Forced into unity," we both laughed over and over again. "Forced into unity . . . and not really minding at all."

"The roof hasn't fallen in, has it?" the cardinal chuckled.

"Wish it would—it might finish off our captors!" I added and laughed.

Our jocularity brought Beppe with his rife. "Shut the fuck up, you two bitches."

The sight of his weapon made us remember where we were. I suddenly felt as if I might be going insane.

That thought, coming from some childish yap way back in my skull, was farcical, yet as soon as Beppe vanished like a phantom I told the cardinal my doubts about keeping under control.

"Pray with me, Rupert! We both . . . we must ask the Lord's pity that He give us strength."

His Eminence dropped to his knees, and I with him. Our oneness in the face of possible death was total. We both bowed our heads in silence, and then each spoke his mind, one after the other, one after the other, one after the other. It was the most soothing litany I ever heard. We let ourselves be enveloped in the courage gained from our prayers and our tears. I don't recall what words we used, only the sensation of calmness that followed.

Both of us apologized to the other, and to God, for our reticence to pray together till that moment. It wasn't long, there on that floor on our knees, before we were propelled by the Holy Spirit to pledge to say mass together, regardless of any doctrinal differences existing between the hierarchies both of us had come from. The threat of death made differences seem sins.

The threat of death . . .

"Death."

The word as stated by the cardinal made me shiver. I said I feared it, feared those who held us hostage, feared we wouldn't be released. Yet Monsignani admitted fear, too, and this soothed me. Then he began a prayer to all the martyrs to Christ he could think of—the list was long, very long. Those who died for their faith—it made me so sad that I shook, then wept.

"Never," I protested, "never could my faith in Christ come close to the verity of those who died believing."

This was the first time I expressed such doubts to this stalwart prince of Mother Church. I had wanted to say these things before, during the two weeks that I knew him. But reticence, in order to retain professional distance out of courtesy to the archbishop, my superior, seemed the only way to deal with a cardinal so close to the pope. I was Anglican and he was Catholic, after all.

But being locked in that cell together, with no knowledge of how long we might have to live, changed everything. My professional reticence vanished from me that afternoon, as did the hauteur of Monsignani.

I remember thanking him for not chastising me for my doubts about my faith and embraced him when he too admitted having doubts in recent years—even in his high position! The man's humanity kept revealing itself by love, and I felt a calming of soul which prepared me for the atrocities to follow.

The cardinal stood and helped me up. He said he was resigned to die. He admitted, whilst looking off in space, that he really did know where we were being held—and who had organized our captivity—but something in his Eminence's voice forbade my asking questions.

Food arrived, but our calm was shattered as we realized the bearer was Iacopo, looking diabolic. He snarled: "The Vatican, the government, the queen, the president, every maniac of power in the sick capitalistic world is hounding us for your release. Fuck them all. You *talk*, Arcadio, answer my questions about Vatican finances . . . and . . . about internal security of the pope."

"Never!" cried Monsignani emphatically. "Do you think my name's Judas?"

"I don't give a damn if your name's *dog*. Tomorrow my questions get answers, or you get your just reward."

We picked up our plates and ate in silence. Both of us left our bread and our wine. I tried to concentrate on eating the pasta with salami and tomatoes, but I was unable to control my thoughts. All sorts of faces of people I'd known and loved or hated passed before my mind's eye.

This cast of acquaintances and adversaries was disquieting. My appetite waned. The cardinal, ever sensitive, sensed this and stood, and with no transition at all converted this meal into the mass. I then stood with him and we each said parts of the Liturgy in our own languages. It was so moving to be saying this mass together, notwithstanding that our unity had been forced, that when we came to the celebration of the Eucharist we both felt as happy as if the room were bathed in sunlight. For us, it was as if we were officiating at Communion in a basilica of Rome. The rough red *vino di tavola* and the thick, spongy, unsalted bread of Lazio never tasted better to us than during that night of thanks and of prayer.

7

Friday brought trouble. The cardinal was taken away before breakfast, and I was left alone to worry over my friend's fate. His Eminence was gone all morning and afternoon. When the two animals herded him into our cell, he looked more dead than alive.

I had heard nothing. Wherever they took him, whatever they did to him, I didn't dare ask. I began to shake, but I went to him immediately for he was staggering and I put my arms around him to help him into bed. I wanted to scream out in rage against the criminals who were committing this outrage, but some sickening lump gagged my throat. All I could say was, "My God . . . my God . . . how you have suffered."

I moved my bed next to the old man's and sat for hours, holding his hands, being by him, showing him I cared. It was some time before it registered that poor Arcadio's fingertips were burned. They had tortured him.

Some hours later he roused as if from a nightmare and muttered, "There's more . . .more . . . up the stairs . . . a very deep voice . . . a voice . . ."

"But why? Why won't they take *me*? I'll offer myself. You can't take any more of this evil!"

I began mumbling dreary things. The cardinal passed out into sleep.

Somewhere near midnight Iacopo clomped into sight. "Tell *Reverendissimo Eminentissimo* that tomorrow at midnight a friend of his will come to pay respects. He'd like a *private* audience. Don't forget now. Tell him!"

Then he vanished.

Hours later I fell onto the cot with my clothes on and dozed. Sometime later I was startled to wake and see the cardinal already up, and revived—indubitably by the intervention of the Almighty. He was on his knees, saying an Our Father.

He noticed me and came over to me, then apologized. He begged my forgiveness for making me worry, then said, "We'll get through this with the strength of the Lord." I then recalled the message of the *brigatista*, and told him.

Beppe brought coffee and said we looked green, an agreeable greeting. He left and Iacopo sprang into sight with a chair—like a lion tamer in a circus. All he lacked was a whip. "You know," he began, "we really don't hate you at all. We just think you priests are totally unnecessary for humanity."

"I'd be loath to envision the world you'd construct," I said calmly.

190

"Don't worry. You won't be a part of it."

"You and your kind are disciples of Satan!" declared Monsignani. "But as John says in Revelations: 'Fear none of those things which thou shalt suffer. Behold, the Devil shall cast some of you into prison, that ye may be tried; and ye shall have tribulation ten days. Be thou faithful unto death, and I will give thee a crown of life.'"

"Do you honestly believe such trash?" the leader asked and crossed his legs in order to sit comfortably.

"I am a cardinal of the Church. I am no charlatan."

"It's Saturday. Tomorrow is a day of rest. We have a special Sabbath surprise for you." On that note of warning Iacopo pulled a paperback from his trousers and pretended to read. We both looked at each other and wondered how long the madman would sit by the gate. He was obviously doing this to irritate us.

Soon enough he swore and cursed the lack of light in the passage. "How can I read in this fucking hole?" He stood to face us. "Here. Something to exercise your intelligence." He tossed the book through the bars. It landed at my feet. The cover portrayed a naked whore having sex with three young men. "You both can read it, and toss each other off."

"Please let me have some water? I asked you yesterday—you must let us wash," His Eminence beseeched.

"Scared of a little dirt? Well, don't soil your pretty fingers! You'll end up looking like the working class you hate so."

"How do you know what we hate?" I queried.

"Don't worry—just read your book."

"Bring us water. Please?" the cardinal begged.

"Don't he look nice, Rupert, with a stubble? Makes him almost look a worker," Iacopo joked.

"Please, can't we wash?"

"What'll you give me for water? Your holy *blessing*?"

There was no answer, so the fiend turned to leave us alone. The chair remained by the gate.

191

"Yesterday . . . there were others, three I think, in those masks. They said the Brigade have been beating about the bush, but now they were going for the prey," the cardinal whispered. "The prey, they said, is the Roman Catholic Church, which they intend to abolish. Their new tactic is to attack the Church instead of making demands on the State."

"Sick," I concluded, "but predictable. They've shown how vulnerable, how easy, is the apparatus of the State, more so than the apparatus of industry in this violence-prone country. Where else can they turn now, but on the Church?"

"The surprising thing is that the Brigade took so long to make their first attack. I know I represent a symbol to them—of all the Church of Rome ever stood for, good or bad. Vast is the hatred against the Church in this country, Rupert," said Monsignani as he shook his head. The cardinal then bent down to grab the book that was thrown, but flipped through its pages with a sly smile on his gaunt face. "Look. Another trick. Not a page of print. All blanks."

He gave it to me and said: "Use it. Take short notes. Use a code. Each day put something down. Go back to Sunday and record something. I'll help you to remember. You shall survive this, Rupert. You shall live to tell the world what we've gone through. I won't. They will kill me, Rupert, but you . . . you shall live. Promise me, promise me you'll write about this? Do you promise?"

I squeezed the book tight in both hands and promised His Eminence I would do as he bade. Then I ripped off the obscene cover, shredded it into bits and threw them in a dark corner under the cardinal's bed.

"Do you have a pen?" he asked.

"I don't think so."

He reached into his cassock and produced a plastic ball-point. I took it in silence. The coded notes I took during our captivity are open before me now. When the

192

brigatisti shot us, for some reason they left them on my person.

8

The light was switched off and we slept. At midnight—between Saturday and Sunday, the ninth and tenth of July—the light flared again and a gruff "Wake up" forced us out of bed. I was completely shocked when my eyes focused to see a figure robed completely in black yet utterly recognizable as Ercole Roseazzini.

Monsignani's nephew was seated belligerently outside the gate, legs spread far apart, balancing a machine gun on his knees. Quickly I glanced to the cardinal for his reaction, but he was groaning to himself at the revelation. Then he said semiaudibly, "I knew it was you. . . . I knew you did it . . . . I knew you . . ." He was on one elbow, squinting, staring at his nephew, this accomplice of terror. I felt truly ill at that moment.

"Get up—I want to see you both," Ercole ordered bellicosely. The machine gun was pointed toward us. We were both in our underwear. We swung out of the cots and sat up. I felt dizzy—and couldn't imagine how mortified Monsignani must have felt. One of his own relatives a *brigatista* . . .

"It's a vendetta, isn't it?" the cardinal asked, composing himself somehow. "My own sister's grandchild . . . Do you realize what shame, what horror you're causing those who've loved you, who've watched you grow up? Do you . . . Ercole?" The cardinal's voice broke with emotion.

I could say nothing. The whole thing was so utterly astounding. I thought, So this is Italy! The history of so long a struggle, going back millennia, where all too often great families were torn apart by internal feuds, now

193

seemed so believable. But recollection of recent familial strife between Fascists and Partisans in the last war made the situation credible. But truly, the sight of Ercole, our *enemy*, beyond those bars, made us both feel nauseous.

The cardinal was visibly shaken, but he tried all the harder to control himself. At that moment, at midnight, I realized that I would have to try to come to grips with Ercole—if humanly possible—and try to get him to talk if not return to our side.

He seemed to read my mind, for he growled: "Don't look so pleased, Broxbourne. None of your evangelizing games are going to work. I'm miles away from the repugnant hypocrisies you gloat over. We don't agree with your values—we're beyond them. We're liberated from your insane world."

"You dangle in the abyss of your own insanity, boy," his uncle said.

"Don't you dare call me *boy!*" He stood and pointed at us demoniacally.

I sighed and began the impossible task to try to reason with him. "Ercole . . . tell me . . . how long have you been with this group?"

"Why do you ask?"

"What're you *doing* with these maniacs!" the cardinal yelled. "They're just using you. You're a slave. Can't you see sense or are you so far gone you don't even realize what you're doing?"

"I don't even hear you, Arcadio."

"You haven't for one whole year."

"That's right," said the nephew, sitting down again.

"It's impossible," the cardinal said dolorously, mainly to himself. "You—from such a valid heritage of this schizophrenic country—millions would give anything for just one day of your background, let alone a place secure within it. You discredit your whole heritage, your ancestors, your family. Ercole—see justice for the sake of Christ—think of your poor mother. This will *kill* her!"

194

"So?"

"You have no heart. Truly you're possessed. Oh to Jesus we'd had you exorcized before you—"

"Stop spouting rubbish. You old fucking bag of puke. You and your witch-doctor superstitions. People like you don't deserve to live."

"Then over fifty percent of Italy doesn't deserve to live. You know how superstitious at heart are your very own people."

"Then half of Italy *doesn't* deserve to live."

"You're mad—mad, Ercole," the cardinal whined.

"Do you, by chance, know where you are?" Ercole changed the subject suddenly. His eerie eyes were sparkling—and frightening.

"What?" I queried.

"Where are you, Arcadio? Shut up, you English cunt."

"You gave them one of our properties, didn't you?" Monsignani asked.

"What *is* property . . . but a weapon against the people?" the renegade responded. "This place's been abandoned for years. Windows upstairs are broken."

"But downstairs in the cellars—"

"Are catacombs." Ercole beamed. "Precisely. We're beneath the house of my aunt Lucrezia Mimabue. The aloof one, the bitch. The sly marchioness who never married . . . the dyke . . . the one with all those diamonds . . . the one who let this perfectly good place for a family of ten go . . . for years . . . sitting here . . . useless. So we decided to liberate it. She never comes here. Uncle Zanobi never comes here. Nobody but rats scale these walls topped with broken bottles. So one day I got the key from her."

"How?"

"Stole it. I always fancied this place. It has historical connections."

"What's he mean?" I asked the cardinal quickly.

"He means—believe it or not—this property is . . . it's

195

behind the wall of the old Appian Way. Yes, these rooms are catacombs, private ones, closed to the public, little known to anyone who doesn't own them."

"That's right," affirmed Ercole. "It's quite possible early *Christians* came down here for clandestine meetings against Roman repression."

"How symbolic for us then," I said sarcastically, but the thought was horrific.

"Lucrezia keeps a skull in her dining room. It came from one of these chambers." Monsignani remarked.

"With luck she may even get yours . . . if you continue to withhold information," growled the teen-ager bloodlessly.

9

His Eminence woke in the middle of the night screaming. A nightmare, no doubt, but the shrillness of the voice plagued me till the bulb was switched on next morning. Instead of Beppe it was Ercole, bearing coffee and a black book which he pushed through the bars and let drop. The book landed on its spine and the binding snapped the pages apart in two sections. Nothing was said. The character vanished.

We drank our coffee and again it was the cardinal who picked the book up. Instantly he crossed himself, kissed it, then pressed it to his breast. Tears came to his eyes.

"The Bible?" I asked.

He nodded his head. He sat, and began reading aloud a few chapters from Matthew. I asked myself: Why would Ercole bring us something of such import to our Faith? I couldn't imagine he did it out of kindness.

The Bible in his hands gave Monsignani strength. He sipped his coffee and appeared tranquilized, as if the Word of God were a palliative for the hurt of being sabotaged by someone from his own family.

This placidity was soon ruptured by the return of the figure in black. Ercole said: "Oh, look—I think I forgot something. There it is—the book."

"No, Ercole. *No*—you mustn't take it from me."

"Give me that damned thing. Give it to me!"

"No." Monsignani whimpered.

"Damn you." Roseazzini raised the machine gun.

I truly thought he'd fire at that instant so I shouted, "Let it go, Arcadio. Let him have it back. The Word of the Lord is within us. They can never take *that* away."

This reached the old man, but he sighed as if dying and passed the Bible to me. I stood to hand it to the fingers clawing through the bars.

"You *monster*," Monsignani snapped. "You filthy swine—you curse to the family—you leper to this nation which spawned you!"

Ercole only chuckled at these words. The cardinal proceeded to have a violent fit of coughing. The figure in black turned to leave.

I went to the cardinal and put my arms about him. But the incident with the Bible had broken him. He turned to me like a child and wept for a long time, so loudly and forlornly as to break the hearts of all but the members of the Brigade.

The rest of that Sunday saw us both in deepest depression. The episode with the Bible worked on me slowly. I felt so thirsty, so weakened, like a pond drained by some vicious kid who had kicked apart the dam.

I must say here that bodily processes of excretion had proven the singularly most disgusting part of our imprisonment. A pot was kept in the corner near the gate but only was emptied once a day—at night when we were sleeping. The cardinal's *berretta* also vanished one night. Needless to say, incarceration wreaked havoc on our internal systems. His Eminence's lungs began to suffer from dampness, and my kidneys functioned excessively.

We rallied somewhat, with great effort, that afternoon. We used our midday bread and wine to say mass, but our hearts weren't in it. We were disturbed by the appearance, midway through it, of the three of them. Ercole, Iacopo, and Beppe just kept staring like hallucinating monkeys at our sacred rite. To annoy us even more, as the blessing of the bread occurred, Iacopo opened the creaky door, stomped in, and took the chamber pot. An unbearable insult. We tried not to think about it, but I found it impossible not to. Iacopo soon came back, banged the pot by throwing it inside, then slammed the gate. The three exited up the passage, laughing.

Soon thereafter the cardinal sank to his bed like a sack of wet rags. I forced myself to speak of something—anything—instead of letting myself grow morbidly introspective.

I wanted to speak about Serafina, but thought better of it. I couldn't help wondering what she was doing now. What was the whole family doing? Had they put two and two together about Ercole's going underground? Or had Ercole actually withdrawn from Palazzo Roseazzini? Even if he had—this being summer—he could have used an excuse such as "I'm off to Capri," and no one would have missed him.

The kidnapping of a family member en route to a christening was too coincidental. Why I hadn't considered Ercole must have been due to a mental block. I honestly hadn't thought Serafina's brother, for all his unabashed abnormality, was so evil.

How were Monsignani and I to deal with the aberration? We came to no conclusion. The subject was so debilitating. God seemed so far away.

For both of us, our faith was visibly shaken. We were ashamed. Our discussions became hit-and-miss. Nothing led to acceptable conclusions, though we spoke about many, many things.

I said, at a very low moment, that I even failed to see how our two Churches of Canterbury and Rome *ever* could come to full Unity. The cardinal snorted and said: "Never mind. Both of us will be dead."

I changed the subject. Again, as one week before, I told the elderly man how I had walked from London to Canterbury after my father had died. But that had little effect, for His Eminence shrugged and said, "Youth has strong legs."

I tried to talk of Canterbury, the cathedral, the archbishop, Becket, but Monsignani seemed millions of miles away, so I desisted. Yet the cardinal muttered, "If he's not the Antichrist himself—then he's certainly an omen of his coming."

"Ercole?" I asked, not needing to ask.

The man changed the subject. "This ancient site's propitious. Do you know where we are?"

The query was like an echo of the nephew's. "Not precisely," I admitted.

"Via Appia Antica."

I told him about having dined at the garden restaurant with Dulcinea.

"We're not far from the Osteria—a kilometer south, at most. This site's Capo di Bove. Above our heads once was a marvelous garden. Lucrezia's mother kept the place for years, a small but gracious retreat. Her garden was famous . . . now run by brigands. Likely it's gone to seed, to weeds. Ruination of culture. . . . civilization *always* is shown by the state of the gardens of a nation. This is true from ancient Egypt to today. Imagine these imbeciles strolling in a garden . . . discussing philosphy, art, space, time, *God*? Some academy of Plato is the bramble patch above . . . barbaric as the briars of their minds. Ercole . . . he's inexcusable. He's known beauty, art, culture, the finest things mortal life can offer human beings. But those others: If from a class not so fortunate . . . *they* are to be pitied. Yet does their deprivation demand destruction of all Good created before they were born? Saint Augustine . . . taught in a garden . . . that of Valerius at Hippo."

Such words made me see my own garden and home in Kent, but the vision clouded quickly. I sank into a mood even blacker than before.

"Across this property's wall, Rupert, on the other side of the Appia, lies one of the most photographed monuments of the area, the Tomb of Metella. Its great travertine cylinder was built for the wife of a son of Crassus in the last decade of the Republic. During the early thirteen hundreds the Caetini family converted it to a fortress and built a Gothic chapel to Saint Nicholas on our very side of the road. San Niccolò a Capo di Bove . . . is a ruin now, just a shell, choked with weeds. Where we are . . . is likely right beneath it."

"Nicholas is my grandfather's and also my little brother's name."

"The name Capo di Bove comes from the marble frieze of sacrificial oxen on the tomb."

"What a place to end up."

"Yes. The basilica of the martyr Sebastian isn't far away either . . . if only we could walk toward Rome."

10

That Sunday night I awoke in the midst of a dream. I was on a road with high brown walls on both sides, no pavements, no lights, no traffic. I think it was some other time, some past century. It was night. Everything was grays, browns, blacks, and blues. I was making pilgrimage—I remember now—to a shrine of Rome. I was alone. A woman's voice, a young one, very tempting, kept urging me to hurry, to scurry up the road before the great gate of the city would be closed. There was no moon, but I was responding to the beckoning voice, trying to hurry. Suddenly—perhaps a hundred meters from the gateway—a bull ox, black and huge, rushed through the rounded arch and charged toward me. Then another, brown, and another, blue, and a fourth bull, gray, succeeded the other and charged. The woman was screeching now. I wanted to get to the city for the night, but of course I had to turn and run like a maniac back down the road which seemed to offer no escape. I was petrified—with four huge oxen behind me, I'd be gored. No doors to the road were open at such an hour, no torches lit the way, no wagon was in sight to jump on, no wall was low enough to scale. I ran and ran and continued to run. Suddenly—on the right a small door was ajar. Thank God! I pushed and then slammed it behind me, panting like a rabid dog. But the oxen persisted and were just outside, and began ramming their horns in the wooden door. I turned wondering where I could hide, yet was startled to see before me a small country church of tan stone, brown in the darkness, which suddenly began to gleam as gold . . . on the tiles on the middle of the portico. Then an angel appeared, who called himself Michael, and I fell on the ground in awe. Never had I been so blessed as to have an angel, let alone an archangel, visit me in a dream. I almost awoke, but the divine spirit would not let me go. "Do not fear. The bulls cannot harm you," Michael said. "But you are lost. You have strayed. Your goal is really not that city. You must confess. Then will you discover the way." Just then the bulls broke the gate and stormed within. But I was already safe inside the church, and the archangel was slaying the four beasts with his sword.

Contrary to most midnight visions, this one was recalled in toto as soon as we were woken Monday morning. I told it to Monsignani as hastily as I could, since I had a premonition His Eminence would be taken away. The elderly prelate just shook his head in understanding, saying: "You shall survive this, Rupert. I shall not. The dream declares it."

I protested and said he too would live. "The bulls will be slain!"

"Confess to me," was all that he said.

Just at that moment, as I opened my mouth to start with the guilt of my doubts, down the hall stomped the figure in black. Ercole. I didn't even have time to begin, but for some strange reason the cardinal felt I'd confessed in my heart. As he stood to go off with his nephew, he looked at me kindly and said, "I absolve you, Rupert, in the name of the Father, the Son, and the Holy Ghost. Amen."

"But I've said nothing," I pleaded. "Oh Christ—where're you going? Don't take him—don't take him—don't take him," I screamed. "Take me! What do you want to squeeze *out* of this man?"

"Let him go—let *go* of him," Ercole shouted and pointed his machine gun at me. I was clutching Monsignani's robes.

"Let go," the cardinal told me calmly. "Let me go. I am at fault, not you."

"He can tell us nothing," snapped Ercole, meaning me.

"But will . . . you'll come back?" I whined, not knowing what I was asking. "Bring him back," I begged. My hands were white as they gripped the bars. His Eminence already was on the other side of the gate. "This is madness—you bastards, you'll sizzle in the hottest depths of hell! Oh dear God, Your Eminence, *Arcadio*," I moaned and sank to my knees on the floor. "Thank you. Thank you . . . for the absolution."

I stared and stared, hoping he'd turn to gaze back. Alas he did and said, "I know you didn't ask to be absolved in the eyes of the Church of Rome . . . but Rupert, I sensed when we first met that you always wanted to return to Mother Church. Now I give you your chance."

202

"Arcadio!" I yelled hoarsely at the top of my lungs, as he vanished out of sight. The light in the corridor went out. I was left alone.

11

In the two-thousand-year tradition of Christianity, as dominant as the urge to conquer, to let blood, to convert for Christ is the urge to submit, to let be, to suffer so to become nearer to Him spiritually. This urge to be martyred is not sick, as modern psychoanalysts would have us believe. It is *natural* to Christians, though it is difficult for nonbelievers to understand.

Before incarceration by the Brigade, and well before the eleventh of July when the cardinal was tortured, I too thought such an urge was just a form of sexual masochism at worst or of folly at best. But that day taught me many things about the Faith.

The cardinal was led away without a struggle—he walked without resistance to the chamber of interrogation. He had a peculiar tranquility about him. It was I who was the blubbering baby, who carried on, who wailed.

I, too, wanted to share what he was suffering. I did not want the Prince of the Church to have to suffer alone. To be left alone—untouched—was torture enough for me. And if nobody would inflict pain upon me, as I kept begging and begging, then I would have to inflict it on myself.

Imprisonment and deprivation had affected my judgment, but I stripped off my clothes anyhow and proceeded to kneel on the stone floor. How long I stayed there I don't know. Hours. I didn't eat. I wouldn't eat. I felt hunger—yes—but refused to eat.

The guards thought this insane. They said I was cracking under the strain. But I was praying constantly—praying for things I never even imagined before, for all sorts of people I thought I detested, for criminals, for whores, for mutants, for maniacs, for the dead. The cardinal was gone anyway—perhaps he was dead—so what use was I? I started to hear things—screams. It was strange, but I was happy; I saw fields, I saw friends, I saw saints, I saw sinners rolling in filth.

I wouldn't get off the floor. The guards got alarmed. They said, "We should shoot you." I said, "Go ahead." They said, "That's just what you *want*." They pointed, they laughed, they said obscene things. They gestured, they poked their rifles at me. But I continued to pray.

Saint John of the Cross described the "dark night of the soul." I tell you—I opened the soul's door and there was night all around. I heard voices. I glimpsed the occasional twinkling of a star.

When was it? Who knows? The reverie, the ecstasy I could not put into words was shattered rudely sometime toward midnight that Monday. Still on my knees I saw two men holding poles with cloth stretched between them. There was something on that litter, somebody, something naked, flesh like myself.

Was I still on the floor?

Who was that? Who *is* that? Where are they going? Those two just brought it—brought *him*—brought . . .

Someone slapped me hard on the face—two—three—four times!

"Get up, you dumb fucker."

Someone else said, "Pull him."

I was yanked to stand, forced to look. There, flung across his cot was His Eminence Cardinal Arcadio Monsignani, naked, fat, green, looking dead. There was blood on many parts of his body. Crosses had been carved into his forehead, his arms, his thighs.

Ercole was standing beside me, looking weird. I couldn't tell if he were revolted or delighted. He handed me gauze bandages, tape, *tintura di iodio*, and went away. The door was locked. We were left alone.

204

I did my best to nurse the poor man's wounds, and was relieved that the cuts were not too deep. I tried not to think of what caused them. I covered the cardinal with his blankets.

On the floor food for two meals still sat near the chamber pot. There was wine, but even though I carried the vital liquid to offer some to His Eminence, I had to drink it alone as Arcadio had passed off to sleep.

12

Beppe brought coffee next morning. I ached all over. The cardinal was snoring. I felt it best to let him sleep but took some coffee for him. Iacopo proceeded down the passage with clothes in his hands, and said, "Step back."

I did. Through the bars he pushed Monsignani's vestments. I caught them and put them on my bed, and dressed. The cardinal slept past noon.

It was the twelfth of July, Tuesday. The nightmarish day before at least forced a solid decision on my part. I waited, though, reflecting on it patiently till the old man showed signs of revival.

He groaned. Obviously I wasn't what he hoped to see. I went to him, asked him how he felt, and told him I'd bandaged his wounds. He thanked me.

This was just as lunch was being brought in. Ercole carried a tray bearing pasta with cheese, boiled fish, and tomato salad. Iacopo held two rolls, some wine. Only Iacopo entered; he was armed. Monsignani turned his cut head.

"Arcadio?" Iacopo queried nastily. "Feel like being civil?"

The leader stood with his feet planted apart, and began an anti-litany of all the things he could think of that were "sins of the Church." I felt like shouting, *Shut up!*

Neither Monsignani nor I really listened to the list. What was the sense? Our feelings on the subject were of no importance to the Brigade. Even had we protested, the *brigatista* would have continued professing the same coarse creed.

The cardinal most definitely was in spiritual and physical decline after the previous day's torture. It was one more vicious tactic, their coming in continually and saying that the Church erred. Some "People's Inquisition," I thought.

"One. The Church's *mortal* sin . . . is its derisive attitude to the poor alongside such passion for the rich. This directly contradicts the teaching of Jesus."

What the hell did Iacopo know about Christ?

"Two. This devotion to money has kept the workers bound to servility for centuries. This is especially true since the Second World War. Three. The Church has been buying control of Italy for the last two generations, financing and influencing the right-wing Christian Democratic party, denying social advancement for the masses. Retaining the repressive and fascistic status quo. Four. The Nazi-style organization of the Church in each village of this poor country has perpetuated its anachronistic philosophy which is: 'Keep the people in chains. Threaten them by Jehovah if anyone thinks along populistic lines.' Five. The Vatican has constantly put a damper on socially beneficial movements already under way in this country by issuing retrograde mandates which put the people in fear. For example, the Apostolic See's stand against divorce, against abortion, against the pleasures of sex."

I shut out his voice totally after that. The list was endless. I started to eat. The cardinal sat up with my help and I gave him his plate, but the food was cold already. We ate it anyway, slowly. The harangue continued. Iacopo didn't even consider it rude that we were eating in the midst of his oratory. Finally he left, like Mussolini, self-assured that his dictates were affidavits of intelligence.

206

Sitting up to eat proved a strain on His Eminence, so he got back in bed and I covered him. Immediately, it seemed, he fell asleep.

My spirits kept sinking. That hellish phrase "sins of the Church" kept playing and playing in my mind, like a slovenly squatter soiling one's house, against every device I employed to evict it.

Anything of import to our release? I wanted to ask, but as no one was in the corridor, I soon forgot.

I feared sleep for some reason. I got on my knees to pray, but they hurt so from the day before that I had to stay seated. There was nothing to do—*nothing*!

Sins of the Church . . .

The evil psychologist Iacopo verily had unleashed a pride of brutish thoughts, awful events of Church history which I couldn't force back. The Black Death of 1348 was the most recurrent of these visions. England's population plummeted from four to two and a half million. Popular dissent against Church wealth reached peaks unscaled till 1538 . . . and Henry the Eighth's horrendous dissolution of the monasteries.

Such ideas chased about in my brain—swarms of diseased rats carrying bubonic plague—as a snide voice inside queried, "Well, maybe the Church *has* really sinned more than she's done good?"

13

To rid my skull of new doubts plaguing me, I went to sleep. Like the cardinal I awoke only to eat the next meal. Even though I thought of saying Communion, the elder prelate seemed only to want silence, so we both slept again till we were awakened on Wednesday.

It's strange, but in such confinement one's usually wide-ranging intellect constricts considerably, notwithstanding the brutal fear of having one's remaining faculties snuffed out by torture. After being startled by the sight of Ercole Roseazzini, I had let my mind gravitate toward the pleasure of the past two weeks in Rome, new vistas shown me, new friendships, and new love with the sister of a *brigatista*.

Rome's high life passed before my eyes as a phantasm. Incapable of reaching out, unable to hold onto one single delight now, I saw the lovely figure of Serafina, in all the scenes I shared with her.

This wretched cell! Even she, even the woman that I loved, now was irretrievable. She was *out there*—in freedom, in sunshine that nurtured terrorists, far from my reach, removed from my heart, hopelessly far.

Serafina did not fade—she just did not come to me frequently.

All that existed was the cardinal and I . . . and he perhaps was dying.

I mustn't let him die!

I awoke. Already he was standing. He was very, very pallid, but he was holding his cup for coffee. The effort was a burden. He retreated to his bed. I thought, Now's the moment. Perhaps I *might* be of use.

I said: "Arcadio, I've been thinking about this for an awfully long time. Just two days ago I . . . when you were . . . I meditated upon it all day . . . . No please let me finish . . . . I decided I no longer can remain the Representative of the Archbishop of Canterbury to His Holiness but . . . but I only withdraw from this position out of a greater belief—that I now must become a . . . a member of the Roman Catholic Church."

Cardinal Monsignani sighed as if ready to weep. He shook his head reproachfully. "Don't you know what that means? Don't you see what you're. . . . Oh my son, dearest Rupert, it gives me. . . . I must think it over."

"Please don't plague your thoughts with difficulties of mine. I've decided, Arcadio. I shall do it, but I beg you for your help. Please perform the rite."

"The Rite of Reception of Baptized Christians," he said, then fell silent. After deliberation he whispered, "You just may be lucky, young man."

"What?"

"You're in Rome as the official Representative of the Anglican—"

"No . . . I'm in this prison—in prison now!"

"They'll say I forced you."

"Let them say what they want. The archbishop, my boss, is in favor of Unity with Rome. I'm only going one step further."

"It's your own decision. I'm sure that it's been hard."

"All my ancesters were Catholic—till Grandfather. I'm just going back—"

"To Mother Church."

"You won't help me? Won't you perform—"

"The rite? Recently . . . I was studying it for the Secretariat for Unity—"

"Then will you please *perform* it?" I had been praying he would say yes, if only to give the man a goal to revive his spirit. A smile at last broke across his wan face. He replied, "Yes, my son, I *shall* perform it."

14

Since that decision, which truly was the most difficult of my life, many have attacked me, Anglicans as well as Catholics, because I "changed allegiance" whilst holding a key post in the Anglican hierarchy. Let me, therefore, explain my motive.

209

I mentioned the premonition that His Eminence would die at the hands of our captors. The cardinal himself had resigned himself to this fate. If he should recover from the brutality and shock to his system from the torture he received, there always was the horrifying chance of his being tortured again. For a man in his seventies, such treatment could prove fatal. A heart attack was no small possibility.

That Wednesday when I told him I decided to leave the Anglican Church, we already had been held captive eleven days. Neither of us knew if more physical torture would ensue, so our anxiety heightened; nor did we suspect thirty-three more days of incarceration lay ahead.

Therefore, due to the agonizing uncertainty of it all, and due to the lack of information given to us by the *brigatisti* concerning any negotiations that might or might not be going on to get us released, my thoughts transferred from worries about friends and family to the sole human being with whom I now was struggling to survive.

Given that the Brigade did not try to extract information from me (I was excess baggage in the car when the cardinal was kidnapped), my health hadn't degenerated as noticeably as Monsignani's (but then, I hadn't been tortured), and my youth cried out to offer some sort of help to this elder who was suffering so dreadfully. I felt it my duty to God, if I had any faith at all, to try to revive the cardinal's waning spirits by the most dramatic and purposeful means that I could.

So I chose to abnegate my own career in the Anglican Communion, to give up my post in Rome, and to embrace Catholicism as a civilian. It was as simple a sequence of thought as that.

"Better to be a sinful Catholic layman . . . than a pitiful Anglican priest," I told Monsignani after he agreed to perform the Rite of Reception.

15

The decision to become a Catholic produced greater anxieties than I had reckoned. For the next two days as Monsignani continued to revive, my "motive" seemed impossible to comprehend. Perhaps it had been an escape route—to bring Serafina to whatever haven I was hungering for in my mind.

I mention her at this point because my journal reveals that she dominated my thoughts. When I should have been concentrating on the psychologies of the captors, especially Ercole's, or meditating on my "conversion" to Catholicism induced by the strain of being held hostage, I somehow could only deal with memories of the beautiful girl. Serafina began to take on qualities not demonstrated during our short time together.

Was my love for her just infatuation?

Did I like her . . . or her body?

At least by my becoming Catholic, we could marry without ecclesiastical dispensations.

Ercole came down the corridor a few times. Obviously I wasn't thinking sanely, because I thought I perceived that he was in the mood to talk. The cardinal, much saner than I, snarled at my bantering with his depraved nephew. "For the love of God, don't bother, Rupert. He's lost!"

Monsignani turned to the *brigatista* and tried to get the boy to report on the progress of our release. "What is His Holiness saying?"

"You have no bargaining power whatsoever, Arcadio. Why do you ask? If I tell you the Vatican's agreed or not agreed to front the money for your release, would it matter, since we're still holding you? When you agree to

211

our terms, then you'll notice differences in the situation."

"Will you free us?" the cardinal asked impatiently.

"The decision isn't ours."

"Whose is it then?" I grumbled.

"Perhaps . . . God's?" Ercole replied with horrid irony. "Isn't His justice complete? Well, it's your way of dealing with Him that brought you here. You both got what you deserve."

The cardinal snapped: "You of all beings of this earth are the least qualified to make the shortest pronouncement about divine theology. You know nothing, so why give voice to your ignorance, which is total!"

Ercole laughed, a kid at a circus entertained by a vulgar clown. "You, Arcadio, haven't improved a bit . . . by being a guest of our hospitality. We shower *indulgences* on you—you'd just as soon kick our balls in. Lots of thanks we get, keeping your sort alive."

Then the maniac turned to me and asked crassly: "Hey, you—Rupert? Did you *fuck* my sister?"

Silence. Ercole chortled and strutted away.

"His fatal naïvete's so complete," Monsignani whispered shortly thereafter, "that he imagines such crude questions bother me. Whether you did or did not have relations with Serafina—"

I didn't let His Eminence continue, as I felt the moment for confession had arrived. "I did, Arcadio. We did, but I'm not ashamed. I love your niece. I do want to— very much I want to marry her."

"Should these walls set you free—you have my sincerest blessing, young man. If only I could live . . . to celebrate the marriage."

"I love the whole family. You've all been so understanding, and it grieves me so to see the results of . . . of having produced such a one as Ercole."

"Do you recall, Rupert, when you moved in, you

212

went to your garden in the night and a cat suddenly fell into the bushes?"

"By . . . Ercole? Damn him—who else!"

"He told Serafina. She told me."

"But why—why could she say at Villa Ferrucci that Ercole had no other friend but her?"

"He had her duped. As children, those two were inseparable. He brainwashed her into believing anything he said. Your appearance was a threat to this, don't you see?"

"My God!"

"I was in favor of your seeing her. I prayed you'd lead her thoughts away from that insane brother of hers, and you did."

"But why would a terrorist continue living at home?"

"The Brigade keeps many members in the 'bourgeois world' as security for *brigatisti*. If young recruits live clandestinely, if too many withdraw completely from the family or whatever environment they spring from, their sudden disappearance of course alerts the police. It's far more advantageous to the criminals if young blood keeps a toehold in the familiar setting. Ercole's case is so simple it's sad. Can't you see, he's just being used by these animals!"

"Thinking about him never made me happy."

"Imagine our past two years then. Ercole's their pawn though he's convinced he's vital to whatever mad new world they'll dare to construct. Yes, as a member of our family he *has* been privy to quite a bit of information many governments wouldn't mind having. We *are* that close to the pope. We've many ties to the Italian government, also. For them to get an impressionable and hotheaded boy like my nephew was just what the Brigade was waiting for. Most of the youth of *Roma Nera* are so wrapped up in themselves they don't have a drop of social conscience. Along comes Ercole Roseazzini who did have a drop and who gets alienated from his roots the instant he sets foot

213

in university. Thus politicized, he's ripe for the plucking. He may be unique of his class, but he isn't unpredictable. It had to happen. It's just a miracle it hadn't happened sooner."

"The disaffected from the working class and from the bourgeoisie—" I began.

"Precisely—then the inevitable fall of one fool from the heights. It's happened in the past, all through Roman history. We should have expected it. But watch—Ercole's just being used, I tell you, used to get a Vatican financial expert captured, used to tell the Brigade all he knows about who knows whom in upper-class Rome, who deals with whom in business, who sits on what board, et cetera, things he's heard in the house all his life, things which have been preparing his brother Oduardo for years to take over his father's activities."

The cardinal sighed. "Once the Brigade's done with my nephew, I predict that neither his being their accomplice in my capture nor his being the supplier of whatever information can spare him his life. Be sure—the boy's days are numbered, as are mine."

This discussion lasted from Thursday into Saturday, as the cardinal spoke at great length about each of the various members of his large family. I also had things to unburden about my own.

Especially, I wanted him to absolve me from the fact that my turning to the Church had been an escape from my family. We discussed my parents, their recent and separate deaths, but I did not yet have the courage to go into some intimate family things. The cardinal hadn't told me much about his parents, so why should I belabor him with mine?

Throughout these three days both of us constantly asked the guards about negotiations. Each time our spirits fell with their response, "If something happens, we'll tell you."

214

"But can't I write to the pope?" Monsignani kept pleading.

"What for?" they kept retorting. "To give him our love?"

Time passed so slowly. Looking back upon it, I believe Monsignani felt that as a Catholic I might be more a candidate for priesthood than for bridegroom to his niece. This is why he didn't immediately perform the Rite of Reception, but kept talking to me, asking me all sorts of questions, judging my soul.

Subconsciously, he was performing a *rite de passage* which would stretch throughout the next week. He was training me to enter the Church in as proper a mental atmosphere as conditions could allow. Thank God we'd found a common ground for our discussions.

16

At midnight between Saturday the sixteenth and Sunday the seventeenth of July, the Brigade woke us up roughly. I was forced to lug my bed to the iron gate. The cardinal and I were told to sit and watch as Ercole, Beppe, and Iacopo proceeded to defame the mass.

We'd been given no bread or wine that evening. Though we'd planned to say the Eucharist after our meal, the *brigatisti* were a jump ahead of us. I shall never forget those faces of depravity which began a long-thought-out attack on the basic rite of Christendom. Staged as but another devious psychological ploy to outrage us, the acts we were forced to watch were so crude as to lie even beyond the bounds of outrage.

I kept wondering as the insanity continued *what* it was they were trying to instill in us? Were the three simply deranged, retrograde children, playing at ridicule, so to show wicked adults they really could be just as wicked? I wondered if they were going through their fetid rite just to prove to themselves they *could* do it—that the presence of a cardinal was no deterrent to their doing it?

Obviously, the defamation was meant for some purpose. I really could not believe that it could be a mere political demonstration of hatred for the basic religious tenets of the whole Western world. The more I watched, the more I was convinced they were doing it to prove to themselves they could do it.

Down the corridor they brought a long wide board and two sawhorses for their altar. They stripped their clothes off and started smoking prerolled joints of marijuana. They sat upon the board nude. Ercole played the priest. From a pocket of his trousers he produced the amber cross and amethyst ring stolen from the cardinal and put them on. He inhaled heavily, began caressing his private parts, then walked around the board blowing smoke in Beppe's and Iacopo's faces, miming the purification incense. The smell was not pleasant. Their creed does not deserve repeating. I shall simply end this paragraph here.

For the First Reading Beppe read the Archbishop of Canterbury's appeal for our release, while the three fondled each other's sexual organs and laughed. Then Iacopo burned the words with his lighter and roared. Then he repeated the pope's plea as the Second Reading. Ercole and Beppe fought over the script to see who could burn it, but Iacopo intervened and lit it himself, telling the two "priests" to be "good girls."

For the Gospel, which shocked Monsignani more than anything outside of his torture, his nephew bent to the floor for a Bible we hadn't seen, the one he taunted us with. Instead of reading Matthew, Mark, Luke, or John, Ercole flipped to Revelation, as he knew his uncle had been studying it of late. He ripped the whole book out of the Bible. Then he threw the rest of the sacred text to the

216

floor and commenced to paw through the remainder in his hand, and to read out snatches which he followed by "No—that's not the one."

This disgusting exercise he repeated over and over. It certainly did infuriate, as well as badly hurt and humiliate, the cardinal.

Iacopo, impatient with Ercole's burlesque, took his hands off Beppe who was now quite erect and said, "Enough Bible bullshit! On with the mass." Then he grabbed the pages of Revelation and began the actual blasphemy of the Lord's Supper.

Iacopo pushed the two off the mock altar. Ercole began to be fellated by Beppe so that he would have company in his tumescence. Then Iacopo jumped upon the board, squatted, and pointed his backside to us. He began to defecate, saying, "This is the Bread . . ."

Then after Iacopo had wiped himself with the last book of the Bible, the two who were masturbating each other from both sides of the board had orgasms on the defecation and screamed, "And this is the Wine . . ."

A triumphant Iacopo then shouted, "The mass is ended," and he stuck a candle he had lit into the slime and departed muttering, "Go our way . . . in *war!*"

17

We must have suffered a mental blackout of what we just had witnessed. After a strangely placid sleep we were woken next morning by the light bulb and by Beppe dropping paper and a pencil to the floor of our cell. As we staggered with our glasses for coffee, the *brigatista* said Monsignani had just one hour to compose a letter to the pope. It would be going out with their second communiqué, to be issued later that Sunday, the seventeenth of July.

Ercole came down the hall as Beppe left. I then noticed that the blasphemous altar had been removed. Neither of the two revolutionaries gave the slightest hint of ever having performed such sacrilege.

Ercole, clutching the machine gun as was his wont, said: "Note the paper. Write your boss and tell him you're alive. Say we're feeding you. Don't say you've seen anything strange in the people's jail. Is that clear?"

His uncle just stared, as if the nephew were from some black hole in an incomprehensible anti-galaxy.

"Don't mention any questions you've been asked. Don't say you've received wounds which you brought upon yourself."

He turned and left. Iacopo followed. He pulled the second communiqué from his shirt. "Here. Read it yourselves." He flung it inside. It read:

> The Leonine Walls of the Holy See are not
> impregnable. The pope is mortal. The intransigence
> of the Vatican these past two weeks is predictable
> and historical. If the Smallest State continues to
> play the girl with the most to lose, then the Brigade
> will rape her. We believe that the Vatican can and
> does influence Italian politics every single day.
> Therefore our demand for Vatican money equally is
> feasible. A small sum of one million pounds
> sterling to be paid in lira—isn't it tiny for the price
> of a Prince of the Church? Time is running out. No
> more private communication will be dispatched by
> us to the Vatican after the release of this
> communiqué. Cardinal Monsignani's life now is the
> responsibility of the man who wears the Triple
> Crown. The People's Inquisition still is in progress.

Two unlined sheets of paper were requisitioned for the cardinal's letter to His Holiness. I don't know the exact words he put in it. I didn't interfere. The old man became

218

exceedingly emotional whilst writing it and I believe that he signed it as a sort of will, in case no other letter would be allowed outside.

At one point Monsignani looked up with tears in his eyes and told me, with the greatest humility, that he was telling the pope that I was alive. He was asking the pope to telephone Canterbury so that the archbishop might notify my sister Samantha, who hadn't gone to Athens.

This, from a man with so many of his own preoccupations to be sent to the pope—struck me as so kind and touching that I vowed to tell the cardinal more about my family as soon as we had a peaceful interlude, whenever the fiends might allow that.

As I was thinking this, Monsignani again looked up. "With your permission, it would raise my spirits so if I could be allowed to tell His Holiness that I shall be performing the Rite of Reception on your behalf."

But I responded fearfully: "*Don't* put that in writing! Who knows who'll get hold of this? *They'll* be reading this too before they let it outside these walls. Such information (and they're shrewd enough) would be used to denigrate us both. Please, just say I'm deeply humbled by any help the Holy See provides for us, that the Holy Father's definitely in our prayers."

Monsignani kept his writing very small and finished it as quickly as he could under the strain of knowing that each word would be double-checked by the Brigade. I honestly don't see how the man could compose his thoughts, but somehow he did, and in time to read the letter once through before Beppe came to abscond with it.

That nobody reprimanded us on Sunday was a sign that the Brigade had found the letter inoffensive. Or . . . had they?

18

At one o'clock Sunday, Ercole brought the midday meal, the usual *pasta-olio* with cheese, a tin of tuna, and a zucchini to cut as a salad. I heard myself sarcastically asking him as he bent to shove the gruel beneath the gate, "Do you often have sex with men?"

He smirked and turned to go, saying: "Why? You get all hot and bothered last night?" Then he started off but his uncle called to him. "Ercole?"

"What?"

"Won't you stay a moment?"

"You get excited last night, too? Don't tell me you've kept a clean cock all these years—with all those pretty-boy seminarians keeping your sheets nice and warm. What about that young *monsignore* of yours? Hey, Arcadio, do you fuck your secretary or does he fuck you?"

"Why can't we speak about—"

Ercole ignored the cardinal and looked at me. "You, Broxbourne—the cardinal didn't let Your Lordship meet his gorgeous secretary, did he? The servants say he spends a lot of time in His Eminence's penthouse. Poor sod, he must be weeping bucketsful—of come."

I told him that the secretary and I never had been introduced.

"Irish he is—queer as they get—but does he look butch as a general, a very *young* green-eyed general."

"Gavin is somebody who works very hard, Ercole, not like—"

"I'm sure he does."

I tried to change the subject. Since the conversation was loose, if nothing more, I thought I'd risk asking about

220

our other captors. "Ercole, what is Beppe's background? Where does he come from?"

"Why? Taken a fancy to him? He's very long, and very tall, but I'm sure you noted his dimensions."

"Is he Roman?" I asked, suddenly having lost interest in the dialogue.

"How'd you guess? I'll tell him you're asking for him. He *is* Roman—yes—from the Campo di Fiori, from a working-class alley off the market called Vicolo della Grotte. Want his number?"

"Tell me more about him," the cardinal said dryly.

"Ho—the *old* goat's taken a fancy, too! Wait till Beppe hears how popular he's become."

"Don't be ludicrous, Ercole. What's his surname?"

"Spadino."

"Parents?"

"Father's a fish vendor, his mother's sold used clothes all her life."

"How—how do you possibly relate to such people?" Monsignani cried. "What can you ever have in common with the working class?"

I think the question registered for a split second, for a look of pain replaced the rebellious expression for a few seconds. But it disappeared as quickly as it had come and Ercole carried on oblivious to the query. "Beppe is working-class. He grew up in the market, working with his father selling fish since he was a boy. The Campo . . . has one of the highest crime rates in the city—it's a slum!"

"You sound like some third-rate propoganda leaflet," spit Monsignani. "What can you say about Iacopo?"

"Iacopo's my boss." The voice sounded light-years away.

"How long have you known him?"

"A time."

"How long have you been connected with the Brigade, Ercole?"

"A time."

"What did you do that first week we were kidnapped? You who organized this nightmare—where were you hiding?"

"Outside. The Brigade put me on assignment."

"Who? Iacopo? Where's Iacopo from?"

"Milano—near Milano—an industrial suburb of the industrial capital of—" His voice was so strange.

"You're sounding like a leaflet again, Ercole. What about Iacopo? The name is Tuscan. What's his family called?"

"Orcagno. I think they're. . . . His parents were Tuscan, near Siena. They left and went to Milano after the war."

"Iacopo's not working-class, is he?"

"Middle-class—*piccolo borghese.*"

"Do you two talk much?"

Suddenly the door from the rectangular room above opened with a whoosh and the leader shouted down like a madman, "What in hell are you three gossiping about, you *cunts*! Ercole—get up here immediately."

Roseazzini left. We were perplexed as we couldn't decide if the whole thing had been staged. Obviously, dementia was in the air, trying to undo us all, *brigatisti* included.

"Just as you can tell what class an Englishman comes from as soon as he opens his mouth, so can I an Italian," Monsignani said to break the silence. "Iacopo had to be Tuscan. The name's most common there—rare elsewhere. His *milanese* also is noticeable, as is his being fairly well educated. Beppe's lack of polish is lamentable. Once there likely was a mind inside that skull. It's so sad—these terrorists once were just children. They grew to be pensive young men, whose questioning led them to some incomprehensible utopia, some new world where they're really only craving to be children all over again. Like children, they see right through the gruesome adult world's phon-

222

iness and games, but like children, if they can't shout and scream the silly adults into compliance, they resort to destructiveness."

After some minutes of silence, the cardinal added: "This infantile *brigatista* mentality catches on so well here in Italy because Italians grow up to become spoiled kids. How else can one explain the millennial lag between the once most powerful and best organized empire on earth and its lamentably late unification again as one nation? Italians *can* be organized if they want to—but like children they usually *don't* want to."

The uncanny logic of the cardinal's thoughts was punctuated by his saying: "The aim of these terrorists is babyish. Simply by sporadic acts of destructiveness—even by your or my murder—they think they can force mankind into egalitarianism. A more stupid theory never coursed through human brains! No theory is so visibly contrary to God's will. If He wanted us all equal, then He would have created the world solely as a patch of artichokes, or perhaps nothing but a bed of oysters. That diversity's the rule, not the exception, doesn't seem to have occurred to the Brigade. After all, they're kids."

19

That evening and Monday morning we saw only Beppe. Both times, after placing the food, he unzipped his trousers, pulled them down, and commenced masturbating. This sick, overt sexuality which hadn't been a part of our imprisonment before the profanation of the mass soon appeared to be just another factor in the Brigade's revolt against all society's norms.

Sex is a basic right of humanity. Under the conditions in which our captors held us, it wasn't consoling to realize that they were using sex as one more way to destroy our

223

sanity. They specifically were aiming sex at that part of our being, at that part of a man of religion who all too often has to sublimate his natural sexual urges: the *mind*, which would rather contemplate things higher.

This new tactic of the terrorists was most disturbing. For me, in particular. My thoughts, which had stayed well away from sex, now were magnetized by it. The anxiety that this caused was just what the Brigade was hoping for, I'm sure.

To allay the pressure, both the cardinal and I talked continuously. He was training me to enter Mother Church, and I was confessing so many things which I thought I'd forgotten many years ago.

"My mother," I began at one point, "must have known your sister well. Princess Aurora spoke of her." ˙

"Unfortunately," His Eminence replied, "I never did have the chance to meet Her Ladyship."

"Mother's *ladyship* caused Father's family much debate!" I told him of her drinking, her concerts I'd seen and not seen, her love for and her conquering of Paris, and her love-hate for her intellectual fans and the stupid snobs of London. "She'd suddenly have intense Greek bouts of devoted motherhood. My God, she did produce five children, and not once did I ever hear a single rumor that they were sired by any father but my own. But then, Mother would suddenly rebel against this brood she produced, she'd curse the large Kent estate and the husband much younger than she—the husband who was so loose with women—and with men. Yes," I admitted to the cardinal, "Father had a craving . . . for something I didn't find out about till late in life. Odd—it was my youngest sister Amy who broke the news to me. Four years ago. Nicholas was nine and a day pupil in Canterbury. At that time, Father had a stroke. He was forty-eight and was forced to recuperate at home. Though Father's father had been dead eight years, my father never had had an extended stay at Dexter Mote. He'd only called on weekends, pre-

224

ferring our Belgravia town house or, more to the point, his women . . . and his men of New York. Mother hated Manhattan, with good reason. She'd go to Paris instead. I think they last slept together thirteen years ago—to produce Nicholas. Four years ago, when Amy came to me weeping and carrying on, she was fourteen and I was home from my theological studies. She . . . she said that Father and Nicholas were 'doing dirty things' in his room . . . that Father . . . had left it unlocked one morning, 'things' which Amy had seen."

The cardinal looked shocked, so I asked if I should continue.

"To rid this from your soul . . . is healthy," he admitted.

"I want to tell you . . . of my parents' deaths."

He said kindly, "I'm listening."

"Father's death two Mays ago was a result of . . . a result of . . ."

"Do you really want to talk?"

"Unnatural sex. This date roughly coincided with the first anniversary of my ordination. There was to have been a special celebratory service for me in my London church. It was canceled because of Father's death . . . because of murder."

That certainly startled the cardinal. "Murder?"

"Mother poisoned him."

"But . . . how do you know?"

"She told me . . . soon before she died. This was roughly seven months later. She was dying so she decided to kill him. He didn't deserve to live, for all his infidelities, after she was gone, she said. She wanted him in hell, she told me, where she could keep an eye on him. I'll never forget the look on her face when she said, 'It was for the best of both of us.' "

"But—" Monsignani fought for words—"but was there no scandal?"

"Murmurs. It happened in Kent, not London. We're

225

an isolated but important Kentish family. What could any-one do? Aldous, my father, had had two strokes already. The coroner reported death due to stroke. That was that. Into the family vault he went. Mother became delirious with anguish as the Mediterranean woman lurking inside her suddenly sprang to full force. Mother *sang*—she sang a beautiful sad Greek love song. My own mother *sang* at the funeral of my father. Everyone was horrified but the family—and even though I secretly was singing with her, it took away all desire I ever had to visit Greece."

"Good God! Her singing didn't cause a scandal?"

"Murmurs. Once the mob got back to London. No-body expected anything but strangeness from Mother."

"But your three sisters? Don't they know the whole . . ."

"Story? I'm the only one. Now, Arcadio, now do you see *why* I joined the Church? I never told the children what Mother confessed to me—what I now confess to Your Eminence and to the Deity, both for my sake and my dear parents'."

The cardinal raised his hand as if to grant absolution, but I intervened saying: "I'm not finished. I must get this out. Did your niece Dulcinea tell you that I told her my mother was dying of cancer?"

"She said nothing, other than she'd known Louise and loved her. It was . . . let *me* confess one thing . . . it was due to my sister and niece that we invited you to move to Palazzo Roseazzini—oh God, Rupert, would that we sat there now—because the two women loved your mother so, they felt compelled by friendship to offer you hospitality and I readily complied."

"I see. Thank you."

I felt I would weep, but carried on. "Mother was difficult, yes, but I accept her reasoning. Father tortured her and never in my life did any gossip get back to me about Mother being unfaithful to my father so for years I believe she kept her composure, stoically, as best she

226

could, being an artist of incredible sensitivity. My God—she was compared to Piaf! People adored her."

"I know. I often heard her songs. Aurora kept after me to meet her, yet I was always working, *working*! It never was to be."

"So Mother poisoned him. He'd been guilty of one last indiscretion, far too unforgivable to condone. Also, she was failing . . . as her cancer, lung cancer—she smoked till she died—drove her to kill herself. She took too many pills—that was all. All that suffering, all that pain, all that guilt, all those songs . . . those songs . . . then suicide."

I couldn't go on. I started weeping in Arcadio's arms for my mother, for my father.

20

Next day, Tuesday the nineteenth, and each day through Saturday of that week of my training to enter the Church, Ercole was delegated to bring all three of our meals, which he brought nude. He would fondle himself for a while, exhibit himself erect to us, then stomp away. It was macabre. He would say nothing to us.

We wanted to ask him questions, but toward Thursday the cardinal and I agreed: What was the use?

Iacopo came that Tuesday as we were saying the mass after lunch. He proceeded to masturbate, with his back to us. After he finished, he faced us again and sneered. "The Vatican's playing hard to get."

We asked him about any progress since the second communiqué and the letter to the pope. "What do you mean 'hard to get'?" I queried.

"Your Cardinal Secretary of State gave a press conference this morning. He says the Vatican's remaining inflexible in its refusal to negotiate on our terms."

227

"Inflexible?" Monsignani asked. "I doubt he used that word."

"It seems the Apostolic See desires only to speak about money."

"How can you possibly expect one sovereign state, the Vatican, to maneuver the liberation of political prisoners in another sovereign state, meaning Italy? Diplomatically it's out of the question. You can discuss ransom, but you can't expect complicity in the affairs of the government of Italy."

"But the money . . ."

"Could be arranged, if you drop your impossible first demand."

"We said we shall not communicate further," Iacopo snickered weirdly.

"Let *me* communicate—by writing on your behalf."

Iacopo laughed. "You're a wizard, but only about money." He pulled a pad from a pocket.

"Do you still have that pen?"

"Yes."

"Then write quickly. Only to the pope. Tell him you and I have spoken. You've given your word that the Vatican *can* front the million pounds in lira. If they do so by . . . by this Saturday midnight then we won't carry out our bombing planned for that same time."

"What about our release?" Monsignani begged.

"Comply. We'll adjust the situation from there. Now hurry—write that note."

"How're you getting these messages to the pope?" I asked, wondering if someone inside the Vatican was an informer.

"Just say your prayers. Don't ask too many questions." Iacopo left us, while Arcadio wrote quickly. For the first time in days, I noted he was smiling.

I couldn't smile, thinking the whole thing a ruse, just another torture tactic to try to dim our minds. If the Brigade should agree to drop their first demand for the release of prisoners, they wouldn't be getting compensation out of us for dropping it. But, it might assure their organization of realizing a million pounds. Strange that they chose pounds, I thought.

Monsignani finished the note to the pope. As he gave it to Beppe, who came to fetch it, the cardinal crossed himself, then kissed the paper before handing it to the thug, a gesture that Beppe profaned by pretending to wipe his private parts with it.

21

We waited all that week for news about the change in the Brigade's demand. For five solid days all that we saw was the offensive nude body of the cardinal's demented nephew. He would leer, but would not converse with us. His miserable silence especially agitated his uncle, who was trying his hardest to appear unshaken.

The old man's wounds were healing, I must say, but that was small consolation. The boy provoked a line from Monsignani, though, which I shan't ever forget: "And what *is* politics anyway—but publicly applauded masturbation—invented by the Devil!"

I can't tell you how sick of the vapid fare we became. Mealtime was no joy. Through Saturday the twenty-third of July, though, we said mass twice daily, almost out of a need for something to do.

We attempted "intellectual" discussions of the latest debates in ecclesiastical circles, but our fatigue, lassitude, bitterness, or incapacity to deal with the issues from prison prevented meaningful exchanges of opinion.

Often I saw Serafina in the midst of our talks. I was

229

dying to hold her, to kiss her. I asked His Eminence if he'd ever been in love with a woman. He wasn't slow to reply. "Yes."

I didn't enquire any further.

He told me how much he enjoyed visiting his titular church in south Rome, in the modern quarter the EUR, named after the Esposizione Universale di Roma which was supposed to be held in 1942 but wasn't, because of the war. His church, built in the fifties, was functional and gleaming inside. There was some way in which the light came through the azure-blue skylights—an odd radiance, a sunburst on the ceiling—which pleased him immensely. He looked forward to visiting it since there never were any tourists at mass, just Romans.

Monsignani had had little experience as a pastoral priest for the past thirty years. This he regretted deeply. The problems of a pastorate, of sharing one's love with God and with the people of one's parish, being the intercessor between the sacred and the profane, was a subject we did keep going back to as I prepared to enter the Church. I should state that the cardinal never once exerted pressure on me to become a *priest* of the Catholic Church. I'm sure he would not have turned me away—had I heard the call. But considering that he had given me his blessing to marry his niece, I sensed that he knew my long-range desires better than I knew them myself.

"The love of a pastoral priest is for his people," His Eminence said sometime that week. "It verges on madness, because the most intense loves of one's life sweep one away as if the brain is deranged. Just look at these creatures holding us captive."

"What do *they* love?"

"Their selves, Rupert, only their selves. I was a student of art history at the University of Florence when I heard the call to be a priest. My father was a famous professor, but through my own studies I was drawn to

230

the Church, and I'm proud to confess that this happened because of art—which was my first love."

"Your transition from art to the Church . . . is so understandable, in such a city as Florence."

"Yes, my son, this is true." The old man slipped off into memories of Tuscany and his youth.

After some time, he revived and said, "When one decides to leave the secular world, where does one step but into the vastness of the unknown? For a young person this is a terrifying experience—leaving many behind, those who expect a different path to be followed."

"Dear God—I know!"

"But Christ died loving, then rose to sit in glory. His example is perpetual—it can only give one strength."

"So often, I've been weak," I admitted.

"It takes a rare strength, a rare priest indeed, to live a spiritual life to the fullest, notwithstanding this world. The Holy Spirit can possess one at the oddest of times, anywhere. One must be open. One must be receptive to the *incarnational*. To be able to say *yes*—as did the Blessed Virgin Mary—is something so awesome as to be beyond the gift of words."

"The Word alone, as a force . . ."

"Must never seem strange . . . though it frighten."

22

Saturday, after we were asleep, we had another eerie midnight alarm by all three terrorists. All were clothed—belligerently smug like the Fates—all were armed. The vision frightened us greatly. I felt our time had come.

We had all but forgotten about the Saturday deadline; this was why we were woken. "Get up," growled Iacopo.

"What?" Monsignani asked weakly.

231

WOKEN ?
AWAKENED?

"News for you two divine bastards. The Vatican's failed to comply. The letter you wrote was given to the pope. He read it and agreed to the amount of the request. The money was given and delivered to Pasette del Biscione at the corner of Campo di Fiori at nine this morning when the market was at its peak. An old woman brought the two shopping bags, then gave them to a younger woman as planned—just like mother and daughter. Yet the pope had told the police. The market was suddenly blocked off. Our girl was armed and fired to break through. A *poliziotto* was killed, the market went berserk, two tourists were wounded, our girl was murdered . . . all this for *you*, Monsignani. Are you proud of yourself? Are you happy? Are you pleased with the way the Vatican deals with the world?"

The cardinal was gray—lips twitching—the cardinal was tongue-tied. Shaking, he tried to verbalize something but could not. I was no better, unable to say anything at all.

"You will pay for this, Monsignani. Tonight, in five minutes, there will be three large bombs going off in your titular church. That's right. Your titular church in the EUR is going to explode. Nothing will remain—*nothing*.

"That's . . ." But the cardinal looked at me totally distraught and started to sob. "That's . . ."

"Don't speak," I said going to him, hugging him, holding him. "Is this true?" I screamed, unable to believe what I was hearing, unwilling to accept it as fact. "Is it? *Is* it! Tell us—for God's sake or Satan's within you all, tell us!"

"This morning's atrocity in the Campo is now all the world's news."

"Show us," I demanded.

"Go," and Iacopo motioned to Beppe who started up the passage and returned with a *Paese Sera*. Sure enough, there was the headline, the story, the photo. The cardinal looked, but this only induced a horrid fit of coughing.

232

"One minute," Iacopo snickered, "and your prize modern church will be just rubble."

"But people might . . . get"—His Eminence coughed and whimpered—"killed."

"Can't you stop them?" I shouted. "Do something!"

They all laughed. " 'Do something'—he screams like a bitchy little actress—'do something!' Do something yourselves! Get ready for bed. It's beddy-bye time, night-night."

They vanished up the dim hall, chortling, as three bombs exploded inside the church of south Rome.

23

As low as the terrorists were sinking in their carnival of inhumanity, our spirits began to soar in a dizzying cry toward the divine. This may sound perverse, but as we imagined the destruction of the cardinal's titular church, we both felt sucked upward, away from the horrors of the world.

I am not just speaking subjectively here, as His Eminence and I later discussed this mutual sensation in depth. It occurred in both of us, and was not unlike the ecstasies described by the saints. It could only have been an act of succor by God.

We both needed strengthening—we both received it. A force intervened in that cell, to prevent our minds from falling into suicidal depression.

Somehow, this uncanny euphoria, was a realization that whatever acts of savagery the Brigade attempt on the Church, they could not be victorious for their weapons were only mundane. They could try and try to conquer, but they would try till they saw their doom. Even should they be guided by promptings from Satan himself, they were destined to fail.

This was the truth which uplifted our hearts at this heinous hour of the night, at such a fearful hour of our captivity.

Even as we railed against the destruction of a building that recently had stood for God's honor, we were in a bizarre state of bliss, and the cardinal said, "Now we can sleep."

Soon we were dozing with no troubling dreams.

24

If someone had told me before that night that he had had such an awesome feeling as ours when we were told of the bombing, I would have replied that such a spiritual epiphany was something I never would be privy to—for all my sins. Indeed, it was easier to picture Cardinal Monsignani open to such a manifestation of the Lord.

I was awake and thinking this when both of us were shouted out of our beds next morning by Beppe, who was neither nude nor armed. He seemed surprised that neither of us wanted coffee. We both had saved wine and bread from the meal before, so he cursed us and walked away.

Monsignani then spoke about the incomprehensibilities, for mortals, of divine love. He said that the dilemmas *were* understandable by embracing the teachings of Christ. "You and I, Anglican and Catholic, already are united by baptism, which no one can ever disunite." He said my turning to Catholicism was not "conversion" as I was not heathen. He said: "Much as the Roman Church has accepted the ordination of *married* priests of the Eastern Church, so perhaps can we accept that the Anglican Church has *women* as priests. Rome herself has caused immense dilemmas of the spirit by positing so fervently the Church as truth, whereas so many conscientious objectors from the Reformation onward have posited the Scriptures as truth."

He was thinking aloud, then added: "Rupert, you and I don't come from such different ecclesiastical backgrounds as many are wont to think. The seven ancient rungs of the Ladder of Sacraments are the same for both traditions, Catholic and Anglican. Many issues for Unity do still need debate, long after I am dead and you are once more among the laity. But the Holy Ghost now is working swiftly. Unity will happen. Such a Rite of Reception which we now do celebrate . . . no longer will be necessary."

The cardinal led the mass. This time I simply partook of his presence. As we had been doing of late, the Readings and the Gospel were pulled from memory. His Eminence recalled the biblical passages in his own words. His sermon was brief: "Your penance, Rupert, which is required for reception into Mother Church, has been this forced incarceration. And I judge you need no more rigorous a trial for your faith. Amen."

The Rite of Reception followed. His Eminence invited me to come, and I knelt before him as he said: "You have come of your own free will to this decision, by careful thought and by the guidance of the Holy Spirit. I now ask you to profess the Faith with me, in the presence of the Lord our witness."

We said the Nicene Creed. Then I added, "And I believe and profess all that the Holy Catholic Church believes, teaches, and proclaims to be revealed by God."

The cardinal then laid his hands upon my head and stated: "You, Rupert, the Right Reverend the Marquess of Broxbourne, the Lord receive you into the Catholic Church. His loving kindness has led you here, so that in the unity of the Holy Ghost you may have full communion with us in the faith you have professed, in the presence of the Lord. Amen."

After we finished the Eucharist, the cardinal asked for my notebook and pen. He flipped to the back and therein signed a formal declaration that he had performed the rite for me on Sunday, the twenty-fourth of July.

25

Ercole left later that day. We don't know where the Brigade ordered him to go. His whereabouts remain a mystery to everyone save the *brigatisti*.

He came down the passage in his black clothing but without his machine gun. He looked glum and muttered to his uncle, "I'm going now."

"What?"

"I'm going."

The cardinal gawked at his relative as if he wanted to say "So what."

"Here," mumbled Ercole as if fearing a sneak attack. He was trembling. As he spoke he quickly pulled something from a shirt pocket and tossed it onto the cardinal's bed.

The old man crossed himself. The object was his amethyst ring.

"But you . . ." His Eminence began.

"Shhh, I'm going . . . can't talk."

Ercole turned and left, as his uncle asked, "Will I ever see you again?"

The boy's action obviously was a sign, albeit small. We couldn't shrug it off as inconsequential. The deed lingered in our thoughts through the remainder of our imprisonment.

The old man clutched the jewel as if it were the very seed of life. Then he stood, walked toward me and shoved it into the pocket of my black jacket, a strange smile of peace on his worn face. The gesture touched me deeply, and I started to say thank you. He covered his lips as if to seal the transmission. I still have this sad reminder with me. It's on my finger now—the deep purple stone which was given to His Eminence by the pope.

As for Ercole, I'll return to him later, but must say now that his disappearance was coincidental with a remarkable period of calm in our captivity. Beppe came down that Sunday with the evening meal, and even lingered to "chat." For some reason known only to him he didn't use this as an opportunity to offend us as usual. In fact, he behaved toward us as if we had just encountered him in a Roman *caffè*: informal, even friendly!

Such nonchalance was just a devious gimmick, a tranquilizer after the shock of the bombing of the cardinal's church. But as we sat there, while Beppe gossiped through the bars, it indeed seemed almost refreshing.

He joked about having worked in the smelly rubbish-littered Campo di Fiori since he was five, and even said with bloodless black humor that he could well imagine how excited the Campo must have been yesterday morning at the shoot-out. "My father, silly bugger, he'll be talking of this one for years!"

"He sells fish in the market?" I asked.

"Ercole tell you?"

"That's right," the cardinal replied.

"Ercole's been valuable to us," he admitted.

"What's your mother do?" asked Monsignani though he was really interested in Beppe's last remark.

"Works near the Campo, a little junk shop selling used clothes. I worked with *her*, too."

"You've worked all your life?" queried the old man.

"All my life! I went to school . . . only sometimes. I hated it, also hated work. What's the sense working in a corrupt world, capitalism destroying all desire to survive. Why work legally, in a system out to chop the balls off its workers?"

237

"Is this why you became a *brigatista*?" I'd wanted to ask this question for many days.

"If you're not born working-class you never understand," Beppe snorted and stood proud. "I was lucky—I had a good brain. I never was afraid to ask questions, say no to authority, spit in the face of a system I saw more and more crazy as I grew up. Why should I have to hustle? Why should my parents slave when rich sons of bitches never lift a finger all their lives? The more I wondered, the more enraged I got. I got into politics at home, but the Communist party of my parents is such a sellout. The people of my parents' generation, the ones who liberated this fucking country from the Fascists, the ones who fought, bled, and died for a new way of life, just sat back and *aged*. They accepted the same old shit, same old feudalism, same old Church, same old double standards as before. So I decided to leave them all behind, to try a better approach, a more radical approach, to create a society of *true* liberation."

"Your parents know where you are, what you're doing?" Monsignani inquired.

"Like Ercole, I see them sometimes."

"Don't they ask you what you're doing?" the cardinal continued.

"I tell them lies. Living the life of the piazza since five . . . they know I lie, they never know what the truth is. Who *knows* the truth these days?"

Tall wiry Beppe with the close-cropped black hair turned on that note and left us.

26

Monday and Tuesday, the twenty-fifth and twenty-sixth of July, were soporific lulls before the next onslaught. For those two days, the strange *estasi* we'd experienced since Saturday midnight continued.

Beppe's word "truth" always was in our thoughts and caused the cardinal to talk more freely than ever. I was most interested in his admission of having come to the Church through art. Tuesday evening he told me of his progression under his father's guidance toward solitary studies of spiritual awareness as revealed unto the many artists of Florence during the height of the city's prestige.

He mentioned a sincere devotion to music—which suddenly brought back a whole realm of things that both of us now sorely missed. He reflected back to his boyhood. "My grandmother, the one so horrified by the nocturnal appearance of the bees, started me playing piano at age five. I carried on for many years. It's my secret love, the piano," he admitted. "I was the one who urged Serafina to play, and to continue to practice and not to give it up." He smiled benignly and sighed. "Few people know this about me. I like to play when no one's around to hear my mistakes."

"I'd love to hear you play," I said eagerly.

The old man laughed. "I miss Chopin. Especially Chopin. I'd be so content to hear a refrain from a nocturne." He couldn't continue his sentence. "Music is the most direct link to God. If the angels need to communicate in heaven, it has to be by music. Oh Rupert, I miss so many things now!" He looked at me for understanding. "What do *you* miss?"

"I'd give anything for a pint of real ale!" I bandied, hoping to make the cardinal laugh.

27

On the twenty-seventh, Wednesday, serenity snapped like a whip on our backs. We were woken as usual at ten but I couldn't believe what I saw standing beyond the bars. It was a naked woman. Either the Brigade was playing tricks again or I'd gone completely insane.

I stared, as did His Eminence. Both of us were telling ourselves we still must be asleep.

She was young, twenty-five at most. She wasn't beautiful, just a nondescript Italian girl like so many others, with black hair, big floppy breasts, a mass of pubic hair, and rather fat thighs.

She didn't look unappealing. Obviously she'd been programmed to play the vixen. Her sudden appearance, though, ruined our illusory peace of mind as quickly as she'd flipped on our light bulb.

"Out of bed, boys," she coaxed. "Come and get it."

She was holding the coffee and milk, her legs spread far apart. She was a tall one.

We got out of bed as if approaching quicksand. She giggled as we neared her. I kept thinking I saw Serafina, that I must be hallucinating, that this couldn't be happening. God alone knows what the cardinal was contemplating.

"*Ciao, bello,*" she said saucily. "My name's Eva."

Monsignani snapped: "That's not your name and you know it! You've just been told to say that!"

"What're you really called?" I demanded.

"Oooh, you're a big one, aren't you, Rupert?" Then, she whispered as she poured me some coffee, "How can you fuck me . . . like a bull?"

I returned to my bed, sweating. Her eyes were green, very bright green.

"I like the cardinal, too. I bet he's got"—and she reached out for the old man's chin—"a *big* cock!" She tickled his now handsome white beard.

Slowly she lowered the vessels onto the floor and set them between her legs. Gripping the bars and bending toward us, she pressed her face between two cold shafts of metal and puckered her lips. "How about a kiss from

His Eminence? Please? Pretty please? Come on, give Eva a nice long kiss."

"You're not . . . called Eva." Monsignani stuttered and turned away.

She giggled. "Oh, yes I am. Just ask Iacopo."

On that cue the leader came bounding down the passage in the nude with a full erection, and right there in front of us penetrated the woman from behind. She faced us all the while.

The visual impact of "Eva's" visit was disturbing, to say the least, but the mental impact haunted us. We could only hope that the nude woman's appearance was a great psychic boomerang aimed at us, which would return to maim whomever had thrown it.

The woman (I'll refer to her as Eva) continued to plague us on Wednesday, Thursday, Friday, and Saturday. Each time we were more undone by her presence. Like the nude Ercole, this Eva only showed up at mealtimes, when she would taunt us. Then she herself would be fed, as it were, by the sex of either Beppe or Iacopo, who seemed to be going it in shifts.

Whether this so-called liberated woman, this revolutionary, felt she was being used by the men or simply contributing her share to the proletarian cause, I don't know. We didn't try to communicate at all.

What else could one think about but sex? There was a groaning woman being pummeled by men three times a day before our very eyes! Neither of us tried to ask the Brigade what it was they were trying to prove with this display. But I must admit, after the bestial couple were spent and departed, we inadvertently found ourselves talking about their insane motives. Again, we presumed them to be more sick tactics.

Gone were our thoughts of God. Even though we tried to make them soar above the dismal sights, what we had to witness dragged them down. Gone, too, were our sentimental memories of things we missed. We just missed them all the more in lonely privacy. Gone was our calm, we felt, forever.

We still said mass. Though I'd become a Catholic, there was little joy in the cardinal's heart or mine. Mealtime maneuvers were destroying us.

Once, out of desperation to talk about something, anything, I tried to ask Iacopo a question just after he and Eva finished. I didn't want him to run off as usual, so he did not, and remained inside the woman.

"Did . . . did you really cause people to be killed in Campo di Fiori last Saturday? Are you telling us the truth or was that . . . was it just made up?"

Silence. They began moving again.

"Did you really get the million pounds? Are you . . . you're just holding us here . . . to *torture* us?"

They were groaning. My head felt tingly, dizzy. Almost four weeks of imprisonment. And there was no answer. The two terrorists just began writhing again.

"Dear God," I whined. "Stop this, for Christ's sake, stop this!"

"Please answer us," begged Monsignani. "What really happened? Did you blow up my church or not?"

"When will we get out of here?" I groaned.

They just groaned back.

"Iacopo, help us for God's sake! Why are you holding us here?" the cardinal demanded stridently.

"Let us go, let us out!" I shouted. I felt delirious, distraught, despondent.

"Why can't you say something? All you do is moan, like the rutting *animals* you've become." The cardinal began beating his bed with his fist.

28

I thought I'd explode under the strain. For the cardinal it, too, was far more debilitating than his physical torture.

Then it peaked. Again, the fiends chose Saturday midnight, a time of the week we were now conditioned to be terrified of. That midnight neither of us was asleep. We were waiting. We heard the gate clang. The light came on. In stepped a very sensual-looking Eva. Whoever was behind her locked the door and vanished.

Hunting for a man, the woman fell back against the bars with both hands gripping cold iron. Then she lunged forward, still hanging on for dear life.

She'd done her hair up, put on earrings, a bracelet, lipstick, eye shadow, polish on her fingers and toes. It was hard to tell if it was the same woman. Her armpits were shaven. Her lips were orange-red. She even was wearing a delicate gold chain with, of all things, a *cross* about her neck!

She said nothing but proceeded to rub her right breast, slowly, gazing wantonly from the cardinal to myself, back and forth. He turned his head. I couldn't.

She planted her feet apart, then played with both breasts, making her nipples erect. By then, I didn't know where I was, except that if I didn't penetrate her . . .

She was masturbating like a fool. The cardinal covered his head with his blankets, then uncovered it and said, "Rupert, *don't!*"

"*I can't help it!*"

I flung off my blankets and was on the woman. It was a rage. I don't know what happened—when or how long the terrorist who called herself Eva was inside our cell. But when someone came to let her out, I was already fast asleep.

243

29

Thank God for spiritual beings. The cardinal had a sixth sense more acute than any human being I ever met. He knew how I felt, late that Sunday. After having let me wallow in putrescence, he threw out a lifeline to save me. "I can feel your guilt way over here."

I laughed slightly.

"But, Rupert, I too have made love to a woman."

That woke me up.

"I'm just a man, Rupert, like any other. You know, these *brigatisti* probably are right."

"Don't *say* that!"

"Rupert, I *could* have been sinning against humanity all these years."

"Stop it."

"We sin the most when we don't even know it."

"I'm the rotten one in this cell!"

"Rupert, let me tell you something. Listen to me. This tribulation—your being here is only by accident of your knowing me."

"Ercole set this up! It's your sick nephew's fault."

"Pray for his soul."

"It's damned—he's damned!"

"Still he needs prayers."

"What are you saying?"

"Rupert, you're a young man."

"So? You're a holy man."

The silence was awesome.

"Hear me, Rupert. I need to confess something."

"I can't give you absolution, can I?"

"Once a priest, always a priest. You are a priest, Rupert."

I felt humbled.

244

"This has to do with Ercole, with Serafina, with me, with you. I . . . I hadn't the courage till now. But, you know that Serafina was ill?"

I swallowed. Would he say she was dying?

"Do you know why?"

"No."

"She . . . she had a false pregnancy."

I couldn't respond.

"It was false though . . . she wasn't pregnant after all."

"Then she's . . ."

"Not a virgin."

"Who was the . . ."

"Father?" He took a deep breath. "Ercole."

"Her brother? You mean, she and *Ercole* . . . ?"

"He raped her."

"Oh God!"

"Three months before you got to Rome, in March."

"Kill him . . . I'll kill him—the *bastard!*"

"He'll likely kill himself. He's not worth bothering about. Sad but true. Serafina . . . she was suffering a sort of morning sickness when you arrived."

I stared at the man.

"How do you know this?"

"She came to me in March."

"How did she . . ."

"Mid-June of last year. I was in Guadagno's. Everyone but the children was away. Serafina and Ercole were alone in his bedroom. I was passing by and overheard them, Ercole I mean. What exactly was going on, I don't know. Ercole was moaning, saying he loved her and wanted to sleep with her."

"What did you do?"

"I knocked and pretended to be looking for Oduardo, who'd just left my rooms a few minutes before. Their brother was en route to Egypt. I said I wanted to say good-bye."

"And?"

245

"Serafina came out, very upset, and followed me to my terrace. She told me what Ercole was doing. It was then I presumed the boy was possessed."

"Did you tell his parents?"

"This is why I'm confessing to you now. A priest commits a sin if he sees sin is imminent but does nothing, out of fear, to avert it. I *tried*, Rupert. I made a scene and said Ercole was bedevilled, which is why his mother refused to talk to me for weeks. She came round, though, in mid-August, when her son quit university. As months went by, Ercole obviously went deeper and deeper into political activities, secretly, while continuing to reside in the palazzo."

"His father kicked him out, didn't he?"

"Once on Christmas Eve for not going to mass at Saint Peter's with the family, and once this past Lent for telling his father he hated him."

"And Serafina?"

"Ercole finally got his way in March, and raped her. Serafina . . . she was traumatized and experienced the false pregnancy, which, thank God, she recovered from."

"When I showed . . ."

"She loves you, Rupert!"

"Because I was a new man in the palace?"

"Don't be bitter. She loves you. I know my niece. I'm sorry, this must be a shock to you. But imagine how I feel, having to tell you this, here, in this. . . . Do forgive me, please?"

The humility of the cardinal disarmed me. "There's more," I asked, "isn't there?"

"Rupert, this will sound mad."

"Everything here sounds, looks, *is* mad of late. What's the difference—your tales or theirs?"

"A month ago Ercole came with that bloodthirsty glint in his eye and tried to blackmail me."

"What?" I whispered, not wanting to hear.

246

"He said his sister was pregnant, pregnant by an 'immaculate conception' he called it."

"Oh, stop."

"That's just what he said."

"Oh, Arcadio!"

"See? I was prepared—for anything from him. What other being but a maniac would come to a cardinal and say without a sign of remorse that his very own sister was pregnant by an *immaculate* conception?"

I just shook my head.

"I was appalled. I began cursing him for such mean blasphemy but he didn't flinch at all."

"What did he do?"

"He told me I had to notify the pope. He said it was a miracle. Such an event, he said, had to be reported."

"Raving mad!"

"Possessed is the word. All those months since leaving school Ercole just was playing at being a moody rich boy, a superstar of Rome's golden *gente perbene*. Satan curse him—he just was a depraved hoodlum of the Brigade, using his own sister as his scapegoat. It was beyond anything I ever had heard or read about."

I could say nothing.

"Ercole kept on, though—I'll take that snide stare of his with me to my tomb. He said he needed money."

"For what?"

"I don't know. I told him to jump off the balcony, I was so furious! *'Be damned,'* I said, *'I'll take your sick case before the inquisition.'*"

"Oh no . . . so that's why . . ."

"He's determined to use that word . . . yes."

"But no one calls it that today."

"It's now the Sacred Congregation for the Doctrine of the Faith, yes, but it still does exist. It was the first congregation founded, therefore it's also called the Supreme Sacred Congregation."

"And the Holy Office."

247

"That's right. Ercole's case would be perfect for them. He knows it. You must seriously consider introducing it. Give me your journal and I'll sign a coded note for the cardinal prefect."

I stared at the elderly man, as he signed the order to commence an inquisition, as the weight of the whole horrifying situation pressed upon me.

"Ercole ended his visit with this: 'Either you tell the pope your niece is the new Virgin Mary—or I'll kill you.' Yes—he used those exact words. So I knew . . . something dreadful was on its way."

The cardinal paused and stared at me. I could say nothing.

"I've one last thing to tell you, and this is the most difficult yet. It's a sin on my own part, and it involves your feelings for Serafina."

"Go on," I said hesitantly.

"You, Rupert, I saw at once to be someone who could . . . who could save Serafina's sanity, her very *soul*. Therefore, I worked behind your back to make the girl fall in love with you."

I was too confused, couldn't respond.

"Do you hate me, Rupert? Just tell me if you do. I beg your forgiveness." His Eminence began weeping on his bed.

"Don't," I shouted. I stood and raised the old man up. "Don't." I embraced him and told him I loved him as a father. I began to cry. I think I realized at that moment, for the very first time, that the cardinal likely would die soon at the hands of the Brigade. Then, as he was pleading for it, I placed my hands upon his lowered head and granted him absolution for his sins.

30

The woman returned on Monday, saying: "It's August. Aren't you happy?"

Gone was her sex-kitten purring. Now it was a bullish voice, authoritative.

"Roman?" Monsignani asked.

"Roman," she confirmed.

"Are you really named Eva?" he inquired.

"Just hold your coffee glass."

She looked severe. Her black hair was yanked back tightly. She wore a khaki uniform of some foreign army. She turned to go as quickly as she came.

At lunch she returned with six bumpy rolls and a bottle of white wine. *"Buon appetito."*

"Where's our pasta?" I demanded.

"You're not getting any," she retorted. "Bread and wine from now on. We're running low."

"How in hell do you get bread in this madhouse anyway?" I burst out in anger. "Bake it yourselves? Or does the bread man come with deliveries?"

"You ask the stupidest questions," she answered bluntly.

"How do you expect us to live on buns?"

"Who says we want you to live?"

"Bread and wine—nothing more?"

"You're lucky it's not just water."

"You're just doing this because of Saturday night, aren't you? Aren't you?" I was losing control.

"Pretend it's Christ—eat *Him*," she snapped and stormed up the passage. We heard arguing in the main room, then the door slammed.

"We can't eat this," I whined and threw the *panini* down on my bed.

249

"The Lord will help us," began Monsignani.

"Like hell! Just like He helped weeks ago, letting us end up here? Some bleeding deity—this Jesus!"

"Rupert, it could be far worse."

"How much worse?"

"They could be torturing us right now."

"They are torturing—what in hell do you call this treatment here—*dolce vita*?"

"It's food, Rupert. Something to keep us going."

"Yes, sustain us till the inadequate Italian police force can search and search and never find us. Sure, sustain us till they shoot us, since they'll have to get rid of us somehow. *Brigatisti*—even snakes don't like being holed up forever. If only to shed skin, snakes have to surface to the sun."

"You must eat. The food at least is fresh."

His Eminence sat and began chewing. I refused, and waited some hours until my hunger overwhelmed my pride, whence I wolfed the remaining rolls and said nothing.

31

The miser's diet finally got to Monsignani, too. He fell into depression. I didn't help. Later on Monday I snapped at him, "Are you sorry you confessed what you did to me?"

It was a cruel question, for which I am ashamed. The cardinal, reacting to my cantankerousness, retreated into a very black agony of introspection.

The cardinal's slip into his own abyss made me feel hopeless. The continuing menu of bread and wine, bread and white wine, made me feel drunk, constantly drunk. A huge stone was tugging us, pulling us beneath the surface of humanity, ever farther down into hell.

Was it Wednesday? At one point, Iacopo slipped into

sight and told us: "The police were searching the Appian Way. They've even gone through the abandoned villa up above us to no avail." Then he said with puffed pride, "Italian police are such idiots." His barrel chest flared in excitation. "Here we sit, right below their nose, and they can't even detect we're here."

"Self-contained, eh?" I queried.

"Self-contained," he replied with glee and left.

So were *we*, I felt, wishing Iacopo would stay a bit longer. Just to hear another being's voice, even if the being were inhuman.

But was I evil, too, I wondered?

Was the cardinal evil?

Maybe Monsignani was truthful to admit sins against humanity. Perhaps the cardinal *was* debased . . . as debased as I? This prince of the Church now sat sulking on his beddy-bye . . . aw poor thing . . . he'd made confession to someone his equal in lowness.

Then I heard a voice inside me asking: What good does confession do between those whose spirituality is so negligible?

32

Monsignani sulked through Wednesday. I amused myself by fantasizing about Serafina, and by having nightmares all pertaining to food.

On Thursday, August the fourth, the cardinal awoke, and spoke. He'd literally said nothing since Monday.

"I just had a dream, Rupert, a most hopeful, a most marvelous dream. Winds were blowing from all four directions. I stood by the sea, as the sun set into it. The waters were calm. Not a single wave moved. Tide was out, and a lavender mist hovered above the sands, which were moist and shone like mirrors. Across the sea, from

251

the sun, a gigantic wash of orange-red light stretched to my feet, and a voice from the sun called out to me. Just at that instant my feet left the beach and touched water . . . when the sea turned to a great lake of boulders, pink and rounded with age. No boulder was larger than a man. The sky was a palpable rainbow of hues, and reflection from the heavens to the rocks was a true delight . . . incredible. And so I walked, stepping from boulder to boulder, as the sky grew darker and darker. Yet the stars had come out and gave enough light, so I wouldn't lose footing or fall. The night was warm. Music, as if the chorus of children, began to call to me to continue onward. The boulders turned into white soil. Then the white soil turned into a paved road of white marble, which glistened from a radiance beyond a great gate. The music of the choir continued ever more sweetly, higher, past the reach of mortal hearing. The voices were sweeping me upward, when an angel with wings like rare emeralds caught me on his back and flew me higher. Ever higher we soared inside a dome of pure gold, embossed with the deeds of the saints. And before I knew it, we were going straight through a circle at the apex of the dome . . . then coming to rest in the presence of a throne, before which was the calf of an ox. The beast then raised itself to its height, like a man, and was garbed in a vesture of cloth which shimmered like opals that continually moved, as if they had been liquified. From the small ox came a soft voice that said: 'This is the throne of the Creator of all. This throne sits now near the earth. This has been prophesied. The last war will be fought, but the forces of evil will not be the victor. Glance behind me.' Behind the throne, which was now within a white cloud that dissolved it, was the Holy of Holies of the temple of Jerusalem, and its veil was rent in twain. The four winds of the world kept blowing the fated fabric in diverse directions, and I stared to see what the Holy of Holies contained. But only a lamb, with the radiance of the force that created the universe, stood still behind the cloth and the winds and said: 'I am the sacrifice and that which performs the sacrifice, the earth and what quakes the earth, the rock and what rends rock to sand, the grave and what opens the grave. The saints will rise again and reign in triumph. The tribulation of those who die in my Name is not to be eternal—as he who has faith in Christ Jesus, in me, will be restored in glory, though he decay now in death.' "

33

With the incessant bread and wine diet, which continued till we were shot, it seemed that the cardinal and I were living an eternal Last Supper. We soon grew accustomed to the thought of not having anything but liquid and grain.

I must say, I began to look forward to breakfast—the coffee and milk—more and more. I felt happiest in the morning, and that is an apt choice of word, since the mornings found His Eminence and I holding our glasses as if they contained mythical nectar.

Thursday, Friday, and Saturday, the fourth, fifth, and sixth of August, we were virtually left to our own devices. We were brought a ream of paper, a dozen pens, and a handful of envelopes by the woman who challenged: "See how much you can write. Write as much as your fingers can stand. The cardinal's go only to the pope, yours go only to the Archbishop of Canterbury."

So we spent three days writing letter after letter, each to his superior. I estimate both of us wrote thirty apiece, perhaps ten a day. The labor was tiresome, but passed the time. Between paragraphs we would occasionally look up and laugh aloud about some remark, then recount the anecdote.

Drugged by the diet, wretchedly tired from the writing,

we were too haggard to ask our captors about negotiations for our release. As far as we were concerned, negotiations had ceased. The Brigade was merely debating when they would have to kill us.

Disregarding this intimation, Monsignani and I withstood the eerie silence, whilst our rapport continued to grow. As our anecdotes proliferated, so did our tendency to gossip. I remember joking about the "glamour world" of Cinecittà, which His Eminence never had known. He began telling funny stories of his own "glamour world," Saint Peter's.

Come Saturday evening, when our post was collected by the woman, the strain was getting to be too much. It took very little to make us snap. The woman simply had to say: "In four hours it's midnight."

"Midnight? Damn you all—why do you always do your dirty work at the most despicable hour? What is this—a coven?"

"Don't provoke her," begged Monsignani.

"She doesn't need provocation."

"That's right, boys. Keep it up." She winked, "and I'll put on my makeup and rape you again."

"Rupert, don't," whined the cardinal.

The woman turned and left.

"Where's our supper?" I shouted. "Where are those rotten rolls?"

"Why do you even speak with her?" the cardinal complained.

"Bloody hell—why not? Don't get your blood pressure up!"

"Stop shouting at me."

"I'm not shouting!"

"You are . . . you are," the old man whimpered and began to weep.

The strain, the unendurable strain, now was beginning to tear us both apart.

34

Saturday midnight. They flashed the naked light bulb in our faces. We were wide awake, awaiting it, but not without trepidation. The figure beyond the bars was male this time, fully clothed, blank of expression. It was the cardinal's nephew. Neither of us was astonished.

"Who'd you expect?" he asked. "The pope?"

"Where've you been?" the uncle wondered.

"None of your business."

Iacopo and the woman came down the passage and stared at us like baboons. "Read the third communiqué," the leader told Ercole. Then to us he said, "He's been on sabbatical—studying—haven't you, Ercole?"

The boy beamed.

"He came up with a persuasive document," the bullish figure continued. "Read it to them."

Ercole read what he'd composed. "The People's Inquisition continues. We have come to the conclusion that if Canterbury and Rome heal their differences, the lives of the Catholic cardinal and the Anglican priest will be spared. You have exactly one week to heal the divisions of two thousand years of repressive Christianity. Long live the people!"

"*What?*" both Monsignani and I exploded together.

"Why in hell do you people even *care* about Unity? Why stick your nose where . . ." I shouted.

"Who's this addressed to? Where's it going?" the cardinal was white, shaking his head.

"Impossible . . . impossible . . ." I moaned.

"Two thousand years in . . . *one* week? You're mad!" snorted His Eminence.

"Who says we care?" Iacopo retorted. "We only want to see the pope jump quickly for a change. The Vatican's notorious for stalling, so now they've got an easy deadline they can't fail to notice."

"But, you don't even know the issues, the problems involved, the differences between Roman and Anglican!" I shouted.

"Who's this going to?" Monsignani asked again.

"To the pope, to the Archbishop of Canterbury, and to *Corriere della Sera*. The press must know about this."

"You've no idea what you're asking," snapped His Eminence. "It's taken years to get the ecumenical dialogue to the point it's at today. There's still so much ground to cover."

"Then what should we ask for?" Iacopo queried. Obviously, Ecumenism was out of his range of knowledge.

"Ask for recognition of Anglican Orders as valid," I stated.

"And for intercommunion between Catholic and Anglican," Monsignani hurriedly added.

"Put those two demands down," Iacopo ordered. "Now, we'll see how fast the Vatican's *able* to move."

35

After five weeks of stalling, as if the Apostolic See had exemplified the tactic, the Brigade sprang their devastating surprise on the world. Given that the press and investigatory agencies involved in our case were unified in their belief that the Brigade wasn't joking about the one week deadline, the third communiqué was recognized by all as a shrewd one—diabolic but shrewd.

The issues were of such magnitude for such an enormous percentage of the world's population. How fiendishly ironical—we two men of the religious life, whose job to promote Christian Unity had brought us together, now would likely die together, as sacrifice to the cause we were seeking to promote.

Now I can see why Monsignani said early on that his nephew had the most brilliant mind in the family. It was brilliantly black. Had the boy's interests been properly aimed, he could have triumphed as a diplomat. The twist of this communiqué was almost too subtle to have come from an infamous, brutal terrorist organization. Due to Ercole's wording, the document was shifting their own blame onto our two Churches, should the two demands fail to unite the Churches and to save our lives. An ingenious ploy, it was meant to divert attention to the megalithic churches in order that the Brigade could go free.

With this third and last communiqué certainly, our minds snapped back in to working order. Instead of tossing and turning fitfully that night, the more I thought about the communiqué (if it weren't a fabrication), the more I saw hope between its lines.

In the dark the cardinal and I discussed it. The strangest factor was that the Brigade hadn't mentioned the previous demands. If the revolutionaries had, as discussed, stuck to their agreement for Vatican money, then they supposedly would have dropped the demand for the release of political prisoners. But if they had lost their runner in a shoot-out in Campo di Fiori, then they didn't get the money they were after. This seemed unlikely, since now they weren't asking for any money.

We concluded that they really did get the money. Monsignani believed most fervently—as he had asked the pope to agree in secrecy to the payoff—that His Holiness indeed had done so in secrecy. Thus we fell asleep reassured that negotiations weren't deadlocked, and felt less pessimistic about our chances for release.

That Sunday morning the cardinal awoke determined to find out the truth of the matter. Ercole brought coffee, and while receiving it, his uncle said without hesitation, "Ercole, we know the Brigade got the money."

"Oh," returned the boy, not impressed. "What money?"

"The ransom. For us. From the Vatican. The million pounds sterling in lira."

I continued, "If your group did get it, that means no shots were fired in the Campo."

His uncle added: "If none were fired, your woman receiving the money got away safely. Therefore, it seems sensible to say nothing happened at the market in Rome, nothing appeared in the papers."

"You made those stories up. The newspaper was doctored, wasn't it?" I queried.

Just then Iacopo stormed down the passage. "Gossiping again, Ercole?"

"I was telling them about the money the cross and the ring fetched."

"Oh," Iacopo relaxed, convinced. "Ercole's useful to us," the leader emphasized for our benefit. "He's clever enough to get a good bargain. No pawnshops for our young prince."

"What did you do, hock the things?" the uncle asked, making no mention of the ring still in my possession.

"I went out of Rome to a jeweler's."

"I bet he went to Milano," his uncle joked but Iacopo stared, unamused.

"You can go now," Iacopo ordered. Ercole obeyed. Alone with us the leader mumbled, *"Sette millione*—not bad for an amethyst and a cheap amber cross. The cross was . . ."

"Mediaeval," the cardinal answered.

"Looked it."

"It was in my sister's husband's family . . . centuries."

"Papal family?"

"Correct."

"Too bad the modern popes are going working-class."

"What do you know about popes? Are you even Christian?"

"I'm even Catholic." And he displayed a vulgar

258

toothy grin. "We're all Catholic in my family. What else?"

"Your mother's alive?"

"Daily on her knees for me. She lives in church."

"When did you last see your mother, Iacopo?"

"Years ago. Why?"

"She knows about you?"

"She knows too much. She also knows ... how to keep quiet."

"And your father?" Monsignani wondered.

"Enough of this—*basta*—*punto*!" Iacopo retraced his bootsteps up the passage.

36

Sunday the seventh of August was memorable for an argument in the "reception room" up the narrow hall. Ercole, Iacopo, and the woman were screeching at the top of their lungs. We could catch only the odd word seeping down to the cell.

Ercole soon was racing down to berate us. Acting like a rabid ape, he grabbed the bars and shook the gate violently, cursing us: "You fuckheads—rotten slimy meddlers! I curse the day I was born to the filthy class you two glory in and will die from!"

"What's wrong, boy?" his uncle stood and was not feigning empathy. It was obvious the boy's relationship with the *brigatisti* was at the crisis point. "Ercole," Monsignani began to whisper, "Ercole, my son, I love you. Go—get out of here. Get out of this place before ... "

Iacopo shouted down, and Ercole began his abuse. "You laugh, don't you! You laugh that I'm *possessed*—because I left the gaudy luxury, bitchy servants, houses like museums, private parks, bulletproof cars. You laugh and say 'Well, Italy's Christian name is Contradiction ... and her family's name is Lawless.'"

Iacopo came closer. He was laughing, but armed.

259

"What have I really left behind? What is behind the pretense at nobility? Dogged retention of tradition? Upkeep of the family's old name? The class I come from *pukes*! I could have stood up at any number of boring balls for impossibly stupid girls I know and told the whole lot how assinine they were acting, how their lives were going nowhere. They would have applauded politely and said I was 'being funny' or 'playing rather bold.' The nobility of Rome says things and says things, but nobody ever listens to anybody, nobody ever says a single thing of value. People just babble nonstop till they die a glorious death, till they go and rot inside their family's marble vault with other sorry corpses, all of whom did the same."

Then he turned to Iacopo. "You, Iacopo, can't even imagine how these people live! Oh, now they're in traumas, all of them: for the first time in centuries they realize they've got to go out and work, got to leave the palazzo and find some job, just like the rest of the world. Then they discover they're being treated just like shit. Can you imagine how shocking this is? So . . . they quit. Again they retreat to their splendid baroques, to fret about when the Revolution's going to gobble *them.* But the most incredible thing is that as soon as you dare to ask one of the fretting noble beings what they're doing tomorrow, they get irate that you have the cheek to think to ask the question in the first place. Oh their lives are scheduled to the hilt, gorgeous dinners, trips, but if you ask a simple question, it's as if the world's just exploded. They've so much that's so inane . . . they think it sounds less frivolous to answer: 'Do? I don't know—I never know what I'm doing from one day to the next.' Satan forbid they *admit* knowing a thing! It's so much more English, they think, not to be interested in anything. Let the vulgar lower classes do the trivial actions civilization labels as interesting . . . that's why the masses were put on this earth, to keep the gentry halfway amused."

"And so you joined the Brigade," his uncle said.

Ercole ignored him and pointed his finger at the cardinal. "Your class knows its time is coming. *Roma Nera* is being pissed on by the pope, like some bonfire being doused by a thick deistic prick. And what do you do but shout *'Viva il papa—Viva!'* when it's *Papa* who can't wait to do you in. Answer, Arcadio. It's true, isn't it? I've heard you say it yourself—changes are too unseemly rapid, aren't they? Soon . . . all the ties the Vatican ever had with the patricians of Rome who spawned it will be *cut*—like a baby's cord is *cut*—then the kid will be left gasping in its own incubator of plastic. Yes, the plastic modern world is coming—coming even to Rome—and nothing's to be done to stop it! The rich kid won't have *Papa* to turn to. There won't be a papal shoulder to cry on anymore. *Papa* will be just some queer old bugger across the Tiber, who now and then steals the kid's piggy bank, to do some more filthy old tricks."

"Enough," Monsignani shouted.

"*Basta!*" cooed Iacopo. "*Bravissimo.* You can go now, Ercole," the leader stated like a schoolmarm talking to a brat. Then he smiled and followed the boy, saying, "Thank you," and he patted the young terrorist on the backside.

37

The woman woke us next morning with a cheerful greeting: "Six days till your deadline. Care for coffee?" She grinned, "It's in all the papers today."

We wanted to say "Show us" but thought better of it. Within an hour of breakfast Ercole returned and peered through the bars. "You two . . . you're fading away . . . . Is the bread and wine—"

"Ercole, for God's sake don't talk of it. Let it be. Save yourself. Get out of here," His Eminence said almost inaudibly.

Ercole grabbed his head in his hands and shook his whole body, as if saying "No, I can't."

"You need help, Ercole. Go the the Vatican—the Via del Erba office of the Secretariat for Promoting Christian Unity. Ask for Monsignore Algranati. You know him. Tell him—under the seal of confession—tell him where we are! Phone the Cardinal Secretary of State. I pledge you amnesty—you will be protected."

"Stop," the boy shouted in a whisper. "Satan rules the world—sin rules Satan."

"Ercole, leave us. If we die, you must get out. Don't worry about us. Let the Lord take care of our souls. It's your own that's crying to see the light."

"The world's the realm of things of evil."

The fellow's voice was so strange. I didn't recognize who was speaking. It was so frightening—yet the cardinal seemed in control.

"Out in the world, Ercole, is light."

"Your sister my grandmother's causing a storm. The old wicked woman must die!"

"What's she doing?"

"Talking too much . . . talking too much . . . talking too much . . . just like *me*."

"Ercole?" A growl filled the passage. It was Iacopo, shouting to find out what was happening. "Get up here."

"Go," his uncle urged, then broke out in a sweat as Ercole vanished.

The scene took a lot out of the cardinal. He had wrestled with the demon in control of the youth.

Ercole slunk up the passage and was beaten by Iacopo. We could tell this was what happened as the door remained open. We thought from the sound of things that others were in the room. This was likely, as the cardinal had seen others during his torture.

Soon the fearsome bulk of Iacopo was charging toward our gate. The woman followed. "Cover me," he shouted, unlocked the door, and stepped inside. He held a pistol, she a machine gun. The leader stepped to me and punched me brutally in the guts. I collapsed and was slapped across the face, then he slapped the cardinal repeatedly while saying: "I should kill you now—it'd be easier on us all—far easier! I *should* kill you now."

His Eminence was bleeding from the nose and the mouth but managed to say, "Then . . . do."

"Keep your sick opinions to yourself. Leave the confusions of that nephew of yours, *Eminence,* to us. Is that clear?"

"He . . . needs help." the cardinal moaned.

"Who doesn't nowadays?" the woman snapped.

"Shut up, woman," Iacopo retorted. "Just shut the fuck up." Then he said to us, "Ercole's all right—too many days of basic training—his nerves are frayed. He'll be all right. He just got melodramatic when the radio wired us with quotes from the papers today."

"You let him hear them," the woman interjected.

"Will you drop dead, you bitch."

"What did . . ." the cardinal began.

"Your sister, notorious Princess Aurora, is causing chaos in Rome! After the communiqué was released yesterday she called a press conference and blamed the whole thing on her grandson."

"She . . ." But the cardinal couldn't go on.

"She demanded, and got, a papal audience last night, then returned to have still another bout with the press."

"Tell them her big quote," the woman dared her boss.

"Look, you." Iacopo gave her a murderous look but she didn't flinch.

"Tell them! It's funny."

"The papers are in ecstasy," Iacopo said loudly, still glaring at the woman, "because your stupid sister said, 'The Italian police are so incredibly idiotic that a *brigatista* could be a cop and nobody'd ever know the difference!'"

"Sounds . . . just like her," Monsignani muttered.

263

There was silence. The balding leader appeared to be pondering something, then asked: "How much . . . *is* your sister worth?"

The cardinal said nothing.

"Worth enough to be allowed to live? Or . . . shall we let her die?"

38

After lunch that Monday, the eighth of August, Ercole returned, prodded down the corridor by Iacopo. He was wan and seemed hypnotized, muttering more to the slime of the walls than to us, "I'm going away for a few days."

"Will you be back?" the cardinal asked sympathetically and stood.

"Stay on your bed, both of you," Iacopo ordered. "Carry on, Ercole. Finish the announcement."

"And . . ." he fumbled, "and . . ."

"And what? Tell them!" the leader commanded.

"And someone . . . has to be . . . be killed . . ."

"And who might that be?" prompted Iacopo.

"Principessa Aurora Roseazzini." Ercole could hardly be heard.

"And who is she?"

"My . . . my . . ."

"Stop this! For God's sake, why are you torturing this boy? Haven't you succeeded enough? Haven't you brought him to. . . . Ercole, listen to Uncle Arcadio. Ercole, for the sake of your soul I command you in the name of Christ Jesus to hear me. Though your ears have been shut, your heart hasn't—that I know. I see you. If, and I can't imagine why they'd trust you beyond these walls, but if you're allowed outside—"

"Shut up, shut up!" Iacopo was enraged.

"Iacopo," The voice of the woman was hysterical. "Iacopo, *control* yourself. Put the gun down. What's the difference, now or later? Can't you wait?" She now was beside the leader, pulling him up the passage.

"But he's saying things to this idiot!"

"So what? Ercole's no use to us, either. He's got no more to tell us."

"His pissing uncle's giving him hallelujahs!"

"Well if you believe in that rubbish you're a sorrier man than—"

"Than what?" Iacopo turned and struck the woman on the face.

"Swine!" she screamed.

Others came to the passage, but it wasn't lit and we couldn't see how many for all the confusion. The Brigade seemed incapable of dealing with their own strain.

"Pig! How dare you hit me like that." The woman, her fists flailing, was being restrained and pulled up the hall. "You cocksucking motherfucker!"

"That bastard of a cardinal," Iacopo was shouting.

"Let him tell Ercole all he wants. The boy's remaining *here*," some deeper, calmer, more authoritative voice was declaiming, a voice that shut Iacopo up immediately.

"The . . . the Inquisitor," His Eminence mumbled and retreated instantly to his bed.

Ercole still was staring through the bars, eyes in space. The deep voice ordered the woman to fetch the cardinal's nephew. We were left alone at last.

The experience was terrifying, the first and last of its kind during our captivity. Monsignani seemed so shaken by the sound of the deep voice, which brought back the horrors of his torture, that he could only sit and quiver. Seeing the old man's naked fear totally undid me.

During times of the greatest duress, one's most consciously guarded secrets suddenly can come pouring out.

Tension finds release. This is what happened to me now, a result, I'm sure, of Iacopo's order that Ercole must murder his grandmother.

The cardinal was locked in his own gloom, and I felt the need to pierce it, to reach him. I might regret what I was about to do, but once I began, I couldn't stop.

"Arcadio, I lied to you before. Perhaps it wasn't a lie. Is it a lie to hold back in confession and tell only the easy part of one's sin?"

He gave no response.

"I lied. I didn't tell you all the story that time you listened, when I said there were problems within my family. You, too—you've problems, I know—so perhaps hearing . . ."

He opened his eyes, nodded.

"I mentioned twice that I walked to Canterbury from London. Now I must tell you why."

His Eminence laughed an odd laugh. "Town of the *Tales* . . . the Frankeleyn . . . the Reve . . . the Somonour . . . the Wyf of Bathe . . ."

"Let me tell you! I walked to Canterbury because— because I wanted to do penance for a sin so mortal. . . . It's what . . . it's what drove me to the Church."

I looked at the cardinal imploringly for understanding.

"Go on," he said and exhaled heavily.

"My . . . my father seduced me when I was just leaving school to go up to Cambridge."

"Your father?"

"My father—yes—had sex with me when . . . I told you he fancied women and men. Those in Society thought he was. . . . Fifty percent of London adored him, the other fifty loathed the ground he. . . . He was diabolical, cultured, urbane, very depraved. Behind my back everybody in England snickered and said, 'Well he *is* Aldous's son, after all.' "

"How did it happen?"

266

"How can people comprehend such a thing as 'I've had sex with my father!' So I never told a soul. Can you understand that?"

"Did you want it?"

"Probably! It was summer. No one was at Dexter Mote but the two of us. He was leaving soon, off again to the States. We wouldn't see each other till Christmas. It was his big chance to 'get to know his boy,' to talk to me 'man to man' so . . . so into the library we went, spending hours drinking, talking, I never felt closer to him in my life. It got sloppily sentimental. Father. . . . He said he loved me, wanted all the best he could provide for me, loved me more than all the others as . . . as I was his first, his heir. This was ten years ago."

"Continue."

"We got drunk. We were on the sofa and Father had his arm around me and . . . and then he suddenly grabbed me . . . between the legs and was . . . unzipping and kissing me and . . ."

"God in heaven!"

"We were naked—both of us—and something in me said 'What's the difference—it's pleasure—no one's being killed.' And before I knew it he was guiding me into him, telling me to make love to him as hard as I possibly could."

"You didn't."

"So what—of course I did!"

The cardinal refused to look me in the eye.

"Next day he was gone. We didn't see each other till December, but never a word was said or . . . as if he didn't recollect a thing. Father had one personality by day, but another completely different one by night. It was terrifying. I never knew which one married Mother."

"Did she ever know this?"

"I'm getting to it. Eight years went by. All my young manhood was haunted by what we'd done."

"Wasn't he just showing his love for you?"

"He only loved himself—Aldous Broxbourne! No one

else counted. Why do you think Mother spent so much time in Paris and in Rome? Mother lived her own fantasies writ large. Her role as marchioness was just another part to play, one more song to sing. But she lost control at the end—due to *me*. But let me retrace so you understand."

"Of course." His Eminence now was calm, whilst I was sounding delirious.

"Mother, no Father forced me to make love to him one other time. Forced—why do I say that? I did it because I *wanted* to! And it occurred on the eve of my ordination."

"No . . ."

"Again I was home—for my ordination in Canterbury Cathedral. Late that evening the butler said Father was calling. Though I was praying, I went to his room. He was in bed, reading. He had me pour Scotch. We toasted my ministry. He'd had two strokes as I told you. He wasn't well and asked if I'd rub oil into his back. I said yes, then he pushed the covers away."

"You don't have to go on," His Eminence said to my relief. "I understand."

"With the taste of the seed of the man who made me still in my mouth, I went to the altar of Christ to become His priest! I pledged my life to the Father, the Son, and the Holy Ghost—when I'd just made love with my *father*. After that, even sin had nothing more to do with me."

"What do you mean?"

"Eleven months later I called on Mother in Kent, when she was organizing her concert tour of Greece. Her cancer was killing her, and she knew it, but she refused to give in. It was spring, April. How can anybody accept they're dying . . . when the land is coming back to life? We took a walk. Mother's pain was making her worse than miserable, she had low tolerance and she took it out on me. She blamed my priesthood, my *God*, of being incapable of helping her. Instead of being understanding, I couldn't cope with the fact that Mother was dying—I refused to accept it. We started arguing by the brook near the woods which feeds our moat. Masses of daffodils were in bloom. Neither of us saw them, though I've been haunted by their beauty ever since. Mother began complaining about Father—I still don't know why I told her—but I suddenly heard myself saying, *'Do you know what he had me do to him—twice?'* "

"Why, Rupert? Why did you have to tell her?"

"I was a priest—or so I thought. How would *you* like to live with the horror of having told nobody, not even your confessor, the Archbishop of Canterbury, of being guilty of incest?"

The word was in keeping with the grime of our cell, our unwashed bodies. The sound of the word, slid off the walls like so much slime.

A beatific smile came across the old man's face. A mad thought made me think that perhaps he'd always seen this perversity deep inside my soul, perhaps he knew all along, perhaps he was urging my involvement with Serafina because he knew that she too was an agent of incest. Likes . . . attract likes.

"Why didn't you go to a confessor you didn't know?" Monsignani finally asked.

"I'd made a secret vow of chastity to God when my ordination occurred, on the spot in the Cathedral where Becket was martyred. But I broke the vow, broke it within a week."

"With a man?"

"A very young girl. I've never had sex with any man but my father."

"Are you homosexual?"

"No."

"Do you fear being homosexual?"

"No."

The cardinal sat in silence.

I continued, "I made the pilgrimage to Canterbury just before being ordained, to rid my soul of the guilt of

269

the first time I'd . . . but then as soon as I got there, the second time occurred, as if to undo what goodness I was trying to preserve."

"Oh, dear Rupert, I can see how this has been torturing you."

"But when I told Mother, she laughed like I was some carnival freak. I couldn't make her stop laughing so I . . . I heard myself saying, 'But Father always preferred *me* over *you!*'"

The cardinal just shook his head in disgust.

"Revolting, isn't it? I'm a monster, I know. You've no idea of the reputation I have in London."

"And you're . . . proud?"

"Proud I put my father in his tomb? How could I be proud of that? After Mother stopped laughing, she . . . said in all seriousness, 'Thank you, Son, for telling me, but you know your mother's *Greek*. And we have ways of dealing with tragedy!'"

Monsignani said nothing.

"And . . . one month later . . . she poisoned my father."

The cardinal crossed himself and then came to me to give me absolution.

I fell on my knees and began to cry. "*Now* can you see why I told nobody but Mother? My telling her caused my father's death."

"Don't speak. It's brave of you to have been so honest with me, Rupert. Never mind this, my son. Never mind. All of this has brought your soul so very much closer to God."

39

Not until I returned to England did the world reaction to the Brigade's third communiqué become apparent to me. But that Tuesday, the ninth of August, only five days before the deadline, we did have news of some reaction.

First Iacopo came, complaining about the wide range of opinions in Italy alone about their "demand for Unity." He boasted: "Lots of papers are saying the whole thing's a hoax. But just as many others feel that for once we're demanding something that actually might be beneficial to society." He laughed as he said that, and turned to leave. We tried to ask questions, but he ignored us.

Later the woman came and reported: "Ercole's being given therapy. I pity him. He does need deprogramming, more than the rest of us. His upper-class childhood certainly warped his values."

"You're holding him prisoner like you're holding us," Monsignani fearlessly said.

"He's too confused to go outside yet, especially now that the press is reacting so strangely to this last communiqué."

"What are you planning for my nephew?"

She ignored the query. "Lots of people, including your bigmouthed principessa sister, are saying the Vatican must join with the Anglicans. The Brigade couldn't give a damn, it's just an easy way to take the heat off us."

There. She admitted it.

"So that's why the Brigade sent the communiqué?" I asked. "Just a smokescreen?"

She refused to comment any more, and turned to leave.

A couple of other such visits occurred that Tuesday, with no more conclusive reports than I have mentioned. But the next day, late in the morning, Iacopo appeared and said that world opinion had become very inflamed: a fifty-fifty pull between those who felt it was worthwhile (to give in to the demand for Unity, as it would happen sooner or later—at least, if sooner, perchance it could save our lives) and those who vehemently felt Unity should be avoided at any cost.

Had such a situation occurred while I was at my desk

271

in Rome, I would have been directly involved in discussions to resolve this problem. Given that the Archbishop of Canterbury no longer had a Representative yet needed one desperately, Iacopo told us that the Anglican Bishop of Gibraltar (whose see is the cure of all Anglicans of continental Europe) had been working in my stead for some weeks. The bishop was seeing His Holiness daily now.

The issues were so complex and involved the energies of so many people—not only the Vatican's Secretariat for Promoting Christian Unity—that by late Tuesday evening the Archbishop of Canterbury himself grew so frustrated with the lack of progress that he announced that he was flying to Rome that evening. So when Iacopo came Wednesday morning, he took us by surprise when he reported, "Your boss, the archbishop, is seeing the pope this minute."

I asked as many questions as I could but was answered tersely. I wanted to know where he was staying, how long he'd be in Rome, and if I could write him a letter?

"You just wrote a bagful! No, keep your stupid questions to yourself. No letters. Get on your knees and pray your two chiefs agree to our demands by Saturday midnight. The clock's ticking, you know."

All Wednesday we tried asking as many queries as we could, whenever they brought us the wine and bread we'd grown to hate so. We were living only on hope.

Both of us had lost a lot of weight. The wine very likely was drugged—we felt so sluggish, so dreamy. But the woman who brought our food, if it could be called that, refused to talk except to instruct, "*Mangia*! Stuff yourselves."

On the eleventh, Thursday, Iacopo woke us. "The pope's announced he's offering his life for you two!" The leader peered at our bearded, emaciated mugs and chuckled uproariously: "You two dumb fuckers! Imagine anybody thinking you're worth the life of a pope. Who's that silly shit think he is, God? He thinks we're stupid? What's he think would happen if we did say, 'Okay, pope, you can come live with us now, we'll swap these two maniacs for your life.' Imagine what that would do for the Brigade. We're not idiots. We know Italy better than that. Why if we even touched the Holy Pope, police, army, millions of middle-class housewives in this insane country would tear the place apart. They'd find us—a posse of bloodthirsty Madonna-mumbling bitches in black—*they'd* find us. Touch a pope? Sure. They'd find us. They'd tear us limb from limb."

It was impossible to tell whether the leader was jesting or not. "What's the archbishop's reaction?" I asked.

"To the pope's playing God's fool? The papers are having a circus maximus. No one really knows what to think. Everyone's whispering that the archbishop is doing nothing but causing trouble. It's not every day an Archbishop of Canterbury goes to Castel Gandolfo, now is it? And this time he's come just to say, 'Damn it, give in to the demand to recognize Anglican priests as valid recipients of the apostolic succession or some such rot you quoted me, give in to the call for intercommunion.' It's all such a free-for-all as far as we're concerned. We believe in none of it. Yet our one little scrap of paper caused it all."

His Eminence then crossed himself piously and declared, "Perhaps *you're* the fool of God, because you don't really understand what you've felt compelled to do."

40

We definitely were drugged that Friday and Saturday, the twelfth and thirteenth of August. Who knows what was in the drink or the food? All we knew—and did—was sleep.

273

I believe whatever they drugged us with wore off as Saturday progressed. Iacopo didn't have to come and shake us that evening—to rouse us to eat—as he'd been doing. Then he told us not to bother trying to sleep that evening. "I'll be back for you two at midnight . . . when the Inquisition begins."

We utilized our meal's bread and wine for a mass. The cardinal celebrated in Latin. He said a moving litany to the souls of those who'd been subjected to injustice by the Church in her own inquisitions of the past, when zealots went to monstrous lengths to exorcize "heresy" from the land. His Eminence especially asked forgiveness from the many Christian martyrs murdered for retention of their faith, albeit not the Catholic Faith.

He said: "Many of the changes of late, brought about by intercession of the Holy Spirit, would be deemed heretical by the most jaded Roman of yore. I ask for understanding by these souls. I plead with you, Lord, for forgiveness of both our own sins. In our hearts we do not rebuke You, for the position we now are in."

Then he quoted from Revelation. " 'He that leadeth into captivity shall go into captivity; he that killeth with the sword must be killed with the sword. Here is the patience and the Faith of the Saints.' "

For the homily the cardinal began to think of the names of family and friend, living and dead, for whom he would say a special prayer at this trying moment. The list was long, but we had time. He began with his childhood and paralleled his distinguished career. Then he asked me to do the same.

It wasn't until trying to do so that I realized how simultaneously painful and liberating it was for the soul.

Then we broke the Bread and ate all of it, and drank all of the Wine which we had. For the rest of the time until midnight both of us prayed—in silence.

They came for us right on schedule. Accompanied by Ercole and Beppe, who'd returned to the prison, Iacopo marched into the cell and bound us together at the wrist, by means of cuffs linked with a meter-long chain; a similar arrangement bound our ankles. Both His Eminence and I were wearing all of our befouled clothing. We were led away.

Foresight had told me to be sneaky.. I prayed to God they wouldn't search us, as I'd cut a hole in my jacket at the armpit in which I'd hidden both the amethyst ring and my journal. Weeks ago I'd ripped out a small section of the notebook, so that the pad wouldn't be so bulky. I'd thrown the majority of it beneath my bed and there it had stayed, untouched.

Now they were leading us up the dark passage, into the room we'd seen six weeks before. Things had been changed. The fluorescent light was off. The Brigade obviously had arranged the room for a drama.

Against the wall immediately to our right was a dais of ammunition boxes, perhaps a dozen, two rows of six. Atop this were two chairs, one raised higher by a couple of planks. We were ordered to sit. The cardinal got the higher seat.

The chamber was lit by candles. Both the doors were shut. Opposite our dais was the same metal table as before; it was lit by thirteen candles. Behind it sat the woman who called herself Eva and someone I'd never seen. His face was hidden; he wore the same skintight black mask that the kidnappers had worn. The recollection of that experience wasn't a pleasant one.

The cardinal turned and said: "The . . . the Inquisitor."

"Correct," the masked man stated in that same low voice we'd heard five days before. "The Inquisitor, and this is the People's Inquisition. To my left is the People's Notary: Eva. To her left, guarding you, is the People's Defender of the Faith: Ercole. I myself am the other Defender. To my right, guarding you, is the People's Witness:

Iacopo. Behind the Notary and myself stands the other Witness: Beppe."

Then to Beppe he commanded, "Put the miter on Monsignani's head."

Beppe carried a fool's cap made of not one but three hornlike cones.

The Inquisitor said harshly, "This, Eminence, is the closest you'll get to wearing the Triple Crown."

The display was horrifying. Both Ercole and Iacopo stood at parade rest, legs spread apart, fists on the butts of shotguns. Beppe had a machine gun cradled in his arms. The Inquisitor began.

"The People's Inquisition commences. We've now had one and one half months to view you both, to form opinions of you, to ascertain your guilt. Of course it was known that both of you would be in Monsignani's car that Sunday, and we brought you both here for a cause. Monsignani was most useful for strategic reasons, but Broxbourne as Representative of the Anglican Communion to the Papal See has proven useful as well, though we believe in neither of your organizations. As for Monsignani, twice we asked him things, quietly, and twice he objected to the nature of our questions. Because of his refusal to give certain information to the people we had to punish him slightly. Broxbourne did not possess any information which we sought, so we did not waste his or our time."

The Inquisitor then asked for exhibits. Beppe bent down and handed a metal pail to the table. The man behind the mask reached in and pulled out a handful of letters.

"These disgusting objects, written by Monsignani and Broxbourne in a fit of anxiety last week are either addressed to the pope or the Archbishop of Canterbury. They're not fit to be read by human beings. Whatever these letters were trying to express, they only show how worthless these two men are to society. The contents of their letters are their condemnation."

276

"Are you going to read none of them aloud?" Cardinal Monsignani asked.

"Your mind is so lost you don't even recall what you wrote," the Inquisitor remarked, to the amusement of his aides. "No, destroy this contagion!" he ordered and handed the bucket to Beppe. The captor filled it with fluid, then carried it a few feet from our chairs.

Beppe tossed in a match, and a huge flame rose from the pail. The heat made us dizzy. Reduced to ashes, it started to smoke. Beppe covered it and placed it behind the door which led to safety.

"You never sent one letter," His Eminence snapped. "Then—did you send the others I wrote? Did you ever send the communiqués? Or was the whole thing a hoax?"

The Inquisitor laughed deep in his throat and said, "You see how little faith this man has . . . in the people?"

"*People*! Talk about the believers in Christ, the millions unlike you who don't kill people just because they are different from yourselves." The cardinal was enraged.

"Who mentioned killing? You don't fear for your life now, do you? Do you, Monsignani?"

"No!"

"To save us all time, I'll tell you this. The Canterbury archbishop no longer is in Italy. He flew back to England today. He said publicly he's disgusted with the whole situation in this country, and he decried the sloth of the Vatican in agreeing to the two demands mentioned in our last communiqué."

"Then," I shouted and tried to stand but the two guards rushed to prevent me, "then, there's no agreement at all? What's been *happening* these past few days? Tell us!"

"For God's sake please tell us?" begged Monsignani, as Ercole and Iacopo retraced their steps.

"We're giving your two Churches till midnight today, Sunday. No announcement came out of the meetings of your two bosses except that a statement will be issued by the pope later today. Probably he'll say something from

277

his balcony at Castel Gandolfo. Probably...but who knows?"

"But what about us?" I asked nervously.

"That we decide right now," he replied with cool assurance.

There was a long dreadful silence.

Ercole suddenly broke it, with a voice squeaky with strain: "They...they know about the Campo. They know there weren't any shots fired...that we got the ransom, that no one was killed."

Again, a long silence.

"What are you saying, Ercole?" the deep voice inquired. "Does what they think matter to the people?"

"No," he said.

"Since it's been mentioned, we'll tell you. Money was given to us, yes. We got it as we arranged. No problems. But, it wasn't the equivalent in lira we'd been assured by Monsignani we'd get. It was a sum far less—just a million lira—when you promised a million pounds. Therefore we accuse Monsignani of lying to the people, leading the people on, promising what couldn't be realized—just like the Church promises forgiveness when in truth the Church *hates* the people it says it really serves."

"But the money I brought from the sale of the cross and the ring," intervened Ercole again.

"Wasn't enough to buy bullets for a machine gun," the Inquisitor finished. He stood, pounded on the table, smashed a candle to the floor. "Damn you! Remain quiet or you'll regret you ever knew me!"

The mask turned to us once more. "Due to these added crimes—on top of the list you, Monsignani, already admitted to when we questioned you alone—we're convinced your case is sufficiently grave to warrant the most stringent punishment. If the Statement released by the pope at Castel Gandolfo later today is sufficient for the demands we announced last Sunday, then you Monsignani and you Broxbourne will be released as planned. If it is not, then you, Monsignani, and you, Broxbourne, are sentenced to death by rifle."

No one said a word.

"Do our two witnesses agree? Iacopo?"

"I agree," said the armed figure to our right.

"Beppe?"

"I agree," said the aide behind the table.

"Put that down," the Inquisitor ordered the woman, who scribbled in a book. "Now, you Ercole, as People's Defender of the Faith, and someone for whom I've bent over backward in helping to comprehend the aims of the Brigade, I want you to tell us now just what *are* the crimes which Monsignani has committed against the people."

At that instant Ercole's mind seemed to snap. His face was that of a madman. He slunk along the wall toward us. "You want me . . . want me to . . . to go outside there, up there in the dark and, go up outside and murder my own grandmother, don't you?"

He was aiming the gun at the Inquisitor, yet the masked man remained cool and told Iacopo and Beppe not to move, not to fire at him.

"We were just joking," the Inquisitor explained. "Can't you take a joke?"

"Leave me be! Let me alone! You've squeezed my brain for weeks, I'm no longer myself! For God's sake, what are you doing in here? What's this room doing? These candles? Chairs? My uncle, my . . . mask—why are you wearing that stupid mask? If you kill them . . . kill them they won't remember your face?"

"Ercole?" the Inquisitor was shouting. He stood up.

"Ercole," the Cardinal spoke as calmly as possible, though his voice was shaking. "Ercole, don't do anything rash now."

"*Rash*? Everything's rash these days—these nights. Madness—it's all slime on the walls. Bread and more bread and bloody red wine—*Uncle*—what are you doing here?"

279

"You brought him here," screamed the woman, unable to control herself any longer.

The Inquisitor slapped her into submission. She crumpled onto the table in sobs.

"Kill the three now," Iacopo shouted mercilessly. "What good are they? This has all gone on too long. I'm sick of their faces—Ercole's included. He's not one of us—he'll never be anything but a brat of the filthy rich, playing revolutionary."

"Oh, of course, that's all I am. Ring bearer? Water boy? Here's the costliest twosome your damned group's ever had! Many thanks, sir. Plenty of info? You treat me like shit! Bravo, Iacopo! Fuck yourself with a hand grenade. Just be sure you pull the trigger—when it's way up in your arse!"

"Iacopo, don't," the Inquisitor hollered. "Stay put." He bounded to restrain the barrel-chested terrorist. Then to Ercole he shouted, "Boy, where's your allegiance? I *believe* in you. This is your chance to show me where you stand. With us? Or . . . with them?" He pointed a deprecating fist toward the dais and our chairs.

Ercole screamed, *"Here!"*

It all happened so fast I hardly realized what the cardinal's nephew was doing. A shot rang out. Ercole was collapsing . . . dead from his own shotgun. The boy had killed himself. The battle of whatever childhood goodness left in him was a fight to the finish against some demon of violent revolution. And suicide was the only solution . . .

The cardinal started babbling and fell on the body, dragging me with him. The room became chaos. I think I blacked out. I really don't recollect much of what followed.

Somehow someone pulled the sobbing Prince of the Church from Ercole's body. We were pushed as quickly as possible back to the cell for our last few hours of imprisonment beneath the ground.

41

At noon on Sunday, the fourteenth of August, the pope made history by granting Partial Communion to all Anglicans. I have already described what this means. Such a step was inevitable in the advent of Unity anyway.

I'm sure that the Brigade didn't even know what the word *communion* meant. The fact that the adjective *partial* was used, when His Holiness read the Agreed Statement of the two hierarchies at Castel Gandolfo, caused our fate to be sealed as far as the *brigatisti* were concerned.

The Holy Father pleaded with the terrorists for the understanding that centuries of difficulties concerning Rome's recognizing Anglican priests as valid inheritors of the Apostolic Succession couldn't be overcome in one week, that the two Churches were moving as quickly as was humanly possible toward concord. The Agreed Statement was much longer and far more detailed than this, but in essence it said what I say here.

The brigands tired of us. Also their own internal strain had shown more and more—the one thing that showed them to be human.

The suicide of Ercole Roseazzini didn't help our situation. Neither did it strengthen the cardinal's resolve. Both of us were so emotionally drained after seeing the boy die that we'd fallen asleep in our cell without any difficulty, still clothed.

We weren't roused till one, when Iacopo came to say that we would be shot later that night. He blandly reported what I've said above, but even had the Vatican come out with twenty statements of *total* Unity, I'm convinced the Brigade would have shot us anyway. It simply wasn't worth it to them to keep us alive.

I think we had twelve hours left together. Most of it we spent in a stupor. I must say that Arcadio Monsignani confessed fully to me for a period of three hours or so sometime during this interlude, and almost all of what he told me has no bearing on this accounting. That which does I'm bound by the seal to retain. I then confessed things I need not mention herein.

I can say that this was not easy, this waiting or this expurgation of one's sins. Contrary to what the cardinal kept saying, I didn't believe I'd survive the good man who had become such a dear friend.

We still were in chains. They hurt. But what was pain now but something to take our minds away from death?

Was I resigned to it? Probably not. I believe that His Eminence was. His faith was so much more firm than mine. I held him so dear, respected him and loved him with all of my heart.

Then . . . they came to get us. I was shaking so my teeth were chattering and I tried to say something but couldn't. There were only two men, Iacopo and Beppe, armed with pistols with silencers. The woman and the Inquisitor had left the night before with Ercole's body.

"Where . . . is he?" Monsignani asked, as he led and I followed up the passage.

"The Vatican will be notified where he is . . . when they learn about you."

No more questions were asked. I felt nauseous and asked to relieve myself. In the large room used the night before, we both were ordered to relieve ourselves on the floor, by the blood from Ercole's wound. I became ill and vomited.

"Hurry up!" Iacopo prodded.

We were forced up the huge flight of stairs of stone we'd descended six weeks before. His Eminence began saying the "Ave Maria" over and over and over.

We could hardly see, there was just a spot of light

282

provided by a small torch carried by Beppe. Soon he was ordering the cardinal to "Shut up!"

A trap door was pushed up. At last we breathed the fresh sweet air of evening. Its scent, so associative, made us weep.

"Keep quiet," Iacopo ordered, as our eyes were trying to adjust to the moonlight. I recall seeing a salon, abandoned, and a door in a bookcase which we just walked through. Beppe shut the door and said, "Hold those chains."

I bent my left arm and grabbed the ankle chain. Then we were in an entrance room, then out where crickets were chirping wildly. The aroma of pine was truly too much for us to take. There were stars in the sky, and an almost full moon, and we were being led through a gate.

There—straight ahead—white and cylindrical, was the Tomb of Metella looming like a dinosaur . . . across the Appian Way. It looked bluish in the luminescence of the moon. It hurt so, the beauty of its sight.

The locked gate to the villa where we'd been imprisoned opened to a small drive leading to the tomb. On the right of it were innumerable pines, to the left the ruined shell of the medieval church San Niccolò a Capo di Bove. It was to the church that we were ordered to run.

No one saw us. No dog barked. No car passed. The site was utterly deserted, as if it had never known a soul.

Midway along the twenty-five meters of the main wall, a doorless portal opened upon weeds . . . refuse . . . brambles. We were forced in. No roof had covered the consecreated ground for centuries. Used condoms hung from a branch of a small thorn tree just inside the door.

The two were quick. I suddenly had the thought they didn't like what they were doing. I wanted to cry out to something, but to what? I held the cardinal's hand. We both were shaking.

They shot him first.

283

He fell . . . and because he pulled me down, I believe my life was spared.

The silencers did not work.

The pistols were making too much noise and this also saved me.

God alone knows why the silencers did not work.

I was shot, twice in the legs, once in the abdomen as I was falling with the cardinal.

When I came to, I was in the hospital. The police then told me that my dear friend was a martyr.

Conclusion

Ercole's body was found in an abandoned van in the Circus Maximus, at the San Teodoro end of the huge field where many Romans walk their dogs. This wasn't far from the palazzo where the boy grew up. The Roseazzini refused him burial in the vault with the family princes located at the sea. His body's whereabouts is not public information.

His Eminence rests temporarily in a vault provided by the family, awaiting transfer to a crypt in the cardinal's titular church which is being rebuilt at present.

Since my return to England, quite a few officials from various Italian intelligence agencies have called on me for questioning; needless to say, Iacopo Orcagno, Beppe Spadino, the woman who went by the name of Eva, and the Inquisitor, whoever he may have been, as well as others involved in our kidnapping remain at large as this book goes to press.

I admit absolutely no knowledge about the organization of the Brigade other than what is reported herein.

Not once were we allowed to hear or to see anything that indicated that any foreign terrorist group or government were directly or indirectly responsible for those who held us captive.

I have been pressured continually since leaving Italy to say that extreme left-wing agencies behind the iron curtain, or Cuba, were in league with our captors. To say so would be a lie on my part. If it be true, I cannot support such allegations with evidence.

As for their fabricated tale—the "shoot-out" in Campo di Fiori—nothing of the sort occurred. The Brigade manufactured this idea in order to find an excuse to blow up the cardinal's titular church.

His Grace, the Archbishop of Canterbury, never did say that he was "disgusted with the whole situation" in Italy, as the Brigade reported. He departed from the Holy See only after long and meaningful deliberations on the Agreed Statement, which was released the last day Monsignani was alive.

The cardinal especially asked me to say publicly that in no way can it be thought that he or I lost respect for either the Roman or the Anglican Churches. The two Churches' inability to prevent the cardinal's martyrdom does not mean that we condemned their attempts to see us safely released.

Epilogue

That Sunday after the martyrdom, His Eminence was eulogized. I was at Castel Gandolfo, as was His Holiness the Pope, but I had recuperated enough, I felt (though my doctor violently disagreed), to be taken to Saint Peter's Basilica in Rome for the funeral mass of Cardinal Arcadio Monsignani.

The solemn ceremony, attended by the mourning Roseazzini family plus thousands of the faithful of the Eternal City and, I think, forty of the world's cardinals, was celebrated by the bereaved Holy Father.

I was brought by wheelchair and was still under sedation. Even though I do not recall many particulars of the mass—I was too moved to speak during it—I do remember that as a nurse wheeled me beneath the gold ceiling of the Shrine of Simon Peter, the huge throng applauded in that inimitable Roman fashion of true affection, and I was reduced to tears.

When the pontiff himself was carried into the cathe-

287

dral, and then as he ascended to the altar beneath Bernini's ornate Baldacchino, which stands above the tomb of the man called the Rock of Christ, the emotion manifested in the applause of the people most certainly gave us all strength—strength to carry on.

One particular I shan't ever forget. Because of a special appeal which the cardinal had included in his first letter to the Supreme Pastor, an extraordinary request was granted, as His Eminence's last wish. The cardinal had asked that his niece, Serafina Roseazzini, be allowed to play the larghetto of the First Piano Concerto of Frédéric Chopin, instead of having the Sistine Chapel Choir sing as usual during the actual celebration of the Last Supper.

This request—solely for the sad but heartening music to be played while the people came to the altar—was extremely difficult for Serafina to fulfill. However, the woman who will be my wife had the support and love of her family to bolster her and the cherished memory of her dear and departed uncle to inspire her. Dressed in black, her face barely visible through a veil, Serafina slowly walked to the piano at the right of the Baldacchino, beneath the enormous dome of Michaelangelo, and began to play the melancholy music.

After this, I cannot remember much. I returned to Castel Gandolfo, then was flown back to England the next day. Before leaving Italy, however, I too was granted one small request and was allowed to be driven back to Rome before going on to Fiumicino Airport. The chauffeur didn't want to do it, but I begged him to show me the abandoned ruins of the church of San Niccolò a Capo di Bove in the ancient Appian Way.

The car pulled in the gravel drive, beside the building where my friend had been martyred. Reluctantly, the driver assisted me into the wheelchair and pushed me to the door of the old Gothic chapel. I was bearing a great

288

bouquet of roses, white roses, to lay on the spot where my friend had died.

But I was not the first. The *fedeli* of Rome—the warm human beings of this the most marvelous city on earth—had been to the site before me. The ground where both Cardinal Monsignani and I had lain now was piled high with thousands of flowers, of every type the season could provide.

I was touched . . . to the heart. And there, beside the flowers, on their knees, were a very old woman in black and a very young boy dressed in white. The resolute faith of the woman, who was saying her rosary with her eyes shut tight, was in marked contrast to the boy, who probably did not really understand but who clutched her hand and stared straight ahead with wide, wet eyes, then looked startled when he saw me in my wheelchair. I think he knew. . . .

But I pressed a finger to my lips to warn him not to disturb the old woman, and he did not. His eyes did not move from my face as I said my prayer. When I placed the roses amidst the brambles and the brush in the walls beneath the open sky, the little boy crossed himself and I followed, beseeching the protection of the Father, the Son, and the Holy Ghost. Amen.

Author's Note

The manuscript for this book was completed within Saint Peter's Basilica, Johannes Paulus II Pontifex Maximus.